ENDLESS LOVE

THE 4EVER SERIES #3

ISABELLA WHITE

Inferno

FIRE QUILL PUBLISHING
EROTIC ROMANCE

All rights reserved.
ISBN-13: 9781947649200 (print)
ISBN-13: 9781947649163 (e-copy)

To everyone who loved Holly's and Jake's story.

ACKNOWLEDGMENTS

To God, my Savior. Thank you for showing me the way. I struggled for years and years not knowing where I was meant to be, or what it was I had to do. And then You revealed it to me, dunked me into the writer's world, and I'm loving every second of it. Thank you, for always giving me new ideas through everything that is around me—the new people I meet, the ones that make me gape, and those that make me laugh out loud. Your creation has been the biggest inspiration of all. Thank you for giving me the privilege to know You the way I do.

Heinrich, my husband, and my two beautiful girls. I couldn't have done any of this without your love, time, and compassion for my other love. You are never second best, and all that I do, I do for you.

To my partner in crime, Carlyle Labuschagne, for always hearing my crazy ideas and finding a way to turn it into a reality. Your passion reflects mine, and I couldn't have accomplished what I have if you were not there.

To Monique Fischer, my writing hand—cue crazy laughter— you fix all my stories, fix all my grammar, and make my writing from *blah* to way up there. I'm not a writer, I'm a story teller, but your passion turns me into a writer.

To Sandra Valente, my editor, you turn me into an author. Your passion for this series can never be expressed in words. Passion cannot be bought and I'm privileged to know you and to work with you. I always get a taste of how my readers are going to react, what emotional turmoil I'm going to put them through, through you. I love your enthusiasm when it comes to the 4Ever series, and it saddens me that this is the last novel.

To Regina Wamba from Mae I design, the queen of the cover industry. Thank you for creating all my covers in the 4Ever series. It's a privilege to know you and have worked with you.

To Anika, my assistant. You run my house, make sure my kids are fed, and remind me that I need to eat, drink and sleep. Thank you for everything you do, everything you've done, and so much more. I would be in complete darkness without you. Never quit, please.

To my fans. I know the second book took a long time to materialize—thank you for your patience. The third one took only a year.

Thank you for your love of these characters. I hope that they will stay with you for a long time to come.

Till next time,
    Isabella

ONE

HOLLY

She blinked back tears as she scrolled through the photos of Jamie, her daughter, on her phone. Three weeks had passed since she had moved to Zürich, leaving Jamie with Jake. The only consolation she received from the terrible, heart-wrenching loneliness was that she got to Skype with them every night. She missed her little girl so much her heart ached.

Jamie lived with Jake now. The transition had gone smoother than she had expected it to, but he had an amazing support system. Amelia, Gus, and Robin all jumped at the opportunity to help him out with Jamie.

At first, both she and her mother had been hesitant about how quickly and smoothly everything had fallen into place with Jamie and Jake. But when they'd actually thought it through, they realized that for Jamie, Jake had always been in her life, just stuck in a rainbow.

For Jamie, Jake had come home now, so it was natural for

her to settle in as easily as she had. And she had to admit that from what she'd seen, Jake was a great father.

Rodney, one of her best friends and the only male influence Jamie had had in her life for the past almost six years, also checked in on Jamie from time to time. Not that it was necessary, but he was a part of their family.

As for the Peterses, they were giving Jamie whatever her heart desired.

She loved that her little girl would finally be able to go to ballet classes and take part in other activities, but she didn't want her to become spoiled, and that was a big possibility. Jake couldn't say no to Jamie. None of them could.

For once, things in her life seemed to be going well.

Even her mother was happy. Jake had offered Jane a position at Downsend, but she'd gone back to Seattle. Holly had a feeling she was going to try to make it work with Frank again—in her opinion, her mother couldn't have asked for a better man.

Jane had had it rough with her father, and her faith in men had died out after him. But Frank was different. He was a fantastic guy, and he deserved another chance.

Even though everything seemed to be working out well, there were two things she worried about.

The first was Mara. Jake was making it difficult to forgive her.

What Mara had done was wrong on all levels, but Holly had learned the hard way that you had to forgive someone for yourself. The human soul wouldn't survive and truly be happy if bitterness and anger roamed in the heart.

She desperately wanted Jake to forgive his mother, but he was stubborn. He had his reasons, and she couldn't argue with them, but she worried about the animosity he had toward Mara.

The other thing she worried about was Kate. She still felt

shitty that Jake had left Kate to be with her. They'd hurt Kate badly, and she couldn't seem to let go.

Jake hadn't been joking when he'd said Kate was like Mara. She didn't give up easily. She'd phoned him incessantly in the days before Holly came to Zürich, begging, crying, fighting, more begging.

Without her there, anything could happen. He'd been on the verge of marrying Kate; his feelings for the woman couldn't have vanished overnight.

What if he decided to go ahead and marry her, anyway? Jake had shown Holly what he was capable of when he'd cheated on Kate with her, and he loved Michael as if that boy were his own.

But Jake had promised her that nothing would come between them, not this time. Holly could do nothing but trust and hope that she was enough for him.

She smiled at the memory of Jake telling her over and over that she was everything to him, and that he would keep on telling her that until it sank in.

But she couldn't help it. She was still afraid.

She figured her fears were rooted in the married woman from his past. He never talked about her, and she was too scared to bring it up. Scared that she would hear things she didn't want to hear.

Amelia had told her that he'd been devastated over the fact that the woman was married. But then he met Holly and all that seemed to disappear.

What had happened? Had the woman's husband found out about their affair? Had she broken it off because of that? Or, was it something else entirely?

None of his family members knew the woman, had never met her, and Holly was scared that a part of him still secretly lusted after her.

It was one of the reasons why she still felt marginally insecure with Jake.

What if that woman came back into his life and offered herself on a silver platter while Holly was in Zürich? Would she and Jamie be enough for Jake to say no, and would he truly mean it?

Life was too short to spend it with the wrong person, and deep down inside she knew there was a possibility that she could lose Jake, either to Kate, or the mystery woman.

She shook her head. It was no use dwelling on thoughts like that while she was close to 4000 miles away. It only made her worry more.

Swiping through her album, she smiled at the photo of her and Bernie with Jamie and Layla, Bernie's little one.

She'd eventually phoned Bernie, who had been short with her answers. She couldn't blame her friend. She'd completely shut her out, and hadn't bothered to give Bernie a chance to be a part of hers and Jamie's life.

But the day after Holly had phoned her, Bernie and Leo had rocked up at the cabin. She hadn't been ready for the ambush, but Bernie being Bernie, hadn't given a crap about that.

When Bernie saw Jamie, it was an emotional moment, and even more so when Holly introduced her and she discovered that Jamie's middle name was Bernice.

Bernie had glared at Holly, who had desperately been trying to hide her tears.

Sam was almost seven, and he hadn't recognized Holly at all, but then he'd been a toddler when she'd left them all behind.

She was surprised to learn that Bernie was pregnant again—although barely showing—and that she had a little girl, a year or so younger than Jamie.

Jake and Leo had taken everyone out on a boat trip, so she and Bernice could talk.

Bernice was her best friend, and had been since childhood. In the end, she hadn't just left Jake, she'd left Bernie, too.

They'd needed to sort things out.

She remembered that day so well.

"YOU JUST LEFT!" BERNIE YELLED.

Holly looked down and picked at the comforter on the bed. "I know."

"No, you don't. Do have any idea what you put Jake through?"

Holly lifted her head to look at her. "He told me."

Bernie barked out a hollow laugh. "I guess he gave you the subtle version. He was fucked up, Holly. Not even Leo could get him to snap out of it. The punches my husband had to endure..." Bernie closed her eyes and shook her head as she wiped away a tear. "I don't even want to think about it to paint you the picture, Holly. He looked everywhere for you, and I was no use. I never once thought you would go crawling to your father. You never spoke about him or mentioned his name, so I had no clue where you were. For someone who had claimed to be so in love, you sure as shit ran away as fast as your feet could take you."

"I heard him saying—"

"It wasn't him. I told you his mother was a psycho. Didn't you think to phone Gus when you knew you could die? Or when you discovered you were pregnant with twins? I missed all of it. I was your best friend, and you shut me out of your life!" Tears streamed down Bernie's cheeks.

"I'm sorry."

She ignored Holly's apology. "You didn't even phone me. Did I mean that little to you? Holly, I stayed with you after

Jamie's death, I was there when fuckface broke your heart. Why couldn't you just have phoned me? Did I mean that little to you?" Bernie broke down and sobbed. She slid down to the floor and covered her face with her hands.

"No." She climbed off the bed and crawled over to her friend. She touched Bernie's arm. She needed to repair their friendship, and could only hope that her friend would forgive her for treating her like shit. "I didn't want Jake to lose his friendship with Leo, so I gave up ours, okay."

Bernie looked over at Holly, wiping her hands across her cheeks. "He wouldn't have lost his friendship, because I would've fucking asked you where the hell you were. Jake was insane with worry."

"I know that now, but I didn't that day. You weren't there, Bern. You didn't hear her. I didn't want to believe it, but then she begged me to phone him, so I did. And he confirmed it. It was enough for me to know that he didn't want us anymore, so I made a choice. It was a stupid one, I know that now."

Bernie shook her head, but being her stubborn self, they continued to argue. When everything was out in the open and off their chests, Holly apologized again.

Bernie finally stopped fighting. "Just promise me one thing, Holly. Never, ever do that to me, or Jake again."

Holly nodded, and they hugged for a long time.

"I missed you," Bernie said brokenly.

"Ditto. So much, sister."

Bernie laughed through snot and tears and they broke the hug.

"Tell me about Romy," Bernie asked, rubbing her hands over her face.

Holly took a deep breath and told her everything about Romy's short life, her voice thick with emotion.

"That bitch! I didn't want to believe her, because I knew she was insane when it came to Jake. I was convinced she was behind it, but like you said, Mara finds a way to make you doubt everything you believe in. When you never called me, I believed her, Holly. I fucking believed her, while you were in some fucking hospital fighting for your life and your babies."

"It's in the past."

"No!" Bernie yelled. "Don't you dare give that woman the easy way out. She deserves every fucking thing that comes her way. She lied. Do you know how Gus felt when she told him that the shake hadn't worked? He spent years, decades, on that formula, and then she destroyed it all. That lie broke him, made him think he'd wasted all his time, all that effort. Not to mention what she did to Jake and Amelia."

"Amelia?"

"Amelia hated you. That walk against abortion, the one in high heels? Do you think she would have done that if it wasn't a cause dear to her heart? And she spent all these years resenting you for getting an abortion, because that's what Mara made her believe. Not to mention her drinking problem." Bern sniffed. "She couldn't handle any of it, so she took to drinking. It was bad. She's sober now, or so Jake says."

Bernie let out an exasperated sigh.

"That night, after we discovered you were gone, I told Mara she was insane. And she had the audacity to start crying. That woman never cries. Jake was in turmoil; he didn't know what to believe. She chased me out of her house, but only because I knew the bitch had something to do with your disappearance. I knew you would never get an abortion. And I told Jake that. He was really disappointed that you just left without speaking to him.

"Never in a million years did I think Mara was tech-savvy enough to make you think you were speaking to Jake. That woman is pure evil. When I managed to convince Jake that you'd never get an abortion, he decided to look for you. He hired a private investigator, who tracked your car to a bus stop in Atlanta. From there, we tried to pinpoint a location.

"Jake was callous and stressed out. He didn't even care about his residency. He just wanted to find you. We phoned every damn hospital in the country. Gus ran through with us what we needed to say, what your symptoms would be, and then we just waited. But Mara probably had Seattle Memorial on her list of hospitals to phone, and she never made any of the calls."

"You can't say that, Bernie."

Bernie merely looked at her. "She told you he didn't want the baby, or you, for that matter. She told you to get an abortion. She wanted you out of his life. She didn't make a single damn phone call. I'm certain of that, because Seattle would've phoned Gus the moment you were admitted, Holly."

She tried to imagine what those months after she had left had been like for them all. Between what Jake, Amelia, and now Bernie had told her, she had a pretty good picture.

"The leads went dry after the bus stop. The cameras only recorded three days' worth of footage. Jake was livid, and threatened to sue them. Of course, he didn't sue them, but he did leave. He picked a direction and went with it. For two months, he was radio silent—at least with me and Leo. And then he rocked up at our house out of the blue." Bernie shuddered visibly.

"What happened?"

"Mara dragged him back. He was obviously upset with me and Leo, and that was when I really started to think that maybe, just maybe, you had gone through with the abortion."

She nodded, completely understanding why Bernie had believed that. She hadn't phoned her, just upped and vanished.

She wiped her tears with the back of her hand.

"Do you understand why I'm so upset, Holly? You gave

Jamie my name, but you couldn't find it in you to even phone me."

"I know. How many times do I have to apologize?"

"Yeah, it's in the past now. I'm just...it's going to take time to get to where we used to be."

Holly bit down on her lip. "You really still want to be my friend?"

She cupped Holly's face, then tucked a curl behind her ear as tears rolled down her cheeks.

"You're stuck with me, whether you want it or not." Bernie threw her arms around Holly, and rested her head on her shoulder. "I knew you wouldn't do it," she mumbled, pulling back to look at Holly.

"Bern."

"No." She sniffed. "In the end, I believed her, because you couldn't fucking pick up a phone to tell me where the hell you were, or if you were okay. It hurts, Holly, knowing that we could've done something to help you during that horrible time."

"I'm sorry, I just didn't want Leo—"

"Fuck other people, Holly. For once in your life, think about yourself. You deserve so much more out of this fucked-up life, but you don't think you do. I love you so fucking much, but I am still so fucking livid with you. What if he married Kate? What then?"

"I know."

"No, you don't. She's a bitch, I hate that fucking cow."

"Oh, c'mon, she's not that bad."

Bernie looked at her. "You know the woman?"

She looked down at the floor. Bernie didn't know she'd been back in Boston all this time. She sighed.

"How do you know her?"

"I was a resident at Downsend."

Bernie glared at her. "You were in Boston all this fucking time and didn't call me? You became a nurse?"

Smiling, she shook her head. "I wasn't in Boston all the time. Just this past year. And I'm not a nurse."

Bernie gasped. "A doctor?"

"Yep. Still working hard toward my goal of becoming a brilliant one." She laughed. "Seattle lost its teaching status and now that I think of it, I wasn't really safe there, either. Our paths, mine and Jake's, would've crossed eventually, because my mom kinda had a thing going with his godfather."

"What?" Bernie chuckled.

"Talk about a small world, right? When the status was gone, we immediately got the only options that still had openings in their programs. P&E was one, and Downsend the other. So I went to Downsend, and one of my friends went to P&E. Everything that could go wrong, went wrong. For five months, I managed not to bump into Jake—serendipitous, in my case—but as fate would have it, it brought us an impossible case that only he would be able to take on. I was so careful, but in the end, I bumped into him."

"You bumped into him?" Bernie's eyes were huge at this revelation.

She nodded.

"Why didn't he tell us?"

"I don't know." She shrugged.

"Why didn't you say something?"

"I couldn't. I was afraid he'd take Jamie away. I didn't want to lose her. You don't want to know what my bank account looks like, so I kept my mouth shut."

"How did he find out?"

"I tried, Bernie. I really did." She shoved her hands under her butt as guilt spread across her face.

"Tried what?"

"To hate him, to stay away. I knew he was engaged, but he was still my weakness."

Bernie closed her eyes. "Tell me you didn't."

"Can't do that. Sorry, but I'm a slut when it comes to Jake Peters."

Against her better judgement, Bernie chuckled. "How long did this 'affair' go on for?"

"About three months, then Rodney found out."

"Who's Rodney?"

"My friend, the one who took the spot at P&E? He sort of became Jake's intern, assisting him on all of his cases. He discovered Jake was Jamie's father during one of our phone conversations." She chuckled at the memory. "He'd always said that Jake could've been Jamie's father, they looked so alike, but I lied and told him her father's name was Steve. Stupid lie, I know."

"Yeah, I noticed the resemblance, too. You're gonna need to buy a gun or something."

Holly laughed. "I know. She's so beautiful. Anyway, it all went wrong from there. I couldn't tell Jake, but Rodney made it unbearable. He told me Jake was only messing with me, and that he was still going to marry Kate. So, I asked Jake to choose— I wasn't the one he chose."

Bernie huffed. "Because he couldn't put his family through that again. It was the only reason he couldn't choose you. You should've told him about Jamie. How did he even find out about her?"

"Destiny...call it what you will. We did this all wrong. Nothing good can come from doing bad things, Bernie."

"No, I don't believe that anything bad will happen with the two of you. Destiny...it was meant to be. You came back just as he was about to make the biggest mistake of his life."

"Yeah, but that didn't mean I had to screw his brains out."

Bernie snorted.

"I really wanted him to choose me, but he didn't and my life was a mess for two months. I thought he didn't want me. Listening to the wedding arrangements, him moving it to Hawaii...it clawed at my heart. That was why I let my mother bring Jamie. I missed her so much, and he was going to Hawaii. He was supposed to be on a flight when my mother arrived at the hospital. I didn't know he'd gotten called in for an emergency."

"I'm glad you've made peace with your mom. I need to apologize to her for being so rude when I saw her earlier."

Holly touched her knee. "She understands, Bernie. She wasn't there for me when my sister died, but I get it now. And I don't blame her at all. It's not easy. Every day is a struggle, especially having to look at your surviving daughter and only being able to see the daughter you lost. Without my mother..." She inhaled deeply. "She's my rock, Bern. Yes, she flew off the handle all those years ago, but from the moment my daughters were born, she's been there. She's helped me through the toughest of times. There were days where I couldn't bear look at Jamie, couldn't stand being around her, and my mother was there. Not only to help me out of the dark hole I'd fallen into, but also to take care of Jamie when my heartache was just too much to handle."

"I'm happy for you. I'm glad you had someone with you. You would have had me if you hadn't been so damn stubborn."

"I know. But these years with my mother...they have been crucial to our relationship. My dad is still an ass—some people will never change. Anyway, Jake must have seen her when I came out of surgery. I was assisting one of his cousins, and Jamie announced her happiness to the entire hospital when she saw me. I guess he put two and two together when he saw she looked nothing like me. I was terrified when he cornered me, wanting to know who she was. So we fought and he backed off. I didn't see confusion in him, just guilt. I wanted to get away from everything, as far as I could, but my mother refused to let me leave. She told me we needed to sort it out, and now here we are."

"Just like that?"

She knew what Bernie was really asking.

"No, I asked him to stay...and he did. He broke it off with Kate, and the horrible truth finally came out."

"HOLLY." ONE OF THE RESIDENTS TAPPED HER ON THE shoulder, snapping her out of her journey down memory lane. "The heart transplant is starting."

She smiled up at him. "Thank you, Lukas."

She got up from the table and mulled over her memories as she walked. She was so glad she and Bernie had managed to patch things up and were friends again, because if truth be told, she hadn't thought Bernie would ever forgive her.

They'd made a pact that if Jake fucked up, then Leo could go screw himself, because Bernie didn't want to lose Holly's friendship again. Not like that. And Holly promised she'd phone her, no matter what.

She took a seat in the gallery to watch the heart transplant, but her mind was still far away.

Bernie's daughter's name was Layla, and she was a little spitfire. She looked like Leo, but everything else about her was all Bernie.

Jamie and Layla became friends almost instantly, just like her sister and Bernice had become friends so long ago. She'd always felt like the outsider, like she was going to lose her sister to Bernie, but then she got pulled in and the three of them had become inseparable.

Bernie just had that way about her with people. She'd

immediately hit it off with Rod, too, and that had put a smile on Holly's face. It made her happy that her two best friends liked each other.

Rod still worked at P&E, but Jake was transferring him to Downsend. He wanted him back under his wing. Jake thought Rodney had what it took to follow in his footsteps. And the world needed more surgeons who were willing to take chances.

Rod had been so ecstatic about the praise Jake had bestowed on him, he'd accepted the transfer without hesitation. She was glad, because Rod really had the potential to be the best.

She blinked back tears, trying to concentrate on the heart transplant taking place, but for some reason her thoughts refused to stay in the present.

She missed everyone too much. They'd had such a fantastic couple of days at the cabin before she left for Zürich. She had been truly happy during that time. It had made coming to Zürich even harder than she'd thought it would be.

The goodbye at the airport had been the hardest. She'd been unable to hold her tears back in front of Jamie, but Jake had promised her she would see them soon.

When she realized there was no way her attention would be on the surgery—the surgeon's droning voice bored her; nothing like the way Jake taught while he was operating—she put her earphones in.

Perhaps she'd be able to concentrate on the German she was trying to learn. It wasn't easy living in a country where you didn't understand the language. Sure, they spoke English here, but it wasn't the same.

Of course, Jake spoke the language fluently. She hated that he could do almost everything with such ease. She was a little jealous, because she had to work her ass off at everything.

And now, she was thousands of miles away from him.

She really missed him, ached for him. They hadn't been

able to keep their hands off each other in the days before she left, sneaking off for quickies whenever someone kept Jamie entertained, and spending their nights after Jamie had gone to bed entangled in each other's arms, their skin slick with sweat, their breath mingling together.

He was insatiable.

She missed everything about him.

But for now, they sated themselves with phone sex and sexy Skype dates, but she wanted him here.

Three more weeks.

She was sure she could hold on until then.

Jake was struggling to get Jamie's passport, what with her out of the country, it was close to impossible to get it, since Jamie wasn't registered in Jake's surname. But he'd said everything would be sorted out in time for their visit, and she couldn't wait to see them both.

She was counting off the days.

The things she was going to do to him when he got here... Her stomach dipped as she thought about their sexting the previous day. She squeezed her thighs together as the video he'd sent her replayed in her mind. He'd started off talking dirty to her, then he'd jerked off, grunting and groaning her name. It had made her want him so badly, and she needed to show him what torture he was putting her through.

So, she sent him a video back, teasing him with the Ben Wa balls she'd bought to experiment with during their phone sex.

A voice note awaited her when she'd woken up this morning.

I can't believe you just did that. The things I'm going to do to you...be warned, you won't be able to sit for days.

It had made her laugh and blush at the same time.

The images his voice ignited in her mind of what he would do to her, did nothing to dampen the lust swirling in her core. But as she went about her day, that lust had morphed into something more; sad desperation.

She needed Jake more than what he needed her.

He had everything back home—his family, his daughter, friends. She had nobody.

She never should have taken this year abroad.

She was miserable without them. Just ten more months, and she would go home. Ten more months.

JAKE

He sighed, running a hand through his hair. "Kate, please."

"I told you before. I'm not going to keep you from seeing Michael, Jake, but she can't be there."

"She's my daughter, Kate."

"He wouldn't understand it."

"He's fucking two years old. Jamie won't understand it, either, but I'm willing to let her meet him and accept him as part of my life. You're being unreasonable."

"I'm unreasonable?" Hollow laugher reached his ears through the phone. "You cheating on me was unreasonable, Jake. If she thinks that you are—"

"Damn it, Kate. I told you I was sorry, but I couldn't lie anymore. I couldn't live that lie anymore. I cheated on you because of who she is, not because of the fact that she's a fucking strawberry blond. I've given you all my reasons, one of them being that I can't live without her. I felt like a dog, but I'm no longer going to feel like one. My daughter stays. If you can't find it in your heart to give her a chance, I'm sorry. But she's not going anywhere just to soothe your insecurities. Can I please pick up Michael tonight?"

"No."

The line went dead, and Jake swore under his breath.

He wanted to scream.

Michael was only two, and Jake was the only father he knew. He'd changed his diapers, sat with him while he was sick, loved him like he was his own. Kate was being a total bitch. And the more he dealt with her, the less shitty he felt about the affair he'd had with Holly while they were still together.

A message popped up and he swiped across the screen, hoping it was Holly.

To his delight, it was a video from her. He had a sneaky feeling what it would be, and decided to wait until he was alone. If the video was anything like the kinky photos she'd sent him— her breasts, covered in lace, bare; her stomach, with her hand splayed out on her abdomen; her ass, clad in briefs or a thong— he was in for something explicitly sexy.

And he was almost certain she was reciprocating after the video he'd sent her of him jacking off. He couldn't help it—her sexy photos had made him hard as a rock.

She'd cussed at him and told him that he shouldn't mess with her like that. Then she'd gotten teary, because the distance between them was too much for her. That had led to full-blown sobbing, and he had struggled to get a handle on the situation.

She missed all of them so much, which made the thought that she was utterly miserable unbearable for him.

So, he did the only thing he could think of. He booked a flight to Zürich, and was basically just counting off the hours now. He'd hoped to see Michael before he left, but Kate was impossible.

Exhaling, he went to his office and took out his phone.

Making sure he wouldn't be disturbed, he hit play on the video Holly sent him, and a goofy grin played on his lips. She was in a naughty mood.

Fuck, she looked hot. Her shoulder-length curls bounced as she moved her head, and for that added touch, she'd applied sultry, smoky makeup. With the barely-there red dress, she looked every inch the seductress.

He took in a shaky breath. Even from thousands of miles away, she managed to knock the breath out of him.

"If you think I forgot about that sexy and oh-so-hot movie you sent me, you're in for a rude awakening, Dr. Peters." Then she winked at him, her hands running up and then down her body, sensual and excruciatingly slow.

His breath caught in his throat as his eyes followed her hand, locking on her fingers as they slipped deftly under her skimpy dress to slip her panties down her legs.

What are you doing, woman?

With a come-hither look, she crawled on hands and knees across the bed and lied down, grinning slyly at the camera. Then slowly, teasingly, slid her legs open.

Jake's breath hitched, nearly making him choke on his spit when Holly's bare pussy graced his vision with all its gloriousness.

With a shaking hand, he stopped the video—it wasn't the time or place to watch it—and put his phone back in his pocket.

Taking a couple of deep breaths, he willed the images from his mind. As he had other consultations to get to, it wouldn't be very professional of him if all he could think of were dirty thoughts while dealing with patients.

He willed the hours away, desperate to reach for the phone that felt like it was burning a hole in his pocket. All he wanted to do was watch the rest of that video.

Finally, the end of the day arrived. He dropped Jamie and

her myriad of belongings off at Amelia's house—she'd be staying there while he was in Zürich, and he had to catch an early flight to New York in the morning—and gave her a million kisses, before heading back home.

Settling himself on his bed, he eagerly took out his phone, scrolled to the video and hit play, continuing where he'd paused it. He watched with lust as Holly's open glory taunted him.

His eyes locked on her fingers once more, watching them slide through her slick folds as she moaned his name.

He felt himself growing hard, and chuckled as Holly's moans grew louder, her breaths coming out in pants

Fuck, he wanted to be there right now, wanted to feast on her. The hours until he saw her needed to go by faster.

You little minx.

"Jake, I'm going to come," she moaned.

"Holly..." he groaned, gripping his erection in his sweaty hand. Her moaning and breathy sighs were tearing him apart.

He'd never wanted anyone as much as he wanted her. The weeks without her were even harder than the five years they'd spent apart.

His eyes widened as she pulled at a string he hadn't noticed before; a Ben Wa ball popped out as she cried her orgasm.

The pace of his strokes increased as he gripped his cock like a vice when she pulled out the next Ben Wa ball, a scream of pleasure tearing through her body.

Quickly, he replayed the scene, and when Holly reached yet another orgasm, Jake was right there with her.

When his breath had evened out, he sent her a voice note. "I can't believe you just did that. But, be warned, because what I plan to do to you will most definitely prevent you from sitting for days."

Laughing, he hit *send*.

TWO

HOLLY

She opened her eyes, but there was no rush to get out of bed. It was her day off.

Stretching lazily, she got out of bed, anyway, and trudged over to the calendar on the wall to cross off another day.

Her heart hurt just thinking about Jamie. She yearned to have her little arms wrapped around her neck.

And she wouldn't mind being wrapped around Jake, either.

Picking up her phone, she sent him a voice note letting him know she was getting ready for their virtual date.

After a quick shower, she threw on a pair of jeans and a sexy, low-cut top. It was a bit much for seven in the morning, but New York was six hours behind.

If it wasn't for their breakfast-*slash*-witching hour virtual date, she would've stayed in bed.

Jake was in New York. He'd had a meeting there, and his flight was only due to leave later that day.

Lucky for her, New York was a city that never slept, and

Jake had promised to go to one of the busy restaurants that stayed open really late, so it would at least feel like a date and not just a normal Skype call.

Satisfied with her appearance, she grabbed her keys and phone. She was slightly disappointed that he hadn't replied yet, and a part of her was worried that he might have fallen asleep, but nevertheless, she headed over to the small coffee shop around the corner from her apartment. Not only was it far too expensive for her taste, it was already packed that early in the morning.

Patiently, she waited for a table, and once she was comfortably seated, dialed his number. When his face popped up almost immediately, she snuck in a breath and tried to calm her beating heart.

His handsomeness always had that effect on her, always sent the butterflies in her stomach into a frenzy. It still hadn't quite sunk in that they weren't having an affair anymore—he was really hers, finally.

From the background behind him, it was evident that the place he was at was just as busy.

"Morning, sweetheart." He smiled at her seductively, which only further stirred the heat in her belly. He was so different with her when Jamie wasn't around—naughty and enticing.

"Morning to you, too."

He chuckled. "How are you?" His tone dripped seduction, and though she let out a giggle, it made her sad. She so desperately wanted him with her. Not on a screen in front of her.

"Good."

"Don't start sulking, Holly. Things would've been different if you'd told me about Jamie sooner."

"Stop that. How many times do I have to apologize? Besides, this is not the time and place, anyway."

"Just saying." He smiled. "You wouldn't have been in

Zürich. In fact, you would've been spread out on this table as my main meal."

She shook her head in exasperation, just as the waitress stopped at her table.

"Give me a sec," she said to Jake. Then in very sloppy German, she gave the waitress her order.

"You're getting better," he remarked with a smile tugging at his luscious lips.

She just wanted to lean in and take a bite. Damn screen!

"So, how is the princess?"

He laughed. "She's staying with Amelia. So both princesses are doing just fine."

It was a struggle to hold back the tears, so she took in a deep breath as her emotions threatened to overwhelm her, then cleared her throat.

"How are the sessions with your mom going?" She needed to change the subject.

Jake scrunched up his nose, which was something he did whenever he didn't want to talk about something.

When would he get over it and forgive Mara?

She was furious at Mara as well, with reason—hated was the more appropriate word—but Jake couldn't stay angry at his mother forever.

It wasn't good for him. They'd been close his entire life, but as things now stood, he hated her guts.

"So, what are you going to eat?" She changed the subject again, because he clearly wasn't going to answer her.

"They don't have pussy pie on the menu."

"Jake! You're a pig. People can hear you."

"What? They don't understand me." He laughed.

"They do on your side."

He merely shrugged.

Holly shook her head. The man had no care in the world for

what people around him thought. He was totally confident with himself.

"You know you shouldn't say things like that to me. All it does is make me feel as if I'm going to explode."

He laughed again. "The feeling is mutual, sweetheart. Just three more weeks."

"Yeah, except, I won't be able to do everything I want to do to you, because little snip will also be here."

"Oh, we'll find a way," he teased.

Her heart tightened. She couldn't wait three more weeks, didn't know how she'd be able to last that long.

"So, how is she doing?"

"I told you, she's great," he said.

"Don't do that."

"What, talk to you?"

"Don't play coy with me. You know very well I mean that thing you do with your eyes and lips and voice when what we're actually talking about is Jamie."

"What? You're nuts." He laughed. "I'm having a normal conversation with you."

"Oh, yeah? Strange then that your mouth is saying one thing, but your body speaks a different language."

"I can't help what my body does, sweetheart."

Shaking her head, she couldn't help but laugh. This was hopeless, so she pretended not to take notice of his seductive ways as they continued their conversation, talking about her hectic week and everything she was learning.

Moira hadn't been kidding when she'd said that Zürich would be a great opportunity for her career. Not many got this opportunity, and one had to be brainy, competent and astute. The language barrier, however, wasn't helping Holly excel.

But she was learning it fast and was able to pick up a few

words here and there from sentences—still nowhere near as proficient as Jake.

Her breakfast was placed in front of her, and she ate it while Jake waited on his food. It was crazy he was going to have breakfast at that hour of the morning, but he always went out of his way for their virtual dates.

Their virtual dates couldn't compare to him being inside her, though.

"Have you removed it yet?"

"Yes, Jake, I removed it." Holly sighed. "I still don't get why it's such a big deal to you. I don't want to get pregnant again."

His face fell.

"Jake, I can't go through that again. It...it broke me."

"Holly, you won't go through that again. My father will be there every step of the way, and so will I. It would be completely different this time. I promise."

She shook her head, but a smile tugged at her lips.

"I'm not having this discussion with you right now."

"Why not?"

"You're greedy. You just found out about your daughter and now you want more."

"Of course I want more." He gave her a searing, lust-filled look, and Holly wished she could climb into the screen.

Blushing, she hissed, "Stop it." She couldn't get riled up in a coffee shop.

Jake chuckled as his food was set in front of him.

They ate and chatted about his father's research. Gus had destroyed everything he'd worked so hard on after Mara's deplorable lie, but had recently started anew.

Even though Mara had basically caused the destruction of decades of work, in the end, Gus had agreed to see a marriage counselor with her. Had she been the one in his position, she would have filed for divorce. Especially once she realized that the person she was married to wasn't at all who she thought they were.

Sometimes, Holly regretted running away. It didn't really make her much better than Mara, did it? But she had to believe that what she did was the right thing at the time.

Sure, she'd struggled as a parent and a student, and perhaps Romy—her heart clenched at the mere thought of the little girl she'd barely had a chance to know—would still be alive if she'd stayed, but up until this point, her experiences had helped her grow. And the way Jamie was connecting with Jake and his family now...well, if she'd stayed, it would have been different.

However, that thought only made her think that she wasn't that dissimilar to Mara, in a way. Hadn't Mara done what she thought was right in the moment, regardless of the horrifying outcome?

But, no. Holly hadn't lied. She hadn't destroyed lives. All she'd done was run away.

She set her fork down. It was time to say goodbye. They'd connect later and settle for some Skype sex, even though she ached for the real thing.

It was hard to tell him, "See you later," while keeping a smile on her face, but when his face vanished from the screen, tears clogged her throat.

She really missed him, all of them.

Calling the waitress over, she asked for the bill, cringing at her bad German.

But instead of bringing her the bill, the waitress launched into a string of rapid German sentences that she did not understand. All she managed to make out was that the bill had already been paid.

She hated it when men attempted to hit on her.

It had happened a few times already, and it was hard to tell them to take a hike due to the language barrier.

"No, please. I have to pay for my own bill."

The waitress shook her head, launching into more incomprehensible German. Eventually, Holly gave up as she was getting nowhere.

"Who paid for me?" she demanded. She was fuming. "Where is he? Show me." Being rude to the waitress was inexcusable as it wasn't her fault. "And...umm...sorry. Thank you."

The waitress smiled and gestured in the direction of where the guy was standing. Holly craned her neck and readied herself to march right on over. She noticed he was wearing a cap, and when he looked up, she squinted—he was smiling.

It took a split second before her legs buckled and her eyes welled with up tears, blurring her vision.

Was she imagining things? It couldn't be him. They'd just spoken. He would have told her he was here, wouldn't he? She wiped the tears from her eyes and looked again.

He was shaking with laughter.

The idiot!

Jake was here, he was really here.

She almost peed herself from excitement, and struggled to squeeze past the ocean of people that were waiting at the counter for their orders.

When she neared him, she heard his laughter, and shrieking ran toward him, colliding hard with his body as she jumped into his arms.

"You asshole," she said, planting her lips on his before he could get a word out.

She couldn't fathom the thought that he was truly here. The entire fucking time, he'd been sitting right here. That was why he'd been overly mischievous and flirtatious with her.

Satisfied, she finally tore her mouth from his, and that's when she noticed every eye in the room was on her. Not that she gave a shit. All that mattered was that Jake was here.

"Good surprise?"

"I don't know if I want to kick you, or rip your clothes off."

He let out a deep, hearty laugh. "Let's get out of here first."

They left and went to her apartment building, walking hand in hand.

"You were there the whole fucking time! Where's Jamie?"

"With Amelia, as I said. I'm still waiting on her passport, it should be ready soon. I promise. But she sent you many hugs, so I'll just give it to you in my own way."

She blushed, but rose onto the tips of her toes and kissed him.

"You have no idea—"

"No, *you* have no idea. I purchased a fucking ticket after your little homemade video."

"Good surprise."

His chuckle sent a thrill up her spine, igniting the heat in her belly.

In the clunky elevator, Jake pushed her up against the wall. His hands skimmed down her body until he reached the front of her jeans where he fiddled with the button, popping it open.

"What are you doing?" she asked against his lips.

His reply was a grin as he unzipped her pants to slip his hand into her panties.

"Jake!"

"There's no one here. Where's your sense of adventure, Holly?"

His finger slid into her, his reward a gasp from between her lips.

"Oh, yeah," he teased, his breath warm against her ear as his fingers stroked that sensitive spot inside her. "You like that?"

Their lips found one another's. Never before had Holly wished the elevator would hurry the fuck up more than she did now.

Breath escaped her in short bursts as he increased the pace, his fingers swirling and circling, stroking every sensitive spot. Her body ached and she bit down on his shoulder to quiet her moans. The moans turned to whimpers as her body tensed against his.

He captured her earlobe between his teeth and suckled on it, his tongue tracing her delicate flesh in circles.

The elevator ground to a halt, and on a groan, Jake's hand slipped out of her jeans.

Holly willed air to enter her lungs in an attempt to calm her heart rate as they waited for the heavy door to squeak open.

Jake snorted. "This building is falling apart. Please let me get you a better fucking place." He nipped at her ear and she wriggled out his grasp with a low shriek.

"No," she said, just as the door opened. As they walked to her apartment, her fingers fumbled with the keys until they reached her door. She was so worked up, her entire body trembled. It took a few tries to get the key in the lock, so she took a deep breath to steady herself and twisted the key, bumping the door hard with her hip to open it.

The apartment was small, with only a tiny oven, a sink, and a kitchen counter in one corner. A bed and television took up most of the rest of the space, and through a door was her bathroom—a shower, sink and a toilet.

As soon as she closed the door, Jake reached out and pulled her to him.

"I did warn you there'd be consequences for what you sent me."

"Hope you keep that promise." She cocked an eyebrow as his lips descended toward hers.

On a groan, he picked her up, and her legs wrapped around his waist. He slammed her back against the wall, his hunger matching her need.

Blood rushed in her ears in a delightful melody she never wanted to fade.

Unwrapping her legs from around his waist, he waited for her feet to touch the floor, then started tugging at her jeans. She toed off her shoes and wriggled her hips, helping him to ease her jeans down her legs.

Her hands moved to his pants, eagerly unbuttoning them until she felt his straining erection against her palm. All this done with their lips still locked.

Hooking his thumbs into her panties, he slipped them down her legs to her feet where she stepped out of them. Watching him from under hooded lids, she followed his every move as his hands traveled back up her legs, massaging her calves, squeezing her thighs, until finally...finally, one found her core. He rubbed her swollen, sensitive flesh, palming his cock with his other hand. Abruptly, he gripped her hips, lifting her up against the wall, then rammed his cock into her opening in one single stroke.

She whimpered as her muscles stretched around him, then let out a groan when he grunted and pumped into her with hard and fast strokes.

He slid a hand between them, finding her sensitive nub as he broke the kiss and rested his forehead against hers. Casting her eyes downward, she watched as every stroke connected them. A loud moan coursed through her, and she pressed her lips into the crook of his neck to stifle the sound.

Fuck, she'd missed this. Missed having him inside her.

"Oh...fuck." That telltale fluttering was growing inside her.

"Your pussy is so fucking wet," he grunted in her ear, making her chuckle through raspy breathes.

"Stop talking and fuck me."

Pulling out, he stepped back and lowered her to the floor until she was flat on her back. Crawling up her body, he peppered kisses on her skin until he caught her lips with his, his hips rocking against her before he rammed into her.

"Oh, fuck, Jake," she panted. "I'm coming!" Holly gasped, screaming as she unraveled.

He stilled above her, grinning down at her. His chest heaved with every heavy breath.

She swatted sluggishly at him with a shaky arm.

"It's not fucking funny. Do you have any idea how worked up I've been? I've gone from fantastic sex to nothing."

"I was only grinning because you being loud is music to my ears. And a big ego boost."

"You don't need an ego boost, mister."

He chuckled. "But I'm still not done, Holly."

"Score!" She giggled.

Jake winked, but his gaze was heated as it roamed over her. Softly, he brushed his lips over hers, and Holly sighed into his mouth, happy that he was here.

JAKE

HE TOOK HER AGAIN IN BED, NOT ONCE SLIPPING OUT OF her, as they fumbled with their remaining clothes. Holly ripped at his shirt, the buttons popping off and scattering across the floor.

Her lips caressed his chest, leaving his skin flushed with goosebumps.

Using her feet, she pushed his jeans clean off as he pounded into her.

Jake in turn tugged her shirt off, pulling her up toward him so he could unhook her bra, and as soon as the straps slipped from her shoulders, he tore the offending piece of fabric from her body, flinging it over his shoulder. His eyes feasted on her breasts for a short moment before he lowered his head and took her nipple into his mouth, pulling her hips closer to his.

He kneaded the flesh on her hips as he rocked into her, savoring the clenching of her muscles. Her chest rose and fell frantically and he moved up to her lips, their panting breaths intermingling.

She rolled him over, the movement causing him to slip out of her wet heat. He groaned at the loss, and then she was on top of him. His hands gripped her thighs as she took his cock in her hand and guided him into her.

She was so tight that he moaned as she lowered herself onto him. He stared at her, naked on top of him, a sight he loved. He brought one hand to her breast and cupped it, pinching her nipple between his thumb and forefinger, his other hand gripping her hip and guiding her movements. He rocked his hips up as she bounced down on him, hitting every nerve end inside her. She gasped and bit down on her lip.

That image, he committed to memory, as his hand left her breast to circle her clit with his thumb. His muscles tightened, and her heat clamped down around him. His orgasm was close —he was certain he would die from the sheer pleasure.

"Fuck," he grunted and sat up, swiftly turning so that their positions changed and she was now flat on her back. Without wasting a second, he turned her over onto her stomach, quickly gripping her hips and pulling her backward until she was on her knees, ass raised up slightly. And then he drove his cock home, running his hands over her ass as he pounded into her.

Holly screamed into a pillow, then turned her head to look at him over her shoulder. "Fuck, Jake. I'm going to come."

"Almost there," he grunted, the sound of skin slapping against skin making a loud clapping noise.

When she screamed out of pleasure, he felt her pussy

contracting against his cock. He moved faster, and on a guttural grunt, released into her, his teeth firmly yet gently biting her shoulder.

"Damn it, pull out. What are you doing?"

But he didn't. He wanted her pregnant, and he wanted to be there for it this time.

"Jake." She let out an exasperated laugh as he slipped out of her.

"Relax." He slapped her ass, chuckling as he collapsed next to her, pulling her closer so her body was flush against his. "Your hormones need time to stabilize. You won't get pregnant right away."

"I swear to you, Jake Peters, if this is another one of your schemes—"

"Oh, shush." He pressed his lips to hers to quiet her protesting, and felt her melt again.

He'd never get enough of her.

THREE

HOLLY

They spent the day fucking, then making love. Not a moment passed where their lips or bodies weren't fused together.

He went down on her in the shower, and she was certain she would blackout as another orgasm rippled through her. She'd lost count of how many times she'd come, but she wasn't about to complain.

He was giving her enough so she could hold out for another three weeks, though she wasn't sure it would tide her over.

When their stomachs growled, they decided to go out to dinner. Holly wore the red dress from her video, and high heels that showed off her shapely legs. She drank him in as he fastened the last button of his white shirt. His black pants clung to his mouthwatering ass, and she looked away when his eyes raked over her.

"Wait, before we go," he growled in her ear as he stepped up to her. "Where are your Ben Wa balls?"

She laughed. "Hell, no."

"C'mon, Holly. Please," he begged.

"We're going out to dinner, Jake."

He shrugged.

"Fine, they're in my drawer. Black box."

With determined strides, he walked over to her closet.

She closed her eyes. She'd never worn the Ben Wa balls out in public, and she wasn't looking forward to it.

As he made his way back to her, he removed them from their box. Pausing to make sure she was watching him, he sucked them into his mouth, his gaze hot on her. She flushed, her stomach doing that dipping thing it did whenever he looked at her like that.

Kneeling in front of her, he lifted her leg over his shoulder. She reached out and held on to his shoulder, the sudden move making her lose her balance.

Trepidation filled her belly.

He pushed her panties to one side, eliciting a moan from between her lips when he slid a finger into her, twisting it, then pumping it in and out for a few short strokes.

"We were going to get food," she bit out on a growl, but Jake merely laughed around the Ben Wa balls that were still in his mouth.

Ball by ball, he pulled them out of his mouth, and the next thing she felt was Jake pushing them into her, one by one.

She took in a sharp breath as her skin broke out in goosebumps. The balls now filled her empty passage, and her muscles clenched around them, her legs trembling.

Jake continued his torture by flicking his tongue across her slick folds, to finally sucking her clit into his heated mouth.

Holly's nipples tightened, and she was desperate to grip his head and hold it there for eternity. But instead, she smacked him on the top of his head.

"Jake!"

He pulled his mouth away with a mischievous grin. "I'm not going to apologize for something that's so fucking hot. Let's go, so we can come back quicker."

She laughed as he removed her leg from his shoulder and stood up. He walked over to the door and wrenched it open, a sulky look on his face. As he walked out, she patted her dress into place, then followed him.

With every step she took, her muscles clenched around the balls. The feeling was indescribable, causing an aching need to pulse through her, but she wouldn't let Jake see how it made her feel. No, tonight she was going to pretend she walked around with them inside her every day.

Turning, she locked the door, making a conscious effort not to rub her thighs together.

Jake smirked at her.

"Do not look at me that way," she said.

"What way?" he asked innocently.

"You know very well in what way. But we do need to eat."

Chuckling, he pulled her into his side.

She felt his lips on her head.

"So, how do you feel?"

"Same as any other day of the week."

"You work with them?"

"Maybe."

"Oh, and who helps you out at night?" The teasing note in his voice was gone.

"Bennie, the tofu in my drawer."

Jake barked with laughter. "Still preferring tofu over meat?"

She couldn't help it and laughed, too. "No, but this time, I don't have a choice as the meat is millions of miles away from me."

"It better stay that way."

"Seriously, Jake? I'm not that type of woman."

"Oh, no?" he teased her again as they got into the elevator. "Then what were you doing with me a few months ago?"

"Oh, shut up. You know that was different."

"I'm just joking. Besides, you weren't the cheating bastard. I was."

Whenever he brought it up, a pit formed in her stomach. She didn't see him in that light, knowing that it couldn't have been easy on him seeing her again right before his wedding.

"Is Kate still giving you shit?"

"We can talk about that later." He dismissed her question by changing the subject to the upcoming medical trial he would be taking part in at the hospital she was working at.

She couldn't wait for it to start, because it meant that not only would she see him every day for at least three weeks, it also meant Jamie would be here, and she missed her little girl fiercely.

It was a struggle trying to listen to a word he said, because she was still thinking about his 'cheating bastard' comment.

Amelia and Bernie had told her how hard it had been on Jake when she'd left all those years ago, and that he'd screwed any woman with strawberry-blond hair in the years after that.

And all because he couldn't get Holly out of his system.

So, it hadn't surprised Amelia when he'd cheated on Kate, or that Holly had had an affair with an engaged man. What had surprised Amelia, was that neither of them had brought up the baby before the day Jake saw Jamie at the hospital.

But she had explained that she'd been scared Jake would take her to court and fight for custody. And Jake hadn't brought it up, because he hadn't wanted to be reminded about what a monster she was.

Apparently, he had tried to remember it in the beginning,

which was why he'd treated her like shit when they started their affair again. But he'd still loved her.

Which was probably why he hated Mara so much now. Mara had made him believe that Holly was a monster, and she had let her because she hadn't stayed.

The fact that Bernice had believed she'd had an abortion, just showed her exactly how manipulative Mara was. She wanted to kick herself for ever believing her.

"Are you listening to what I'm saying?" Jake pulled her back from her thoughts.

"Sorry, no. I'm concentrating on these stupid balls."

He snorted as they stopped in front of a nearby restaurant.

He greeted the hostess in perfect German, after which she led them to a small table in the corner.

They sat down and Jake thanked the hostess.

"Are the balls driving you insane?"

"Not that much, but I'm sure you will drive me insane soon."

"You know me so well."

Not long after they were seated, a waiter came over to take their order.

During that time, Holly clenched her knees together and stifled a moan as the balls shifted inside her.

Jake shot her a grin while he ordered for them. When she reached out a trembling hand for her glass of water and took a sip, Jake's grin grew.

"This was a bad idea," she whispered, as soon as the waiter left. She really wanted to take them out.

"No, it wasn't. It's the best idea I've ever had. Trust me."

Rolling her eyes, she shook her head.

"Are they making you crazy?"

"You are making me crazy. Can we just talk about something else?"

"Fine." He winked at her as he took a sip of water.

The waiter returned with a bread basket.

Both helped themselves to a bread roll, the conversation shifting to their daughter and her school.

Jake told Holly that Jamie had made a ton of friends, and that she was taking both ballet and karate. The poor thing was so busy during the day that she was exhausted when bedtime rolled around.

It made Holly happy that Jamie could finally participate in everything she'd wanted.

According to Jake, she was adjusting well, and loved that everyone took turns watching her and driving her to her activities. It made it easier on Jake because of his erratic work hours. And it filled Holly with joy that Jamie was happy—the joy in her eyes whenever Holly skyped with her confirmed it.

Jake's phone rang, interrupting their easy conversation.

Reaching for the phone in his pocket, he pulled it out and looked at the screen. "Speak of the devil."

It was early afternoon and probably time for school to end.

"Hey, honey bear." Jake laughed at whatever Jamie said. "Okay, don't speak for too long," he said.

Holly glared at him as she took his phone. "Hey, baby girl, how are you doing?"

"Mommy!" Jamie shrieked, so loud, that Holly had to pull the phone away from her ear for a second. "Did Daddy give you all the hugs I sent with him?"

"Yes, he did, and I will send you some back. I miss you so much. Tell me about your day."

Jamie launched into a babbling ramble about her day, talking about her friends and ballet, which she loved the most.

"There is this other sport that Aunty Ams thinks I would do great in. Can I, please, Mommy?"

"Sweetheart, it's too much. I don't think you should—"

"But, Mommy, it looks like so much fun. Daddy said it's fine, but said I should talk to you. Please, please, please."

"Oh, he did, did he?" She glared at Jake, who was shaking with laughter. "Okay, sweetheart, I'll think about it and send you my answer with your father."

The waiter placed their starters in front of them.

"Thank you, Mommy! Love you. I gotta go."

"Love you more." Jamie was gone.

"What other sport does she want to do now?"

"I have no idea."

"She said you do."

"Well, I think she's pushing her luck."

"Jake," she said in what she thought was going to be a scolding tone of voice, but it came out as a needy moan when the balls inside her shifted.

"Fun, isn't it?"

"No, it's really not." She inhaled deeply.

"Liar," he said mischievously. "I'll speak to her. She wants to do everything. I can't keep up."

Ignoring his first comment, she said instead, "You should say no."

"I can't."

"I knew leaving her with you would be the biggest mistake."

"No, it's not. She absolutely loves every second."

"Yeah, I can only imagine. So, can we talk about Kate now?"

"Do we have to?"

"Yes."

"It's just...it's stupid. I should've known she was the bitter type of person. Actually, I need to thank you. If I'd married her, I don't think she'd have ever signed divorce papers."

"You would've married her when you were already thinking about divorcing her?"

"Yeah, just shows you how fucked up I am when it comes to you."

"Gee, thanks."

"I didn't mean it like that. I was just blind to the signs. Kate and I were wrong for each other from the start. You have no idea how happy and thankful I am I missed my flight and got to meet my daughter. I don't even want to think how catastrophic it would've been if I'd gone ahead and married her."

"Yeah. How did you think you were going to get me back again?"

"No idea, but I would've thought of something to make you crazy for me again."

"You would've been married. Do you really think it would've worked?"

"Honestly, no. But I would have continued to have hope."

"So, what's going on with Kate?"

He shook his head. "She doesn't want me to see Michael when Jamie's around."

"What?"

"Don't worry, I set her straight."

"That bitch! He's only two years old, he won't even remember a time without Jamie. It's Jamie who..."

"Relax, babe. I told her that."

Holly sighed. "I'm truly sorry."

"Don't be. I hope no one else ever asks me to choose between Michael and Jamie. It would put me in a spot that I don't want to be in. But Jamie is my flesh and blood, Holly, she'll always come first."

She smiled through the tears in her eyes.

"Don't cry."

"You have no idea how long I've been waiting for those words. When you told Ty that day you had a two-year-old"—she took a deep breath—"I was on the verge of asking you what this boy had that my daughter didn't. But then I saw you and Kate with Michael, and I came to my senses, deciding it was best not to. I should have asked you the next day, but by then my mind had already made up so many shitty stories, that I thought it was best you were not a part of our lives. Jamie's fairytale would've been ruined, and I refused do that to her. Now, whenever I think about it, I can't breathe."

"Hey, I'm not going anywhere. I meant every word I said when you asked me to stay." He blew out a gush of air. "I know who I can live with, but I also know who I can't live without. And believe me, it's not Michael and Kate. I've thought back to how my life was without Jamie, and it gets more difficult every day."

"I know that feeling."

"You are stuck with me, sorry about that."

"I'm not complaining."

By the time their mains and then dessert came, the conversation turned to Mara, but they quickly dropped that subject. She knew Jake wasn't going easy on Mara, because he was waiting for his mother to tell him what he wanted to hear. Holly had no idea what that was, but it had to be important to him, otherwise he would have forgiven her by now.

She tried to focus on their conversation, but the balls were driving her insane. And every time she moved, she let out a moan, which made Jake laugh.

"It's not funny."

"I agree. It's driving me crazy," he whispered.

"Can we please just get the hell out of here?"

"Yeah." He nodded in agreement.

Jake called for the bill, barely able to contain his giddy grin.

The walk back to the apartment was excruciating. She took fast, deep breaths to ease the ache, and clung to Jake's arm as if her life depended on it.

"Holly, it can't be that bad."

"Next time, we'll put these up your ass and see what you think."

"I don't think that's what they are meant for.

She rolled her eyes, but relief surged through her when they reached her building.

The elevator was shared with others, so Jake couldn't even ease her aching need, but he took the keys from her. As they exited the elevator, he lifted her up over his shoulder and walked to her apartment.

Once inside, he set her on her feet and devoured her mouth, but he didn't touch anything else, which was what she wanted.

Instead, he picked her up again, and walked with her to the bed, gently setting her down.

Her legs opened as he settled between them, his mouth never leaving hers.

Excruciatingly slowly, Jake moved down her body, stopping here and there to plant a kiss, or nip at a part of her body, until he reached the apex between her thighs.

Hooking his index finger into her panties, he shifted them to one side, then stroked his thumb over her swollen sex.

His tongue and lips replaced his finger, sucking gently until she bucked against his mouth.

"You like that?"

"Fuck, yes." She tugged at her hair, her chest heaving with every stroke of his mouth.

He slipped her panties down her legs. She yearned to have him inside her, but he had other ideas.

His mouth descended to her throbbing pussy, licking and sucking and nibbling.

She clamped a hand over her mouth, biting into her skin. Her other hand reached back and grabbed a pillow to replace the hand she was biting into to muffle her moans.

"I'm going to come," she whimpered.

"Come for me, baby," he urged, as he pulled on the string of Ben Wa balls.

She groaned and her toes curled, her body shaking as he inched the balls out of her.

"Fuck, Jake!" she screamed, flinging the pillow to the floor. "Oh...fuck." She ground on her teeth, breathing hard.

Her legs tensed around his head and he pulled back, just enough to remove his pants.

Then he slammed into her, eliciting a cry.

He moved slowly, every stroke causing her toes to curl further, if that were even possible.

"No, please, don't do this shit. Don't go slow. Jake, I need you. I need you to fuck me. Hard."

He roared and moved faster and harder, like a well-oiled machine.

She gave herself over to the pleasure, screaming when the orgasm hit her.

Jake covered her mouth with his hand as he continued to pound into her, and all she could think of was that this was so fucking right, so earth-shatteringly amazing.

Tears burned her eyes as her orgasm subsided and her emotions overwhelmed her.

She barely noticed when he flipped her over and pounded into her from behind. But she did feel him still as he came, and then he collapsed on top of her.

The thought of getting pregnant fluttered through her mind, and she closed her eyes, praying that it wouldn't happen. She didn't want another child, not now, not so early in their relationship. They were still just figuring things out.

They fell asleep fast. The day's activities had taken its toll on them.

When she opened her eyes and saw her sleeping hunk next

to her, she knew that it was going to be so hard to say goodbye to him.

She was working an early shift today, which meant she didn't have the time to take him to the airport.

They did, however, have time for a quickie in the shower, and then shared a cab. Its first stop was right in front of the hospital. It was almost six in the morning, and the goodbye had to be a fast one.

She kissed him a few times, and then cried openly.

"Get out before you make me cry, woman," Jake teased. "I'll see you soon."

"Okay," she sniveled. "Love you. And be good."

He chuckled. "Love you more," he whispered in her ear, giving her a hug, then a soft kiss that tingled in the nape of her neck.

She got out and didn't look back.

This felt so fucking wrong, but she'd made her bed and now had to lie in it. Fucking Zürich.

FOUR

JAKE

"That's what truly happened, Jake," Mara said.

"You're wasting my time," he spat and got up.

"Jake," Blair cautioned, holding out a hand.

"No, Blair. This woman lied to me for five years, she lied to my father. And all she can say is sorry? I want an explanation! I lost a child because of her."

"Calm down, Jake."

"That isn't fair!" Mara yelled.

"Not fair?" Jake scoffed. "Don't talk to me about what's not fair." He sighed and looked at his mother. "You keep telling me you're sorry, but you don't mean it. This is the eighth session. We only have two left. Two more sessions, and if you don't tell me what I need to hear by the end of this, you will be removed from my life."

"What do you want me to say?" Mara sobbed. "Just tell me, because I do not know, Jake."

"That's the fucking problem. Right now, I don't want

anything from you. You made my life a miserable hell hole. Time's up." He stormed out of the room and past reception.

Cido, the receptionist, still attempted to make another appointment, but Jake just ran out the practice and down the steps.

He was fuming.

Sorry. That was all his mother had to say? As if that would change anything. But she was only sorry for him. Not once did she mention how sorry she was for what she'd done to Holly. For what she'd done to Jamie. Jamie had spent years without a father. He wouldn't believe a word she said until she owned up to the destruction she'd caused.

He knew she was just saying all the things she was saying to get him to forgive her, but until she accepted that Holly was a part of him, there would be no room for her in his life.

At least there was a positive to look forward to. Jamie's passport had arrived and they were leaving for Zürich in a few days. He'd get to see the love of his life again, and they'd be a family. He had to admit that not having Holly here was hard.

He climbed into his SUV and drove back to Downsend. His phone rang and he answered the call via his car's Bluetooth.

"Jake," he said.

"Hi," Jane greeted. "How is that granddaughter of mine?"

Jake smiled. He knew Jane missed Jamie; none of them had expected Jamie to transition so well, but he figured it was because of the story Holly had told their daughter—the one where they'd all been stuck in a rainbow.

"She's with Amelia. I was at counseling."

"I see, how did the session go?"

"Okay, I guess."

"She still hasn't said the things you want to hear?"

"Nope. She's not feeling any remorse, Jane."

"You can't say that, Jake."

"Yes, I can. She never should have done what she did, and you know what she did was extreme. I mean, why was it so fucking hard for her just to accept it?"

"I know, but it's in the past."

"No. For fuck's sake. Romy is dead because of her lies. If my father had been there, I would've had two little girls running around, not just one."

"I know, but life isn't fair, Jake. But that's not why I called. Have you spoken to Holly today?"

"No, why?"

"Just...phone me if you do."

"Jane?"

The line had gone dead.

He wasn't happy that Jane wanted him to phone her once he'd spoken to Holly.

Horrible scenarios went through his mind as he parked the car at Downsend's designated parking area. As he walked up the stairs, his mind was churning.

What if it was bad? He couldn't imagine a life without her, and...whatever it was, they would deal with it.

Once in his office, he stalked over to his computer and opened his Skype app, desperate to talk to Holly.

Her face popped onto the screen.

"You okay?" It was evident she had been crying.

Her lower lip trembled and she covered her eyes with her hands.

"Holly, baby, speak to me."

She shook her head. "I'll speak to you in an hour. I have to go, Jake."

"No!" he shouted, but it was useless. She'd already disconnected the call.

He tried to phone Jane, but she didn't pick up.

Why would Holly have been crying? He knew it was hard on her to be away from Jamie, but this felt like something else.

What if she'd met someone else? What if she'd cheated on him?

The thought was driving him insane and he was itching to buy a plane ticket and check up on her, but he needed to trust her. Though, if she had cheated on him, he would beat the fuck out of whoever it was. Holly was his.

He sighed. It would fuck him up for sure, but he knew he would forgive her.

A knock sounded on the door before it opened.

Rod appeared. "You coming?" he asked.

Jake frowned.

"The two consultations."

"Oh, yeah. Wait, have you spoken to Holly."

Rod looked at him confused. "Not in the past few days, why?"

"She just hung up on me. She was in tears."

"Hey, what is going through that mind of yours?" Rod asked, concerned.

Jake smiled. There was no reason to bother Rod with his insecurities. "Nothing. I just hate being thousands of miles away from her." He got up and followed Rod to his next consultation.

His phone rang during one of the consultations, and he left Rod to alleviate the patient's fear. Patients were always apprehensive when they saw how young Jake was. But he was fucking good at his job.

His heart raced when he saw it was a video call from Holly.

Guilt riddled her face.

"Holly, please, talk to me."

She was sobbing, the tears streaming down her face, and he ran to the elevator so he could get to his office for some privacy.

His heart felt like it had shattered, certain his worst fear had come true. *Hold it together, Jake.* "Whatever it is, we can work through it, okay? Promise."

He walked out of the elevator that opened out on to reception.

"Work through what, Jake?" Holly hissed.

Aggie gave him a stern look.

"Just hold on, I'm almost in my office," he said, opening the door, and then closing it behind him as he stepped inside.

He switched the call from his phone over to his laptop and found her glaring at him.

"I don't know. But you are scaring the fuck out of me. What is it?"

She shook her head, her eyes not making contact with the camera.

"You met someone?"

Her head snapped up. "Oh, my word, is that what you are thinking?"

"Then what?" A relieved chuckle blew out of him.

"I'm not a cheater, Jake."

He cocked an eyebrow.

"Jake, let's get a perspective on this. I had an affair with you, but I cheated on no one as I was with no one. You, on the other hand, cheated, because you were with someone else. "

"Okay. I get it. Relax, will you? What's with you today?"

"I'm pregnant, that's what's wrong!" She covered her face with her hands, and her shoulders were shaking.

He froze as the word washed over him. "What?"

"You fucking asshole, I told you to pull out, but you were all 'Don't worry, it's going to take time, your hormones need to stabilize, Holly,'" she mimicked.

"You're pregnant!" He grinned.

"It's not funny. I had a fucking bad experience—a trip to hell and back—the first time and I'm shit scared."

"Baby, calm down. It's not the end of the world, sweetheart. You're not alone this time around. I'm over the moon."

"Well, I'm not. You have absolutely no clue!" She groaned. "I can't speak to you when you're like this."

His screen went blank, but he let out a gleeful laugh, nonetheless. He jumped up and hollered with joy.

His door opened and Aggie rushed in, with Sue hot on her heels.

He was still so crazy ecstatic, the jumping up and down was still in full swing.

"Jake?" Aggie had a huge grin on her face.

"She's pregnant, Aggs!"

Her eyes grew wide and she shrieked, "You're going to be a daddy again."

"Yes, and nothing, nothing is going to mess it up this time."

"Congratulations," Sue offered, as Aggie wrapped her motherly arms around his waist.

"I can't say when last I saw you this happy Jake, truly happy."

"Oh, I am. And nobody, not even my mother, is going to spoil this for me. I need to phone Amelia."

His sister was overjoyed with the news, and so was his father. Their lives would be filled by little feet and baby cream.

They peppered him with questions, wanting to know why Holly wasn't excited. When he explained that she was scared, Gus assured him that he would be there to monitor the pregnancy, and help every step of the way if need be, and that her experience this time would be a heck of a lot different to what she'd previously gone through.

Later that night, Holly phoned again. Jake was having a hard time containing his joy, but he tamped it down as he could see she wasn't happy.

The tiredness in her voice was something he picked up on

right away during her conversation with Jamie. He was preparing dinner, but his ears were alert. When Jamie said goodnight, he rushed over to the laptop.

"Are you feeling better?"

"No, I feel sick."

"Holly, my father is sending you the first dose of his formula. He also gave me some other meds to give you. It will help. I promise, you are not alone in this."

"Shh!" she hissed.

"Calm down, Jamie isn't near."

She shook her head. "I'll speak to you later."

Yet again, she was gone. She was really angry with him but he, on the other hand, couldn't be happier.

He couldn't believe his luck. He'd truly thought it would take months to get her pregnant, but luck was on his side.

Holly was his meant-to-be.

HOLLY

She was livid with Jake. And not because of what happened.

Spreading her legs and constantly teasing him, begging him to fuck her, had led to her getting pregnant—that was a no-brainer.

All because she was addicted to sex with Jake.

What she was livid about, was the fact that he'd had the audacity to ask her if she'd met someone else.

The man had to have been born under a fucking rock to ask her that. He was one of the smartest men she knew, but so fucking stupid at the same time. Why on earth would she screw someone else when she had him?

It had pissed her off.

She wasn't like that. Obviously, indulging in an affair with him when he'd been engaged to Kate had warped his view of her. She should have known it would happen.

But she would never cheat on Jake.

He was her everything, and if either of them were to doubt the other, it should be her.

He was the sex maniac, not her. He just pulled her into his addiction.

But she'd have to put that thought aside until Jake and Jamie visited. Right now, she needed to concentrate on the coronary bypass surgery she was assisting on. Bypass surgeries were becoming increasingly easy. Almost like breathing, but she still wasn't allowed to do one on her own.

Dr. Somers had taught her so much, and his reputation was world-renowned. And because of her association with Dr. Somers, Dr. Ahlgren gave Holly many opportunities. Ahlgren was the head of cardiology here, in her early forties, and an attractive woman with blond hair and piercing blue eyes.

It seemed like all the women here were blond and blue-eyed, each one sexier than the other, which worried Holly. She knew the neurology residents were excited to learn from Jake, but she also knew that they were all going to throw themselves at him—and honestly, he could have his pick.

She sighed inwardly. Her insecurities were going to drive her insane.

When surgery was over, she felt drained. She trudged off to the cafeteria to the sound of her stomach churning, feeling somewhat dizzy. Getting food into her body was a necessity.

Nobody here knew that she and Jake were in a relationship. Calling Jake her boyfriend didn't sound or feel right. What they had was so much more than what that word implied.

Husband wasn't right, either. For one, they weren't married, and two, they'd never discussed it. She doubted that he would ask her so soon after breaking off his engagement to Kate, anyway. But she knew he was special to her, as she was to him—something he told her every time they spoke.

And then, he had to go and ask her if she'd met someone.

It had pissed her off more than it should have. But she'd blame it on the hormones.

She was just over four weeks pregnant.

With Jamie and Romy, she'd only found out she was pregnant when she was seven weeks along. But this time, because she was feeling exactly the same as she had with the twins—horribly sick—she'd wasted no time in taking a test. It had turned out to be positive.

Fucking Jake.

He was so fucking happy, though.

But he had no idea what she'd gone through with her first pregnancy. What if Gus wasn't able to help her this time?

Her phone rang, snapping her out of her thoughts. It was Gus—almost as if he'd known she'd been thinking about him.

"Hi," she said.

"Congratulations are in order, I hear," Gus gushed. He sounded just as over the moon about it as Jake had.

"Please, don't."

"Too soon?"

"Way too soon."

"I'm sorry you're not feeling the same way we are. We're all super excited and—"

She barked out a woeful laugh, cutting him off. All she felt like doing was crying.

"You okay?"

"Not really. I'm scared shitless."

"Jake told me as much. Don't worry, Holly. I'm sending you some medications with Jake. You can try them out and see if they make you feel better. They're all safe and good for the baby. And you."

"Yeah, let's just hope the baby doesn't multiply like the last time."

"However many there are, we'll all be with you every step of the way. You are not going to do this alone. I promise. Even if I have to work day and night on this formula, you will be okay, Holly."

"Thank you, Gus," she said in a teary voice.

"So, my granddaughter really wants this dollhouse and I said I'll try to make her one."

Holly laughed. "You're turning her into a spoiled brat."

"She's my first, Holly. Let me, please."

"Yeah, sure. Make her the biggest dollhouse a kid could ever dream of. I know you Peterses, nothing is too damn much."

He laughed. "I'm glad you're starting to make peace with that. Now, stop worrying. We are all here for you, Holly."

"Thank you, Gus."

Gus and her father were complete opposites. Where Gus was a naturally happy man, Charles was naturally mean.

One thing she was not looking forward to was what her father was going to say when he discovered she was pregnant again.

Jake had tried. Heaven knew he'd tried to thank Charles Scallanger for being there when he hadn't been, as well as pay him back, but all her father had done was tear up his check and tell him that nothing he did would ever bring Romy back.

It'd hit Jake harder than she thought it would, because it was true.

Charles did not believe that Mara had been behind it, and the more Jake tried to explain, the meaner Charles became.

But he'd kept his cool, not losing his temper, until Charles started fighting with Holly about her dumb decisions; wanting to become a doctor, and for letting Jake into Jamie's life. Then, he'd threatened Jake with a lawsuit, one that would prevent Jake from ever seeing Jamie again.

And Jake had snapped.

She shook that Jake out of her head.

You could trample all over him as much as you wanted, and he'd just sit back and take it, would even go out of his way to prove that he meant everything he said, but if you trampled on his child, or threatened her in any way, you would come off second best.

They settled out of court—it hadn't been a strong case to begin with—but Jake had seen it as a way to pay her father every cent he should've paid from the beginning.

She'd really thought her father would somehow manage to change Jake's mind about him being with her as it was way too much drama, but it had only brought them closer together in the end.

And then, she'd left for Zürich.

And now, well...now she was pregnant, and hormonal, and her insecurities were nagging at her. She was grateful that Jake was back in her life, where he always should have been, but she still didn't trust him fully. Especially not when he had a bevy of beauties to choose from.

Her insecurities stemmed from their affair, from the fact that Jake had cheated on a woman he'd committed to. She knew that. And she also knew that the coming months wouldn't be easy—they'd be working long hours, the pregnancy would take its toll on her, if not try to kill her, and the women would be throwing themselves at him...

No, she had to stop these crazy thoughts.

This was what Jake had meant that night in the car. She would make up her mind, because of her insecurities, and the result would more than likely not be the right choice.

Giving someone the benefit of the doubt was by no means an easy thing to do, but deep down she knew Jake wouldn't do to her what he'd done to Kate.

Jake had much more to lose than she did—Jamie, Holly, and the new baby.

She had to believe that he wouldn't do anything to screw it up.

FIVE

HOLLY

SHE WIPED HER MOUTH AND SAT BACK DOWN ON THE floor. Morning sickness—freaking all-day sickness in her case—was a bitch.

Her checkup with her new gynecologist, Bianca, wasn't for another week, and luckily Jake would be present to help her voice all their concerns about the pregnancy.

They were due to arrive tonight. As she was working, she would only get to see them after she knocked off.

Jake had rented a house instead of an apartment for the duration of his and Jamie's stay, and Holly couldn't wait to soak in a bath again.

She should have taken Jake up on his offer to get her a better apartment, then she wouldn't have been suffering the way she was every morning. The tiny apartment made her claustrophobic, but she didn't want to take his money. Mara thought she was a gold digger, and she wasn't going to give her the chance to prove that theory.

She loved Jake for who he was, not for what he had. She didn't care about his money. Even if he lost every single penny, she would still love him. No amount of money would ever make her stop loving that man.

Pulling herself together, she hauled herself up off the floor, washed her face, and returned to the OR. She was up in the gallery, watching doctors perform a heart transplant, among other things.

The patient had cancer, which had caused the deterioration of most of her organs, and that meant that multiple transplants were taking place.

There had been cases like hers before, but not as severe.

"You okay?" Lukas asked. He was a head taller than her, with pale blond hair and blue eyes. He was always helping her understand the medical terminology. Eve, another resident, teased her, saying that Lukas was interested in more than just friendship. But he knew she was not available. And she knew that the moment he saw she was with Jake, he would back off. Nobody was a match for Jake.

Nodding, she took out her notebook to write down notes. The surgery was long, but with the technology assisting the doctors in this hospital, it was more thorough and more successful than it would have been at any other hospital she'd worked at.

This was the future.

Eventually, a doctor's job would be replaced by machines, but for now, she wanted to learn as much as she could.

Technology could fail, too, and then it would fall back on humans to treat people.

After hours and hours of surgery, where the patient was monitored in order to make sure that everything was working as it should, she was wheeled off to ICU. There, she'd receive the care and treatment she needed.

Holly looked down at her watch, taking steadying breaths, because she was still a tad dizzy. A smile spread across her face, though, because only five hours remained before she got to see the two people she loved most in her life.

All residents were called into one of the lecture halls—it reminded her so much of home. This was where the doctors relived a case that unfortunately didn't end up a success.

That was where she learned the most, and even though she still struggled with certain medical terms, it was an immense help.

Once everyone was settled into seats, the chief of surgery, one of the doctors who part-owned the hospital, got up.

"Thank you all so much for being here, I really appreciate it," he said, welcoming everyone. He was very polite, and she knew he was one of the best—his status preceded him. Jake had told her a number of things about him.

"I'm so delighted to be able to start with this new journey. We have a project, presented to us from a brilliant neurologist living in the USA, who will be present here from time to time in the upcoming years."

Holly frowned. It sounded as if he was about to introduce Jake. If he'd arrived early and not told her, she would kill him

The audience applauded.

"Dr. Peters," he said, taking a step back from the podium to make way for Jake who was walking up onto the stage wearing a white coat.

Holly moved to the edge of her seat as Jake began speaking in German.

He was here, meaning Jamie...she jumped up, grabbed her things, and ran out of the building.

Her little girl was finally here.

She made her way to the childcare facility and caught a glance of Jamie's black hair as she walked past the window.

She was here, she was here! Finally.

Holly opened the door, and Jamie spotted her immediately.

"Mommy!" Jamie ran straight at her. Holly crouched down so Jamie could run into her open arms.

"I missed you so much." She breathed Jamie's scent in and planted kisses all over her face.

Jamie cackled. "I missed you more."

"Not possible. I missed you this much." Holly spread her arms wide to show her how much she'd missed her.

Jamie babbled in that fast way only six-year-olds could, telling her everything about their flight—they'd flown first class —and about the house. Then she told Holly that the people talked funny here, but that she knew some words as Daddy had taught her.

It didn't surprise Holly that Jake was already teaching her German, and she wouldn't be surprised if it was one of Jamie's extra lessons.

They probably spoke it in the evenings.

A picture formed in her head of Jake teaching Jamie German before bedtime, of them laughing as Jamie said words over and over, sometimes getting them right on the first go, and other times totally wrong. Her heart clenched from home-sickness.

She'd hardly seen Jamie before leaving for Zürich. It was damn hard not being able to see her daughter every day.

She stayed with Jamie, making art and laughing over Jamie's silliness, until her beeper went off.

Groaning, she said, "Mommy has to go work, sweetheart, but I will see you later, promise."

"Okay, Mommy. Love you." Jamie wrapped her arms around Holly's neck and squeezed.

"I love you so much."

Jamie giggled.

Holly got up and walked to the door, pausing to look back at her daughter. She didn't want to leave her, but she had to go make her rounds with the rest of the residents.

At least her shift ended in two hours, and then she could go home to the man she loved and the daughter she adored. The two people she'd missed terribly.

Her life was finally perfect again, even if it was only for the next three weeks.

───────

THE ROUNDS TOOK ABOUT AN HOUR, AND HER QUEASINESS made her head to the cafeteria. She had to snack the whole day to keep the sickness at bay.

When she reached the cafeteria, her eyes did a scan, hoping to find Jake, but when she didn't see either him or Anna Belikof, one of the doctors who was collaborating with Jake on the project, she assumed they were still discussing some of the details.

She grabbed a salad and took a seat next to Lukas.

The group at the table were teasing Eva and Petra, who were both gorgeous girls. One was tall and slim, with dark hair and almost purple colored eyes, the other had light blond hair, and reminded her of Julia, not her personality but her pettiness.

As far as the German language went, she only understood some of what was being said. But on hearing Jake's name, she sighed. That sigh was followed by another when she made out the word *wet*.

Oh, boy. Just her luck.

"Where did you run off to?"

Smiling, she replied with, "To see one of the most amazing people in my life."

Lukas laughed. "You really do love your job." He misinterpreted her reply, obviously thinking she was talking about a patient.

"I'm going to get a cup of coffee."

"You sure it's good for the baby?"

"Ha-ha. It's making me tired, and why I have to drink coffee," she said in German.

"It's a baby, not an *it*," Eva said in German.

"It feels like an *it*."

Leaving them chuckling, she headed to the coffee urn.

From the corner of her eye, she saw someone heading her way, but she didn't look up.

But then she had to turn to pour her milk.

"Thank you. You are not allowed to drink coffee," Jake said from beside her, taking the cup out of her hand.

"I'm allowed to have coffee, and if you don't give me that cup, I swear, there will be no sex tonight."

"I'll take that chance. No coffee. Here, have some juice, instead." Winking, he walked away with her cup of coffee, while she barely managed to catch the juice box he'd tossed at her.

"Juice, seriously?"

The group at her table were silent when she walked back to them and took her seat. Her eyes followed Jake as he walked right on out of the cafeteria. Giving herself a mental shake, she turned back to see everyone looking at her.

"You know him?"

"Who, Macaroon?" she teased.

"You lucky fish! You worked with him?"

Holly laughed. "Yeah, something like that."

Eva squinted. "What are you not telling us, Yankee?"

"I don't know how to say it in German," Holly teased as she got up. Pulling the wrapper off of the straw, she jabbed it into the juice box and left them staring after her.

JAKE

Being this close to Holly, working with her again, felt like home.

And tonight, he'd have her next to him in bed, and depending on how Jamie slept, preferably naked.

He sipped the coffee and grimaced. It tasted nothing like the coffee Holly used to make at Downsend. This was horseshit. He placed the cup on one of the food trolleys outside a patient's room, his nose wrinkling in distaste, then headed to his meeting with the residents who had been assigned to the program.

Rodney would be perfect for the program, but it had already been a bitch to get him transferred to Downsend. There was no way he'd get it signed off to bring Rod to Zürich.

The women ogled him, especially Anna, who seemed to be undressing him with her eyes. He hated that they were looking at him in that way. It would take weeks for them to settle down and get used to him, if he was lucky.

But he didn't even spare them more than a glance. The only woman he cared about was Holly, and he was beyond ecstatic that he'd be here for her first checkup.

He remembered the first time he saw Jamie and on the ultrasound screen, back when they'd thought there was only one baby. He had been so emotional that day, and hadn't wanted to leave Holly.

But this time, it would be different, because she wasn't going anywhere. She would be close to him and he could touch her belly whenever he wanted to, and speak to his baby whenever he felt like it.

When it was time to go home, he went to the childcare facility to get Jamie. He found her sleeping on the floor and smiled. The flight had taken a lot out of both of them.

Luckily, Jamie wouldn't have to spend her days at the daycare as he'd hired a tutor through a well-respected agency, and the tutor, Victoria, was starting tomorrow. She'd not only tutor Jamie, but also watch her while he and Holly were at work.

Bending, he gently picked up his sleeping daughter from the floor, deciding to wait for Holly at reception.

"Is she yours?" Anna asked when she walked past him.

"She is. And she's extremely heavy when she's asleep."

"Then put her down."

"And wake up this sleeping beauty? Hell, no."

She laughed. "Who is her mother?"

He knew this question would come. The corner of his lips twitched. "You wouldn't believe me if I told you."

"Do I know her?"

"Perhaps."

There was a crash in one of the nearby rooms, and a resident he had seen talking to Holly earlier rushed into the room.

"Holly!" the resident shouted, and Jake's lungs tightened.

Turning, he quickly asked one of the nurses to take Jamie and ran into the room behind Anna, who was already helping Holly—she was splayed on the floor.

He bent down.

"It's okay, Jake, you can go," Anna said, but he glared at her.

"No, don't worry. I've got this," he said, placing his hands gently on Holly's neck, feeling for injuries.

"She's pregnant," one of the residents added.

Jake glared at him. "Get Bianca here, now," he ordered, and Anna passed it on. It seemed like he wasn't going to get rid of her.

"C'mon sweetheart, open your eyes," he whispered, but Anna still heard it.

"You know her?"

"Yes." He looked up as he felt Holly's pulse. It was steady. "She's carrying my child."

Anna's eyes widened, and then she frowned at him.

Just then, Holly groaned and her eyes fluttered open.

"Déjà vu," he said, and she smiled.

"Shit, where is Jamie?"

"Calm down, she's safe. Just stay still. Bianca's on her way."

She tried to look around her, but it was futile, so she closed her eyes. "This is so embarrassing."

"C'mon, it's not that—"

Thwack! She slapped him. "And it's all your fault. I told you I didn't want to get pregnant again, Jake."

"I'm sorry, baby." The corners of his lips pulled up.

"It's not funny," she cried out, tears welling in her eyes.

"We'll sort it out."

Bianca finally ran into the room. "Oh, Holly. Okay, all of you, please get out," she ordered and the room emptied.

A nurse rushed in wheeling an ultrasound machine.

Holly still lay on the floor as Bianca put the sonar over her belly, and a firm and fast heartbeat filled the room.

Jake touched her stomach gently. "See, the baby is fine. Safe in Mommy's womb."

"Shut up," she hissed. "I'm still raving mad at you."

"They always blame the men," Bianca teased.

Holly smiled weakly.

"You can help her up now," Bianca said, seemingly satisfied for the time being.

Jake scooped Holly into his arms and set her gently on the bed.

Bianca did a thorough check on her. Her blood pressure was high, but Holly would feel better once she had Gus' shake in her. Stepping away when she was done, the doctor looked at her. "Call me if you need anything, or if this happens again."

"Thank you," Jake said as he helped Holly off the bed. They walked out of the room, his hand on her lower back.

"That is so embarrassing," she repeated through clenched teeth.

"How many times has that happened, Holly?"

"Same as the first time." Worry laced her words. "Jake, it feels worse now."

"Don't worry. We'll deal with it."

When they reached reception, Holly spotted Jamie sleeping across two chairs and rushed over.

"Stay here, I'll bring the car around," Jake said, his hand still on her back.

"Okay," she replied, her eyes never leaving Jamie.

SIX

HOLLY

SHE WAS QUIET ON THE DRIVE OVER TO HER APARTMENT, where she picked up some clothes while Jake waited in the Audi he'd rented for the duration of his time here.

Her fainting episode had not only embarrassed her, but worried her, too. That was exactly how her first pregnancy had started out. But she felt safe with Jake, and they could phone Gus to ease her worries.

Just then, her phone rang and her father's name flashed across the screen. He must have found out she was pregnant, as he hadn't phoned once since she'd been in Zürich. With one swipe of the finger, she rejected the call and set her phone to silent. That way, Jake wouldn't answer it if he phoned again.

She wasn't in the mood for their arguing.

She grabbed the bag she'd packed and left her apartment, locking the door behind her as she left.

Inside the elevator, fatigue overwhelmed her and she closed her eyes.

Why hadn't Jake listened to her when she'd told him she didn't want to fall pregnant again? But she couldn't place all the blame on him. She'd been the one who had agreed to take out her IUD. Jake was adamant all would be well, and had told her so after she'd voiced her concerns. But what if it wasn't? She wouldn't be able to handle it if she had to lose another child.

Taking in a deep breath, she tried not to think about it—she couldn't bear to think about it. Hurriedly, she dashed her tears away as the elevator doors opened.

The feeling of dread over this pregnancy hovered over her, and she prayed that it was just her brain making her think of a worst-case scenario.

Jake got out of the car as she stepped out of the building and immediately relieved her of her bag, putting it in the trunk of the car while she got into the passenger seat.

Jamie's soft snores came from the backseat, and then Jake was in the car and they were driving away.

She hadn't thought of getting a car while she was here. Her apartment was close to the bus station and within walking distance from stores and restaurants. Plus, she didn't think she'd be able to get used to driving on the wrong side of the road, anyway. But now that she was pregnant and fainting, she figured she'd have to at least think about using Uber, or getting someone to drive her to the hospital and back. She would talk to Jake about it.

What was her life going to be like when Jake and Jamie went back home?

She stared at the buildings flashing by, her mind working overtime as she contemplated the next eight months. If her pregnancy even got that far this time.

At the traffic light, Jake touched her knee.

Jumping in her seat, she turned her head to look at him.

"Sorry. Why are you so quiet?"

"It's nothing. Just worried."

"I'm worried, too, Holly. But you are not alone in this."

"I know. Sometimes, it just feels like you're not listening to me, Jake." Annoyance crept into her tone.

"I really didn't think you would get pregnant so soon. I'm sorry, I should've been more careful."

She nodded and tried to smile, but what she was feeling on the inside did not match the expression on her face. The unsureness of their relationship still gnawed at her, considering they'd gone from one extreme to another.

And still, it hadn't sunk in that he was hers.

For some reason, she still felt like she had to convince him to be with them, even though he was doing everything in his power to show her that he was one hundred percent invested in their relationship.

Why had she come to Zürich? It didn't matter how great it was for her career. Zürich was a mistake. She should have stayed in Boston so they could work on their relationship like a normal couple.

He finally turned off into a street lined with beautiful houses, one after the other.

"We're staying here?" she asked, her eyes wide.

"Yes." He chuckled. "I'm a spoiled brat, Holly. Our daughter is as well."

Playfully, she swatted his chest with the back of her hand. "It's your fault for giving her everything she wants."

"Ow!" He rubbed his chest. "I can't help the fact that I can't say no to the women in my life."

She shook her head, smiling.

It was so easy for him to lighten the mood.

They pulled into a driveway, where a magnificent gate greeted them, and with the push of a button on a remote attached to a bunch keys Jake held in his hand, the gates opened.

The sight that greeted her was glorious. Leaning forward, totally captivated, her eyes took in the Venetian-style house. The grandeur elicited a gasp from between her lips and she looked at Jake.

He was grinning at her. "Don't look at me like that," he said.

"Like what?"

"Like it's too much. Nothing is too much. It's just perfect."

"Are we housing six other couples?"

His smile grew bigger. "No," he said sheepishly.

"We're only three people, Jake. This is too much. Don't get me wrong, it's the stuff of dreams, but it's still too damn much."

"I disagree, it's just perfect. Think of it like it's an adventure. We can chase each other around and never get bored. Can you imagine all the fun we'll have?"

She burst out laughing, but stopped when Jamie stirred in the backseat. "Sorry, sweetheart," she murmured, reaching behind her to stroke Jamie's back.

Jake pulled into one of the garages and parked. He got out first so he could open up the house.

Holly stayed with Jamie. She'd gotten so heavy that Holly struggled to pick up her dead weight.

Jake returned a few seconds later and took Jamie out of the car.

She loved how gentle he was with her.

Getting out herself, she followed him into the house, and gaped when she stepped into the large, splendid kitchen.

The double gas stove and large fridge, and the huge kitchen island and gleaming countertops were all meant for a big family, not just three people.

Jake continued up the stairs, as Holly put down her bag and walked down the hallway that led to a living room.

The wooden floors shone, and the floor-to-ceiling windows complemented the room to perfection.

White linen covered the furniture, and she wandered around the room, pulling them off to reveal gorgeous leather couches.

A huge TV was mounted against the wall, not that she had any time to watch TV, or understand anything, since most of it was in German, but she was sure that Jake had brought Jamie's collection of Walt Disney DVDs.

Black-and-white photos of buildings and cities adorned the walls. She couldn't believe this was going to be home for the next three weeks.

Footsteps rushed down the stairs.

"Holly?"

"In here," she called, as she turned on the floor lamp next to her, bathing the room in a soft glow of light.

"So, what do you think?"

"I don't even want to know what the rooms look like," she said as he wrapped his arms around her from behind. "It sure is beautiful."

"I knew you would love it." He kissed the top of her head and touched her stomach. She wasn't even showing yet.

He was stroking her stomach so softly that it made her laugh.

"What?" he asked.

"You're going to be one of those fathers who can't stop talking to the belly, aren't you?" She looked back at him.

"If you hadn't run away, you would've known it." He kissed the top of her nose.

"Seriously?"

"Just kidding." He kissed her lips. "I don't want to upset you. That was really a stupid joke. Sorry."

"You're forgiven," she teased.

"Go take a bath, Jamie is out like a light. She wouldn't wake up even if a bomb dropped next to her. I'm going to go get us some takeout, and pick up some juice at the store. The agency will send Jamie's tutor and a housekeeper over tomorrow. So we'll return to a house filled with groceries."

"Great. Thank you."

As soon as Jake left, she made her way upstairs.

Jamie's room looked like your typical children's room, but without her toys.

Tiptoeing over to the bed, she tucked her in, then kissed her on the head. She left on silent feet once more, and entered the room next to Jamie's. It was the only one with a light on.

A king-size bed welcomed her. The goose feather comforter lay puffed up on the bed, with eight different sized pillows.

Her eyes roamed the room, landing on both her suitcase and Jake's black one.

Three weeks.

Three amazing weeks.

They'd never lived together, apart from that time they'd stayed at the beach house before his residency started. But it didn't count, because Leo and Bernie had stayed with them.

She was excited and yet super terrified, but at least she would learn what his mannerisms were like.

Opening a door, she came upon an empty walk-in closet. Taking a deep breath, she walked through the closet and into the bathroom of her dreams. A claw-footed, oval tub with shiny nozzles occupied one side of the room.

Jamie was going to love it, that was, if her life hadn't been filled with this kind of luxury already.

Without further delay, she turned the taps on and went back to her luggage to get her bubble bath and other essentials.

Back in the bathroom, she poured the bubble bath into the water and began to undress while waiting for the bath to fill.

She caught sight of her reflection in the huge mirror. Her boobs were sensitive and slightly larger, and her belly sported a slight bulge. Twins popped into her head again and she closed her eyes.

Maybe it was only one.

She could only hope.

Tying her hair into a messy bun on top of her head, she inspected her skin in the mirror. She really didn't like being pregnant, and the minute she thought that, she felt bad.

Amelia would give anything to be where she was right now.

With the bath filled, she turned off the taps and climbed in, sinking down into the warm water.

It was the first time she'd been in a bathtub since she'd arrived in Zürich. She'd missed it.

She cleared her mind and pretended that she didn't hear the buzzing of her phone.

But she looked at it, thinking it might be Jake.

If only it was Jake's name that flashed on the screen.

She was still far from ready to speak to Charles Scallanger.

JAKE

JAKE ORDERED THREE PIZZAS FROM THE ITALIAN restaurant around the corner—one with ham and pineapple for Jamie.

He let out a happy sigh. His life was perfect now, compared to how it had been a few months ago.

It could've gone so wrong if that emergency hadn't made him miss his flight. It had changed everything, preventing him from making the biggest mistake of his life. Now he was over the moon. He had his daughter, he had the love of his life, and they were going to have another baby.

With that thought in mind, he pulled out his phone and called his father.

"Jake, everything okay?" he asked.

"Yes, sorry, what time is it?"

"It's around one in the afternoon. How is Jamie?"

"She's sleeping, dead tired."

"And Holly?"

"The reason I'm phoning. She fainted today."

His father was silent. "Have you given her the shake and the vitamins?"

"Not yet, it was in my luggage. I'll give it to her tonight. You're sure it's safe?"

"I wouldn't give it to her if I wasn't."

"I know, I'm just worried about her."

"We all are, Jake. You are not alone in this."

"I know, and I'm grateful for that."

"Where are you now?"

"Quickly ran out to buy something to eat."

"What did Holly think about the house?"

Jake laughed. "Too much."

Gus chuckled. "Send that beautiful granddaughter of mine many hugs and kisses. Tell her that I miss her terribly."

"Yeah, yeah. I'll tell her. Speak to you later."

"I know you are worried, son. But you can call me any time of the day or night."

"I know, Dad. I'm just concerned about what's going to happen when I go back to the States."

"We'll figure it out."

"Okay."

They said their goodbyes just as his order was placed in

front of him. He thanked the woman, paid and headed back to the car.

His stomach grumbled when the scent of the pizza hit his nose. He was starving.

When he arrived back at the house, it was eerily quiet. He set the pizza on the kitchen counter, took one slice, devoured it, and went upstairs in search of Holly—and found her in the bath with her eyes closed.

He noticed she'd closed the toilet's lid so she could rest her phone on it. He also noticed that she had five missed calls.

Curious, he walked over and picked up the phone, then pressed the button on the side so he could see the notifications. Charles' name popped up.

He looked over at Holly. She was ignoring her father and that was the last thing he wanted. Charles had been there for her —however much of an asshole he was—when Jake hadn't been.

He'd tried to make peace with Charles, attempted and failed to tell him his side of the story, even though it wouldn't have changed the outcome of the bad situation.

Exactly what Charles had said.

The man had wanted Jake to leave Holly and Jamie alone, had wanted him to remain absent from their lives, but then she'd interfered and it had all gone downhill from there.

The end result? A battle between them and a huge settlement that Jake felt was reasonable to pay.

He would never forgive himself for ever believing his mother's lies. He should've just followed his heart and walked out of that plane when his gut told him it was the wrong choice.

So close. He'd been so close to her that day.

Putting the phone back down, he quickly undressed, then got into the tub.

Holly's eyes flew open.

"Sorry," he said, and she smiled as she lay back again.

Jake settled himself between her legs. Smiling, she pulled him closer, his back to her chest.

She was so soft and tiny, but having her arms around him felt as if she was the biggest giant in the world.

He felt loved. He felt so many things, but most of all, he felt like he was home.

When her legs wrapped around him, he massaged her one foot.

"Oh, that is so amazing."

"Are your feet sore?"

"You have no idea. I'm never getting out of this bath." Her voice was dreamy.

"Can I ask you a question?"

"Shoot."

"Please don't bite my head off. I'm just a little concerned."

"About what?" She sounded serious.

"Why are you ignoring your father?"

She sighed. "I just don't have the strength to hear what he has to say."

"Maybe he's phoning to apologize, sweetheart."

"Far from it. I can promise you that."

"Then what is it?"

She chuckled. "He must have found out about the bun in the oven and wants to give me his well-educated opinion about it." Her tone was scathing. "Like I said, I really don't want to hear what he has to say."

"You have to make peace with him."

"You have to practice what you preach." She kissed his temple.

"That's different."

"Jake, she fucked up, all of us do from time to time." Holly's voice sounded tired.

"No, there is fucking up, and then there is the horror my mother pulled."

"Is your father still mad at her?"

"We don't talk about it."

"You have to forgive her eventually."

"I will, when she proves to me that she is really sorry. When she shows me that there's an actual heart beating within her chest. When she shows remorse. Holly, I really don't want to talk about my mother now."

"And I don't want to talk about my father, so case closed."

"You should've become a lawyer, instead."

"Why, are my closing statements that good?"

"They are the best," he joked, grabbing her hand so he could kiss it.

He started talking about his project.

Holly listened, and it was something he loved about her. She always listened.

The past few weeks hadn't been easy without her.

He'd had to deal with the therapy session with his mother, finding out about the pregnancy, and Kate, who still wouldn't leave him alone. She phoned him almost every night, wanting to fight about what he'd done.

She was a constant nag and pain, but he endured it, hoping that she would get past whatever stage she was on, get it out of her system and become a human with a beating heart again.

There was nothing he wouldn't do to stay in Michael's life, but he wasn't going to follow crazy fucking orders that no normal human being would even follow.

It was all about punishing Jake.

But, she wasn't punishing him, she was punishing Michael, instead. And how sad was that? He knew the boy wanted to see him.

They washed each other, and while he wanted to take

things further, his stomach demanded to be fed. Reluctantly, he got out of the tub and dried off, then pulled on a pair of pajama pants and headed to the kitchen.

After he'd eaten two slices, Holly joined him wearing sleeping shorts and a tank top.

She opened the pizza box and took a slice.

They ate without using plates, their drink of choice was juice.

After dinner, Jake fetched the formula his father had reinvented and packaged from the car.

He made her a shake and handed it to her.

"Is what your mother did really the reason why he took it off the market?"

Jake huffed. "That's one of the reasons why I struggle to give that woman some rope."

"That's not yours to forgive, Jake."

"I know, but it was a string of lies that made my father pull it. It worked, didn't it?"

She nodded. "My doctor tried everything to obtain more of it, but by then it had already been pulled. As he wasn't given a reason as to why, I naturally thought that there was a flaw." She picked some of the toppings off the pizza before taking another bite.

He knew that. Jane had told him that they tried to get the formula, but notes in this regard had been made in her chart, too.

"Well, there wasn't a flaw. Just another lie."

"You are such a cry baby."

"No, I'm not. Romy died because of those lies, Holly. I never got to hold either one of them when they were born, *because* of her lies. I missed important birthdays, Christmases, Halloweens, *because* of her lies. Don't ask me to forgive her, please."

"I won't. I'm sorry," she said, looking down at the slice in her hand.

"The situation with your father is different, though."

"My father is an asshole."

"That may be so, but he was still the asshole that was there. The way he acted...I would have thought him to be a super asshole if he hadn't acted that way."

"Bullshit," she rallied.

"It's the truth. It means he cares about you in his own messed up way. It might be the only way he knows how. Phone him, speak to him."

On that note, he walked out of the kitchen. He hated that she was so forgiving, despite her hard-headedness where her father was concerned. But he knew that if it was up to Holly, his mother would've already met Jamie-Bernice.

The woman was a devious snake—he doubted he would ever have it in him to forgive her. Everything he'd said to her, he truly believed and meant.

She was the reason Romy had died.

Amelia knew it, his father knew it, Robin and Armand knew it.

Why couldn't the woman he'd called *Mother* all his life, grasp it?

SEVEN

HOLLY

Her heart ached for Jake whenever anything to do with his mother came up.

But she'd only brought Mara up because she worried about Jake walking around with the weight of a boulder in his heart.

She truly believed that not being able to forgive tainted one's soul, and she didn't want that for him.

What Mara did wasn't something Holly had ever said was right—far from it—but that wasn't what forgiveness was truly about. You had to forgive someone, not for them, but for yourself.

If only she could get that through to him.

And as far as her father went, she understood where Jake was coming from. She knew her father well; he'd only fight with her, and it would end up with them calling each other names. Not something she had the strength for.

But she dialed his number, anyway, and waited for him to pick up.

"Hello, Holly," he answered.

"Hi, Dad. I see you've been trying to reach me."

"Yes. Is it true?" he asked.

"Is what true?" She played dumb, wanting to delay the inevitable.

"That you are pregnant again."

"Dad, I'm an adult and I'm not going—"

"Then act like an adult, Holly. That guy almost cost you your life. Romy is dead. Do you even remember her?"

"Don't you dare say that! How many times must we tell you he didn't know?"

"Don't give me that bullshit. I'm not a child, Holly."

"And neither am I. But you seem to act like one often enough. Believe me, forgiving you and all the shit you did, was twenty thousand times harder than forgiving a mistake he wasn't a part of." She cut the call and breathed hard through her nose.

Enough with his accusations. She'd had it with him and his stubbornness. She wasn't going to hate her father, because he was so ignorant. It was always black and white with him. There was never a gray area.

Thankfully, she wasn't like that. And she refused to become like that.

Turning off the lights, she went up to their bedroom. But first, she popped into Jamie's room and said a small prayer.

Jake was already lying in bed with his laptop on his lap, typing away, when she entered.

She settled next to him, watching him work.

"I can feel your eyes on me, woman."

She chuckled. "Are we going to become one of those couples who bring their work to bed? We might as well get a TV in the room.

He looked at her and smiled. "Just going over a few notes."

"I'm sure you are." She flipped the screen closed and Jake managed to pull his hands away just in time before the laptop shut.

"Get it off the bed before I chuck it off." She pushed herself onto her knees and cupped his face with her hands for a kiss.

"Yes, ma'am," he said, placing the laptop on the floor as his lips met hers. The kiss deepened.

"I guess you're not that tired, then."

"No, you can thank my father for this extra spike in energy."

"See, I told you he's not that bad."

Snorting, she said, "He is an asshole of high proportions, sweetheart."

"If you say so. I beg to differ."

Flinging her leg over his body, she climbed onto his lap, and Jake immediately adjusted her so that her crotch fit perfectly on his.

His cock hardened when she rocked against him.

It felt amazing being so close to Jake. He was everything she wanted, everything she'd ever wanted. But that could be said for every woman who had ever laid eyes on him.

Of this, she was certain.

She was waiting for his flaws to show, but as yet, there was nothing.

Well, he did have a temper at times—she'd seen it, but it always seemed to disappear when he was round her—which perhaps related to his struggle in being unable to forgive Mara.

Still, no one could be this perfect.

Was he going to break her heart again?

It was driving her insane, because men like him, those who had the entire package, weren't real.

But here he was, the same guy she'd fallen for years ago, only that much more amazing.

Jake suddenly grabbed her legs, turned their bodies and

dumped her on to her back, falling on top of her. Surprised, she laughed softly, trying hard not to wake up Jamie.

They resumed kissing, riling each other up, and then his hand slipped into her shorts to cup her mound. The finger that entered her most private place elicited a groan from between her lips, his touch igniting her entire being.

The stress of the day, of her pregnancy, and of the conversation with her father, melted away when he kissed her neck.

Groaning, she bucked against him, desperately trying to remove his pants with her feet, while he quickly pulled hers off with his hands.

Free of their clothing, she gasped when he entered her with one swift stroke. She bit down on her lip when he moved achingly slow inside her, her moans mounting.

"You need to be quiet, otherwise Jamie is going to wake up."

What he was asking was a feat so hard to control, it was nearly impossible.

The sex didn't stay exclusively in the bedroom.

They moved to the bathroom after making sure that both the bedroom door and the walk-in closet's door was closed.

Jake pressed her back up against the wall and fucked her again before they moved to the toilet seat, where she straddled him, riding him like her life depended on it.

Again, it was a struggle to keep her moans to a low decibel, but to her ears they sounded loud, even with Jake's hand over her mouth. From the toilet seat, he moved her onto the floor, positioning her on hands and knees, and took her from behind, his one hand tangled in her hair, the other gripping her hip, guiding her as he rammed his cock into her, over and over again.

She couldn't put words to the sensations he enticed.

"Oh...fuck, I'm close," she panted, her voice sounding raspy. "I'm close, I'm close, ooooooh...yes!" she hissed between clenched teeth.

That was all the incentive he needed. Summoning whatever strength he had left, he upped the pace, and pistoned faster and faster as she tried to suppress her cries.

With a groan and a jerk, he came, filling her up. Spent, he let go and collapsed to the floor next to her.

Her own limbs gave out and she fell to the side, landing on top of him, sated and spent.

"One of us has to go see if Jamie is in our bed."

Chuckling, she said, "I'm going to take a shower, so I'll leave that to you." After planting a kiss on his nose, she got up.

"Fine, I'll go and look. Good thing you can't fall pregnant again," he said, grabbing a towel to wrap around his lower half.

Trust him to remind her about her condition. Jake had to go and bring that up again.

Asshole.

In the shower, she turned on the water and started lathering her body, only to have Jake join her a minute later.

"I guess miracles do exist."

Without a word, she started lathering Jake's body.

He closed his eyes when she neared his erection and grunted, the water flowing over his face.

"You are going to be the death of me, woman," he groaned as his lips found hers.

Holly felt like purring.

Guess the fun for tonight wasn't completely over.

JAKE

THEY ONLY GOT TO BED AT AROUND ELEVEN. HE WAS GOING to struggle to get up in the morning, but sleeping next to Holly, with her in his arms, was the best feeling in the world.

He knew he'd found his soul mate. He'd known it since the first time he set eyes on her. He chuckled to himself. Holly still didn't know about that, but if he told her, she would know how dangerous she was to him.

If she had to leave him again, it would crush him for good.

No, this time he'd just have to hold on. He'd have to teach her how to fight for what was right, for what she wanted, as he wouldn't want another ever again.

He didn't give a shit about what they would discover about one another, because nothing, nothing in this world was going to make him stop wanting her, or stop loving her.

And even if, for whatever reason, something had to happen and she still didn't want to fight, he would continue to fight for all of them until there was no more fight left in him.

Holly and Jamie were his life, and the baby that was on the way would only make it all that much better.

He said a short prayer, asking God to keep them safe, and then fell into a deep sleep.

When Jamie jumped onto the bed early the next morning, his eyes flew open.

"Okay, I'm up. Let's give Mommy some time to sleep, okay?" he whispered when Holly grunted.

He kissed Jamie on the head, and bent over to kiss Holly on hers, then got up with Jamie in his arms.

On their way downstairs, he asked Jamie how she'd slept.

"Like a rock," she replied, making him bark with laughter.

Who she'd heard that from was a no-brainer. Amelia was such a drama queen.

He heated up pizza and she ate it with the ketchup he'd asked for at the restaurant, then poured her some juice.

"As soon as the housekeeper gets here, she'll do some food shopping for us," he said, grabbing a slice of pizza for himself and taking a bite.

He told her about her tutor, and because he'd been speaking about it with her for days prior to their arrival, Jamie was excited to meet her.

He started speaking in German to her, and she answered him. She'd learned the language quickly, which astonished him at how good she actually spoke it in just two months.

Holly joined them a while later, and the first thing she did was kiss Jamie on the head.

"Look, Mommy. We are eating pizza," Jamie said in German.

Holly frowned at Jake.

"You've been busy. Any other languages I should know about? English please, baby. Your mommy is a bit of a dummy."

"You are not a dummy," Jake teased her. "Nobody in this family is a dummy."

"Oh, shush. I can't do happy with you two. It's too early," she said, planting a kiss on his shoulder.

Chuckling, he poured her a glass of juice as she helped herself to a slice of pizza.

They hadn't told Jamie about the new baby yet, and he really felt that it was time, but he needed Holly to be the one to tell her. She was the one who was good at explaining things to Jamie.

"I'm going to get dressed," he said, leaving them to whatever conversation they were having.

He hoped Holly would tell Jamie about the baby, and that if and when she did, it wouldn't make her feel like she wasn't enough.

That was the last thing he wanted her to feel.

EIGHT

HOLLY

THE DOORBELL RANG WHILE SHE WAS TALKING TO JAMIE. She was struggling with how to bring up the new baby, how to tell Jamie that she was going to be a big sister. It had to be done properly and at the right time, because she didn't want Jamie to feel unwanted. At the moment, Holly thought it was still too early.

First trimesters were always unpredictable, especially with her condition, and she didn't want Jamie to feel the pain if she ended up losing the baby.

On an exhale, she shook the negative thoughts from her mind and headed to the front door.

Outside, stood a girl about her age, maybe younger even. She was a big girl, but she was by no means what people would call fat. She had dark eyes and dark hair.

"Good day. My name is Victoria. I was hired as a tutor for Jamie Bernice," she greeted in German.

"Oh, yes. Please, come in."

Victoria entered and immediately smiled when she saw Jamie. "She's a pretty little girl."

"Thank you," Jamie answered in German.

Victoria's eyes widened and she started speaking to Jamie in German.

Just then, Jake came running down the stairs, dressed in black cargo pants, and a light blue button down shirt. His sleeves were rolled up.

He looked really good, and his cologne smelled divine.

"The tutor is here. I'll go get ready for work," Holly said as she passed him.

Jake greeted Victoria in perfect German and started talking to her about the next three weeks.

When Holly joined them again a few minutes later, Jake was still busy discussing Jamie's schedule with Victoria.

The TV in the living room blared, so Holly made her way in that direction. She found Jamie eating Fruit Loops in front of the TV—Cartoon Network filled the screen.

Smiling, she took a seat next to Jamie and kissed her on the cheek. "So, what do you think of Victoria?" Jamie didn't take her eyes off the screen.

"She's pretty."

"Remember, if there's anything she does that you don't like, you have to tell Mommy and Daddy, no matter what she says, okay?"

Jamie nodded.

"We spoke about strangers, and people touching where they shouldn't be touching, didn't we?"

Jamie nodded again.

She hated having this discussion, but if there was one thing she'd taught Jamie from the moment she was able to comprehend the intricacies of this kind of situation, was that she had to tell either her or her father immediately—no matter what the other person said, or how scary it was.

Jamie was a beautiful little girl, and she was growing up in a messed-up world. Teaching her this was the only way to keep Jamie safe.

It would be her worst nightmare if anything ever happened to Jamie, and she didn't even want to think what Jake would do.

"I love you, sweetheart. Mommy has to go to work now, so you be a good girl for Victoria." She gave her a big hug.

"Love you too, Mommy," Jamie said, placing a sticky kiss on Holly's cheek before turning back to her cartoons.

She walked into the kitchen just as Jake finished with Victoria.

"We have to go. I won't be here when Maria arrives, but please give her this list and have her pick the stuff up from the store. We'll be back later this afternoon."

"Go, I've got this." Victoria tried to put them both at ease.

Jake smiled and went to say goodbye to Jamie, but Holly stayed with Victoria.

"Tutor, huh?"

Victoria started to laugh. "You didn't know?"

"Oh, no. I did. I just didn't know how it would all work. Are you happy with only working for three weeks?" Holly went to the fridge and grabbed what she needed to make her shake for the morning. She only drank two a day; one in the morning and one at night. The one she was preparing now, she would take with her to work and drink it on the way.

"I'm working with the agency, so it's nothing new to me. Some clients only live in Zürich for six months and spend the other six elsewhere. I have many students that only need my help for a week or two."

When Jake returned to the kitchen, they said their farewells to Victoria and left for work.

The house was built on top of a hill, and Holly could see almost the entire city sprawled in the distance as she walked out the door.

Strangely enough, she still hadn't seen the house in its entirety, but right then all that mattered was that she was here with Jake.

She sipped on her shake while Jake drove them to the hospital.

"So..." She smiled. "You had the talk with Jamie, too."

"The 'stranger danger' talk?" he asked, without taking his eyes off the road as a grin spread across his lips.

"Yeah, that one."

"I did. I would kill anyone with my bare hands if they ever tried to hurt her, or you."

"I would, too. Ever since they laid her in my arms and she wowed me with her beauty, it has been a fear."

Jake chuckled. "It would not happen without us knowing about it. I checked Victoria out thoroughly—she has no criminal record, and her résumé is as long as my arm."

"Really?" Holly asked, surprised.

"Don't let her age fool you, Holly. She is a very clever and competent woman, and the agency is very strict and takes great care over who they take on."

"You know a lot about this, don't you?"

"My mother and father traveled to Germany from time to time. Amelia and I went through our fair share of tutors, just like Jamie is now. She'll be fine. I promise."

She took a deep breath. "Of course you did."

Holly had an urge to put cameras in the house, but she knew it was just paranoia eating at her.

When they got out of the car at the hospital, Jake took her hand in his as they walked toward the entrance. Once they reached the door, she kissed him goodbye, knowing she probably wouldn't see him all day as he'd be occupied in neurology.

They went their separate ways. Her eyes followed him as he walked down the hallway in the opposite direction. A lovesick puppy was what she was when it came to him.

Shaking her head, she made her way to the lockers, but when she entered, the conversation that had been going on, died.

Eva and Petra watched her the whole time. She could feel their eyes on her back. No doubt, it had to do with Jake.

"So, you know Puff Pastry?" Eva leaned against the locker next to hers. She spoke to Holly in English.

Holly laughed at the name. "Guilty."

"He's really the baby's daddy?"

Holly nodded.

"Why didn't you tell us?"

"Because of this. The way you look at me, Eva."

"I'm just curious. Tell me...what do you do with *that* next to you every night?"

"You really want me to answer that? I thought the bun in the oven would be explanation enough."

Both women laughed.

"Yeah, it doesn't surprise us." Petra put on her white coat.

"What happened to the girl's mother?"

"Huh?"

"You know, the little girl, the one that looks just like him."

Holly frowned slightly, but a soft smile adorned her lips. "You're looking at her."

"She's yours?"

"And his, hence the reason she looks just like him and not me."

"Holy crap. How long have you been with this guy? The last time I heard, he was going to marry Kate Niagelli."

"It's a very long story." Holly downed the rest of her shake, then placed her bag along with the empty bottle in her locker. Shutting the locker door, she said, "Don't look at me like that, Petra. He's my kryptonite."

"Sweetie, I think he's everyone's kryptonite."

Holly smiled again.

"But something tells me you are his, too."

"Oh, shut up. Let's get to work."

After lunch, Holly filled in some paperwork at reception. A new patient had just been admitted and she needed to make sure all the paperwork was correct.

She heard Jake's voice behind her and turning her head, she saw that he was speaking to Anna. She went unnoticed as they entered his office.

Insecurity entered her mind again. She hated that he worked with such beautiful women, and the fact that they'd done certain things behind closed doors didn't ease the heaviness in her chest.

Stop it. Jake wouldn't cheat on me.

His office door opened and Anna walked out.

"Dr. Scallanger, may I please have a word?"

"Of course, Dr. Peters." Holly mimicked the professionalism in his tone, but the second she was in his office, he locked the door and pulled her into his arms.

"Just like old times, huh?" He kissed her and she giggled against his lips.

"Not really, because this time I get to go home with you tonight. So, not fully like old times," Holly purred dreamily as his lips traveled across her skin.

"Stop talking, woman," he murmured in her ear. "I only have ten minutes."

Their lips met and they kissed with a hunger Holly hoped

would never fade. Her back connected hard with the wall in his office.

His fingers fiddled with her pants and he pulled them off, but he didn't let her near his.

"What are you doing?" she asked as he moved back a fraction, taking her hands from his button, while he caressed the flesh at the nape of her neck softly.

"I only have ten minutes," he repeated, going down on his knees.

Hooking his thumb into the side of her panties, he moved it aside and extended his tongue to lick her throbbing sex.

"Oh, fuck," she moaned, as he lifted her leg over his shoulder.

He grunted against her sex, the vibration only enhancing the feeling, and then he sucked her clit into his mouth.

Her hands grabbed his head. "Fuck, Jake," she whispered, trying hard not to moan too loud.

His sucking turned into a kiss, and then he stopped.

"I need to talk to you about something."

"Now? You're fucking shitting me, right?"

Grinning, he closed his eyes.

"Oh, my gosh, you are such a tease. What is it?"

"I want Jamie to become a Peters."

"She is a Peters."

He shook his head. "On paper."

"So, I'm going to be the only Scallanger?"

He chuckled. "Please. It just makes my life so much easier. That's why it was such a bitch to get her passport. If her last name had been Peters, it would've expedited things quicker."

"We can talk about that later."

"Okay, I have to go."

"Seriously?" She groaned in frustration, which had Jake laughing at her.

"It's not funny."

"I told you I only had ten minutes. It takes me about three minutes to get to the other building. I'll see you later."

He closed the door behind her.

Asshole.

Bending, she snagged her pants up off the floor and pulled them back on.

But a laugh escaped her lips.

He was still the same old Jake, grabbing her wherever he could.

A smile spread across her lips at the thought that Jake was finally hers, even though she had rare moments of feeling insecure.

VICTORIA GREETED THEM WHEN THEY GOT HOME THAT night.

"Sorry, we're later than we wanted to be." Holly felt so bad, she inwardly cringed.

Victoria merely laughed. "It's okay. It's part of the job. Jamie is in the bath, but she'll be out soon."

"Can I keep her?" Holly asked, turning to Jake.

Victoria laughed. "I'll see you both tomorrow, same time. Say goodnight to Jamie for me."

"Will do. Goodnight, Victoria."

On reaching the doorway, she stopped and put the strap of her bag over her shoulder. "Oh, before I forget, Maria made a lasagna. I put it in the oven for you. When the ringer goes, just take it out." Victoria smiled at them and left.

Holly looked at Jake, who went over the cupboards in the kitchen, opening them one by one and peeking inside. She could see the cupboards were filled now with groceries where they previously weren't. Probably what Jake was checking up on.

"She's serious."

Jake looked at her. "About what?"

She ran to the oven and opened it. A lasagna was baking. She breathed in the delicious scent.

Jake smiled and shook his head.

"You really are spoiled, aren't you?"

Wiggling his eyebrows at her, he pulled her into his arms. "Just a little. I think it's a beautiful evening to go sit on the verandah and enjoy Maria's lasagna."

"We have a veranda?"

"You didn't explore last night?"

"No. But I'll go check out this veranda now." She gave him a quick kiss and walked away, glancing over her shoulder at him.

"There's a sliding door in the corner of the living room."

She quickened her pace and found the door behind cream curtains, which she opened with ease.

The sight that greeted her made her gasp.

Not only was the veranda enormous, a huge wooden deck was attached to it, sprawling out in front of her in glorious splendor.

There was a stunning table made of steel and wood that could sit at least eight people, with chairs Holly wouldn't have thought to put outdoors.

A few lantern lights hung from the roof.

Stepping out, she walked over to the table and sat on one of the chairs as she looked out at the colorful garden and luscious, green grass.

Tonight was a beautiful night. But soon, winter would be here.

"Mommy!" Jamie ran out the door and clambered onto her.

"Hey, gorgeous." She kissed her on the head. "How was

your day? Did you enjoy your bath? You smell so nice," Holly said, sniffing at her like a dog.

Jamie cackled as Holly continued to sniff her. "Stop it, Mommy," Jamie cried, and Holly finally stopped as Jamie adjusted herself on her lap. "My day was amazing."

She looked just like Amelia when she said that. It was obvious to her that Jamie's aunt was spending all the time she could with her, so much so, she was starting to rub off on her daughter.

Jamie told her about all the places she'd gone to with Victoria.

That brought a smile to her lips. She was glad that Jamie hadn't been cooped up in the house all day.

Jake walked out the door and handed her a glass of cold juice, Jamie a juice box, and then opened his beer.

He sat down on the chair diagonally across from them as Jamie babbled on.

Then Jake joined the conversation, but switched over to German.

Holly shook her head.

"Mommy doesn't understand, Daddy."

"Oh, it's fine," she said and squeezed Jamie tightly. "Mommy needs to go and make some salad." She set Jamie down, then got up and headed to the kitchen.

She was so happy. That was the thought that ran through her head as she took out the fixings for a salad and placed them on the cutting board.

But the heaviness of her paranoia took over. It haunted her. A bad omen was waiting somewhere around a corner, and it scared her to death just thinking about it.

THE DAYS OF LIVING TOGETHER FLEW BY, AND HOLLY learned a lot about Jake. He was neat in regards to himself, but was kind of a slob with everything else around him. He threw his clothes on the floor, made a sandwich without cleaning up after himself, and so on. All those tiny annoying things.

For Holly, that was a flaw, but it wasn't one that would drive her bonkers as it was minor.

However, she refused to clean up after him as she was no one's slave. Thankfully, Maria came in everyday and cleaned, anyway.

That was how he'd grown up, with people cleaning up after him. So very different from her.

As for the pregnancy, she hadn't fainted again, which meant that the shake was working, and she was happy when four more arrived the following week.

Gus spoke to her often, reminding her that she needed to phone him the minute she didn't feel well.

She figured he was doubting himself.

Right now, she was lying on a bed in Bianca's office, waiting for Jake to show up. He finally arrived, out of breath. His schedule was hectic.

"So..." Bianca looked at them. "Do you want to know the sex?"

"Can you see it already?" Jake asked with a hint of skepticism.

"No." Bianca smiled. "Just want to be prepared for when the time does come."

"No," Jake replied, sounding adamant.

"Really?" Holly looked at him, her eyebrows raised in disbelief.

"It doesn't matter what the sex is, Bee Puke. As long as the baby is healthy."

"Well, then I guess we don't want to know the sex."

"Okay, I'm making a mental note of it."

She took measurements of the fetus, and Holly was suddenly hit with a sense of déjà vu. Like the last time, when the check-up on Jamie was done, there had only been one heartbeat. But she now knew that nothing should be ruled out. Romalia had hidden behind Jamie, their heartbeats in sync for the longest time, which was why only one heartbeat had been picked up on the sonar.

"Everything looks great."

"Of course it does. Why wouldn't it?" Jake stated.

Bianca chuckled. "I see your father is keeping busy with the trial on the shake again."

"Yes, Holly is his first guinea pig."

"You look okay, Holly. Do you feel okay?"

"So far, yes. I can't complain."

"I'm glad to hear that. Your blood pressure is stable, which is always a good thing. I think this is going to be a completely different experience for you."

"I hope so," she said in reply to Bianca. And looking at Jake with a playful, yet scolding look, she said, "It better be."

Tears shone in Jake's eyes, but not like it had with Jamie and Romy.

She gave her mom, and then Bernie a call afterward to let them know that the pregnancy was going well so far.

Bernie had laughed when she heard that her friend was pregnant again. True to Bernie style, she jokingly told Holly that she really was a slut when it came to Jake.

They'd been skyping at least three times a week. It felt like the past five years had never happened and that Bernie had always been in her life.

They were giddy that both of them were pregnant at the exact same time. Bernie was in her third trimester, and in another ten weeks she would have a baby boy in her arms.

Holly silently wished that hers was a little boy, too. Then Jake wouldn't be surrounded by girls.

Amelia was ecstatic. They spoke to her every single night because of Jamie. She missed her niece and was counting off the days for her return home. Holly wasn't counting off the days, though.

She dreaded knowing that they were going to leave again, and that she wouldn't see them for two whole months.

Jake made love to her almost every single night. It was different than the usual, since Jamie was in the house, but it was still amazing on all the levels that counted.

At some point, she realized she wasn't scared anymore. At least not about her, another bad pregnancy, or that Jake would leave her. But him wanting to change Jamie's last name was scary as hell.

It should have been a great sign of things to come, but that wasn't how she felt. She'd told him she would think about it, and had to remind him, again, that she was still thinking about it when Jake asked her at least another two times.

Time flew by and before she knew it, it was their last night. It depressed her just thinking about the fact that they wouldn't be here, together, the following night. But she tried her best not to ruin their last night together.

The moments they all spent together warmed her heart. She loved spending every second possible with her little family. Having them under her radar, and looking after them was just how it was supposed to be. She was really great at that.

That evening, Jake took them to a restaurant that had made provisions for kids by way of installing a small play area, which Jamie immediately took advantage of.

Holly was aware that he wanted an answer on the surname issue, and knew it needed to happen tonight.

When Jamie ran back to their table for a sip of soda, Holly

asked her the question. "So, peanut," she said. "Do you want to stay a Scallanger, or do you want to become a Peters?"

Jake snorted. "You are putting her on the spot, Holly. Of course she would say she wants to stay a Scallanger."

"I am speaking to my daughter."

"And I want my daughter to have the name she should've had on her birth certificate a long time ago. Honey, go play. Daddy will sort it out."

Holly sighed. "Jake."

"No, Holly." He looked at Jamie. "Go play."

Shrugging, Jamie kissed her on the cheek and ran off.

She, on the other hand, merely glared at him.

"Don't look at me like that."

"But you are—"

"She's my daughter, too, Holly. In fact, I think she has more Peters in her than—"

"Oh, shut up." She knew he was only teasing her, and all because Jamie was his spitting image.

"Please. I'm just trying to rectify something that should've been done a long time ago."

She sighed.

"You are still her mother, no matter what her last name is. That will never change."

"Fine, what do I have to do?"

"The form is back at the house." Leaning over to her, he kissed her gently on her lips. "I knew you'd come around to your senses."

She couldn't help but laugh at him. He was so serious in a not-so-serious way.

When she sat back in her chair, he placed a gentle hand on her belly.

"You're going to be okay," he said matter-of-factly.

"I know. I feel fine, which tells me the shake is definitely working."

"So...no more worries? Because you know the saying that if the mom is upset the baby is upset, is true, right?"

"Yes, I know the saying really well, and I trust that everything is going to be fine. Thank you."

"My pleasure."

They left after spending an hour and a half at the restaurant. On the journey home, her heartstrings tightened knowing that tomorrow she'd have to say goodbye to them and go back to her shitty apartment.

Jake wanted her to remain at the house, but she declined. He'd even offered to get her a better apartment, but she couldn't.

It was his money, and she would never ask him for a dime. Not for herself, anyway.

They made sweet love that night and afterward, she fell into a blissful sleep in his arms.

NINE

HOLLY

Saying goodbye to Jake and Jamie wasn't easy.

She burst into tears at the airport and had to lie to Jamie when she asked her why she was crying.

She'd see them again in two months, just before Jamie's birthday. Which reminded her of the fact that she still had no idea when Jake's birthday was. She'd meant to ask him, but she knew he would only tease her for not knowing.

"Don't cry, please." He hugged her tight.

She just nodded against his chest.

"I'll phone you when we land." He cleared his throat.

Pushing away from him, she wiped away her tears with the tips of her fingers. They kissed one last time.

Crouching down, she took Jamie in her arms and hugged her, kissing both of her cheeks. "Be good, you hear?" She smiled.

"I'm always good, Mommy," said Jamie with a serious expression on her face. But she gave Holly one big loud smack of a kiss on her forehead.

Laughing, Holly got up and stood with her arms wrapped around her middle.

Jamie took her father's hand.

It was a struggle watching them leave. The sexy giant with the sweetest, dark-haired little person walking beside him, holding his hand.

They waved one last time before entering the gate.

"Love you, Mommy!" Jamie yelled across the expanse that separated them.

"Love you more, sweetheart."

People turned and smiled, but Holly was oblivious to it all. She waved and blew her daughter a kiss, and then they were out of sight.

Back to her crappy apartment she went, and once there began to unpack.

Why did they have to leave on her day off?

She sobbed, ugly tears streaming down her face. Her pregnancy hormones weren't helping, either.

At around noon, she lay on her bed and fell asleep hugging her pillow.

When she woke, it was dark.

She felt utterly alone, and never in a million years did she think she'd miss Jamie and Jake this much in such a short amount of time.

The lack of sustenance got her up and out of bed. She made herself instant noodles, which took her a while to eat. Not long after, she decided to take a shower.

Though she was missing them both terribly, she was also going to miss the baths with Jake, and the awesomeness of falling asleep in his arms.

Before going back to bed, she made her shake, then went right to sleep.

Tomorrow, she would start with crossing off the days of

what was going to be the long wait again.

THE NEXT FEW WEEKS WENT BY SLOWLY. BUT AS SHE GOT busy, learning yet more about surgery, and putting her mind to her work, days passed by faster and faster.

Then her glands started to ache. It was what she hated about being pregnant.

She was feeling miserable again. Her stomach was slowly starting to show as she neared the end of her first trimester.

Texts between her and Jake took place every single day. And she made sure to send a text every night before falling asleep.

It wasn't easy, either, as sometimes Jamie wasn't around. But she tried to Skype with her around her bedtime, which was early morning in Zürich.

She also, finally, found out when Jake's birthday was—October the twenty-second.

She'd been right that he'd tease her about it. Said he found it appalling that she didn't know his birthday when he knew hers. Unfortunately, she was still in Zürich. She didn't say anything to him, but hoped with all her heart he'd fly over to spend it with her.

A week later, she got the call in which he asked her to take the day off because he didn't want to be anywhere else but in her bed...with her covered in cream and cherries.

Happy as could be, she burst out laughing.

Then the worry set in.

She had no idea what to get him, and her budget was tight. Her apartment took almost all of her salary, and then she still had to buy food.

She even asked Eva and Petra for help with gift ideas.

"How do you feel about it?" Eva asked, after a long period of silence.

"Fine, I guess," she answered. Her German was improving.

"Sorry, I didn't make myself clear. I meant, how do you feel when it comes to sex?"

"Oh." She blushed. "Horny?" They all laughed. "I really thought it was only a myth that women could feel extremely turned on during pregnancy, but here I am, proving it right. My entire body tingles from the stupidest things. The breeze, the warmth of my apartment, things I eat. It doesn't even sound normal when I say it out loud."

"Then do something kinky, get a sexy outfit that he'll struggle to take off."

Holly grinned. She could just imagine Jake struggling to take off anything.

It did, however, give her an idea. He loved the toys, and she was going to work him up good.

Eva and Petra both gave her an idea, something they'd read in a magazine. It seemed a bit too much for her, and something neither her nor Jake would do, but that both Eva and Petra would if that person looked like Puff Pastry—their nickname for him.

Holly giggled, remembering the first time they'd used the name. It didn't even fit him, but she knew that the Swiss loved their pastries. And honestly, Jake was so yummy-looking, who wouldn't want to eat him?

Holly blushed as Eva told her what she'd read. There was no way she could do that to him.

"They say that the sex is insane."

"Oh, I can just imagine."

"Think about it." Both women got up to leave. Petra, though, was still laughing at Holly's expression.

She waved them off as there was much to think about. Their

suggestion for one. But uppermost in her mind was the thought of what Jake might do, and that alone made her daydream again.

Perhaps this was exactly what he needed.

Payback for all the messages, the flirting over the phone, not to mention him riling her up during phone sex. It could teach him to not do that anymore. Or not. She'd have to wait and see.

THEY MADE A DECISION TO WAIT ON TELLING JAMIE ABOUT the baby until she hit the second trimester, which would be soon.

In the meantime, she decided to get a gift for Jamie. She had a T-shirt made for her that said **I'M GOING TO BE A BIG SISTER**. Then took it a step further and put together a beautiful German story about a little girl who became a big sister, and how this little girl, Sarah, dealt with it. And that if she felt the same way as the girl in the story, she should write down all the questions she wanted to ask so that Holly could answer them when she came to Zürich again. To end, she added a fluffy toy with a tiny box of her favorite sweets.

Jake would take it home with him when he left after his birthday.

They would be spending Jamie's birthday in Zürich, too, and Amelia and Gus were going to join them, since it would be the first birthday with them in her life.

To say she couldn't wait for Jake's birthday was an understatement. She wanted, needed, to wrap her arms around him. As the date loomed nearer, Holly spent most of her free time online, looking for the perfect outfit to wear.

"I thought you might be interested in this," Eva said, showing Holly a website on her phone at work the next day.

Holly flushed bright red when what she was looking at were strings and scraps of material that supposedly passed off as clothing. Although, she had to admit, the outfits did look kinky —but then, that was the whole point, wasn't it?

The one that caught her eye instantly, looked like it consisted of a ribbon that wrapped around the model's body, with a large bow covering her breasts.

When the package landed on her doorstep a few days later, she tried it on. Utter and complete disaster, even though she followed the instructions that came with it. Eventually, after the fifth attempt, she got it right. She studied herself in the mirror; the slight bulge of her stomach strained against the ribbon, but the bow made her breasts look incredible. She felt sexy and confident in the outfit.

When the time came, it would be put to the test.

THE DAYS SEEMED TO PASS WITH EXCRUCIATING SLOWNESS, until, finally, it was the day Jake was due to arrive.

Hauling out her largest handbag, she put his gift in it, along with a can of whipped cream, a small jar of maraschino cherries, the silk scarves she'd purchased, as well as some clean underwear. It paid to be prepared whenever Jake was around, and she didn't want him to miss out on any part of his birthday present.

When she got off the shuttle at the airport, she was just in time. Her eyes scanned the large area, and as soon as she spotted him in the crowd, she ran straight into his arms. Jake lifted her up off the floor and she wrapped her legs around his waist, their lips crashing together in a heart-stopping kiss.

Out of breath, she pulled back and rested her forehead against his. "Happy Birthday."

"I'm so glad I'm here. I can't imagine being anywhere else. I got us a hotel room. Your apartment is way too small," he muttered against her lips.

She laughed. Good thing she'd packed his gift into her handbag. "Fine, whatever, as long as I can give you your birthday present, I don't care."

"Please tell me it's something kinky."

"Kinky as fuck." She wiggled her eyebrows.

He looked up, closing his eyes as if he were sending a prayer of thanks up to heaven. "I cannot wait."

They went straight to the hotel, even though Holly begged Jake to stop at her apartment so she could get a change of clothes; the only thing she hadn't thought of.

"You're not gonna need clothes," he whispered in her ear.

The minute they entered the room, Jake grabbed her and stripped her of her clothing. He slipped a finger into her, then groaned when he felt she was ready for him. He unbuttoned his jeans, and shoved them down along with his boxers over his ass. Without waiting another second, he palmed his erection and guided it home.

At that oh-so-amazing intrusion, she gasped. He'd barely moved inside her, before an orgasm washed over her. The pregnancy hormones heightened everything, and she came again and again, before Jake spoke to her.

"You better not be faking it," he panted, out of breath.

She laughed. "It's this baby, it's doing things to my body that I can't explain."

"And here I thought it was me." He pouted.

She cupped his face. "Shut up. It's a mixture of both." She smiled and planted a kiss on his lips, which quickly became heated. They picked up where they'd left off.

Sated and drenched in each other's sweat, they took a quick shower and then passed out on the bed.

A while later, Holly woke up from Jake's hand stroking her back, his lips brushing kisses over hers.

"Wake up, Holly. I have a surprise for you for dinner."

Groggily, she hoisted herself up to a sitting position and rubbed her eyes. When she dropped her hands, she gasped at the sight before her—a gorgeous black dress and heels were laid out at the end of the bed.

"It's your birthday and I'm getting gifts? That's not how it's supposed to work."

"I like spoiling my girls." He kissed her again, then slapped her ass as she scrambled out of bed.

"Thank you, Jake. Both are beautiful," she said, grabbing the dress and shoes on her way to the bathroom to get ready. She felt like a million bucks in the dress.

The hotel's five star restaurant was where they ended up, and spent the evening enjoying each other's company before heading back to their room.

Holly flashed him a sultry smile.

"Go take a seat on the bed and wait there," she ordered, while she walked over to her bag so she could retrieve the four scarves.

Jake gave her a questioning look, but followed her orders.

She sauntered back to where he was sitting and bending over slightly, removed his shoes and socks. When she straightened, her lower lip was between her teeth, and her eyes burned with heat. Slowly, she grabbed one of the scarves, and then lifted one of his hands.

Jake looked perplexed. "What are you doing?" he asked, as she bound his hand to the headboard.

"It's a no-touching type of game."

"You're going to kill me, aren't you?"

"Hell, no. I love you too much."

"Thank goodness for that," he said, holding out his other arm for her to repeat the process.

She was grinning as she tied the knot. She'd watched a ton of YouTube videos, and was confident that he wouldn't be able to get out of the knots easily.

"This is really hot, you know that?"

"I find it hard to believe that you've never been tied up before."

"It never felt like this."

She chuckled as she tied his feet.

"You're not gonna undress me?"

"Give me a couple of minutes."

"I swear if you leave me here—"

Laughing, she picked up her bag and went into bathroom. "I promise, I won't." She quickly exchanged the clothes she was wearing for the sexy outfit—if one could call it that.

"Holly, hurry up!" Jake called.

Dang. She'd forgotten to put the fifth scarf over his mouth.

She quickly threw one of the hotel's bathrobes on, then took the whipped cream, cherries, candles, and lube out of her bag, and walked back out.

"Holy fuck, what is all that?"

"A surprise."

She set all her equipment down on the nightstand, except for the scarf she'd wound around her neck, then straddled him.

"I forgot one other thing."

His throat worked as he swallowed. "And that is?"

"There'll be no talking from you tonight, either, mister."

"You've got to be fucking with me."

No, she mouthed. With a sly look, she took the scarf from around her neck and gagged him.

Jake's eyes bulged, and he mumbled against the gag, but she couldn't make out what he was trying to say.

"You can thank your lucky stars it's not a ball gag. Now, be a good boy and shush."

Jake emitted a grunt as she got off him. She shot him a cheeky grin over her shoulder, then picked up one of the candles and lit it. This was going to be torture for him. Heading back to the bathroom, she not only touched up her makeup, she added even more—eyes were now smoky, and her lips a siren-red.

She moved on to her hair, and letting it loose, shook out her curls. She looked like a dominatrix.

A chuckle escaped her.

Let the games began.

JAKE

HE TUGGED AT HIS RESTRAINTS, BUT HOLLY HAD DONE A good job with the knots. Whatever she had planned for him, he knew it was going to drive him insane with lust.

The bathroom door finally opened and she walked out.

Fuck, she looked hot. He let out a long groan and tugged at his restraints again.

She laughed.

Thick, red ribbons crisscrossed over her skin, ending in a bow over her breasts, which threatened to pop out.

He raked his gaze over her, saliva pooling in his gagged mouth. Her panties were crotchless. She looked like a decadent present, and he couldn't even untie her.

Again, he tugged at the knots.

"You're going to fuck up your gift if you try to escape, baby," she purred.

Jake grunted. "Cunh awwn," he mumbled against the scarf,

not that it came out sounding like *come on*, which was what he actually said.

"I can't understand you, so don't bother, Jake. Shall we begin?" she teased.

He nodded eagerly, like a bobblehead.

"Don't make me laugh. If you do, those scarves are just going to stay on longer."

He attempted to say "Oh, fuck," but it just came out all garbled.

Holly practically slithered up his body and ripped his shirt open, buttons popping off and flying every which way. He groaned when her nails raked over his chest.

She bent over him, swirling her tongue around first one nipple and then the other, placing searing kisses down to his navel.

Goosebumps popped up all over his skin, and he closed his eyes when her fingers unbuttoned his pants. She coaxed him to lift his hips, which he immediately complied with.

Hooking her hands into the band of his pants, she slid them down to his ankles in a torturously slow motion, then moved back up to palm the protrusion that stood up at attention from between his hips.

He groaned as she stroked him, but she stopped to rub her body along his.

"Are you ready for your present?"

As all he could really do was nod, that's what he did.

Sliding off him, she got to her feet and stood on the bed, legs apart.

His eyes widened at the same time his body writhed in sexual agony; she was giving him a clear view of her bare pussy.

She moved her hands over her body, stopping to touch herself. His eyes tracked the movements, his cock aching, certain he'd come just from looking at her. His breath came out hard through his flared nostrils, and his heart pounded an erratic beat in his chest.

Her back connected with the steel frame of the four-poster bed, and adjusting her balance, she raised her leg, finding purchase by placing her foot on the inside of her other leg at the knee. Lowering her lids, she ran her fingers over her folds. Her pussy glistened with her arousal. She moaned and he grumbled, tugging at the scarves keeping him captive. He ached to be inside her.

He jerked against his restraints when she increased the stroking on her clit.

"Yes...fuck, yes," she moaned.

He recognized that moan, could see on her face that she was close.

"Oh...fuck!" she screamed as she came.

He was in awe of her sudden confidence. It was so fucking sexy.

She bit her lower lip and let out a sultry groan, then her eyes opened and she pierced him with her gaze.

He was breathing hard, his chest heaving up and down. He wished she'd untie him so he could ravage her.

Dropping her knees either side of him, she straddled his hips, leaning down to kiss his neck.

It was fucking punishment not being able to touch her.

Her lips trailed down his skin, her hands stroking his side. His cock twitched as she neared it.

Her lips and her tongue teased him, and he thought he was going to climax just from her hot breath on him. She took him into her mouth, alternating between fast and slow suctions, her tongue swirling around the head as if it were a lollipop.

When her mouth left him, he thought for a moment that she was going to untie him. But he was wrong. Instead, she nipped, sucked, and licked at the sensitive flesh around his cock. She moved up his legs again to straddle him once more, her wet heat sliding along his hardness, but she didn't let him enter her.

The torture continued when she reached for the can of whipped cream. "You want to do something fun with me?" she panted.

He nodded, so fast it looked funny.

"I told you not to make me laugh, Jake."

"Sowie, sowie," he mumbled. Jeez, he sounded like a freaking child, even to his own ears.

Nodding curtly, but giggling on the inside, she continued to slide up along his body on her knees until her naked flesh was but an inch from his mouth, but not close enough that he could get to her if he lifted his head.

She shook the can, then sprayed the cream directly onto her pussy.

Fuck.

Winking at him, she untied the scarf from his mouth.

"Are you fucking insane?" he shouted on a gasp. "Get on my face, woman."

As she wasn't done playing, she merely shook her head and rocked her hips up and closer to his mouth, only to retreat just before his lips or tongue could reach her.

He wanted nothing more than to lick every last drop of cream off her. "Holly, this is supposed to be a gift. Get down here, before I really get out of these scarves."

"You can try, but you won't succeed."

"I'll break this bed, I swear."

She bit her lower lip. "You're bluffing."

"Bring me my pussy pie, or you will be sorry."

"Promises, promises."

He laughed, but she gave him a look that quickly shut him up.

"Oh, you think it's funny. Do you want the scarf back on?"

"No, hell no."

"Good boy," she said, rocking her hips closer again.

Without warning, she shifted forward and straddled his face, eliciting a groan from between Jake's lips when her delicious scent reached him. His tongue darted out, licking at the cream, then sucking her into his mouth, then lapping at her, until she was clean. His tongue swirled around her clit, and he heard her give a breathy moan.

Just as he was about to take her into his mouth again, she got up.

"No!" he growled

"You are so greedy tonight."

"Can you blame me? You're tortur—"

She stuffed the scarf into his mouth before he could finish his sentence.

He growled at her, pulling hard on the scarves again, only to realize that she was right. He was going to have to break the bed to get free. And that was not going to be possible, either. His mind was already thinking about the type of knot she'd made, and how the fuck he was going to get one wrist out of it.

She reached for the candle that was lit on the nightstand, and slowly brought it toward him, at the same time she placed a block of ice in her mouth.

Fuck, she was doing every possible kinky thing he could think of in one night.

With careful intention, she dripped the candle wax onto his skin. It burned like a motherfucker, but the minute the ice in her mouth touched the parts of him that felt like they were on fire, the sensation was amazing.

She repeated the process a few more times, and each time the feeling only grew more intense.

Reaching over to the nightstand again, she put the candle

down and sat back. She then placed another block of ice in her mouth and with it, cooled his body down.

It was pure agony, but he liked it. A lot.

She trailed down to his cock, and he gasped for air as the cold ice in her mouth hit his erection, making it jerk in response to the coolness.

Then she started all over again.

HOLLY

SHE DEFINITELY OWED EVA FOR PUTTING THIS PLAN IN HER head. She wasn't sure where she found the confidence to do what she was doing to Jake—it was totally out of her comfort zone—but having him helpless to her touch, stirred something inside her.

Her ritual started all over again, and Jake's heated gaze only spurred her on. He was moaning wildly, bucking against the bed.

This time, she used the whipped cream on him, spraying his erection from tip to balls, then licked it off, one tongue lap at a time. He groaned in frustration.

Holly smiled. Eva had said there was no way in hell he'd be able to last a third round. She stopped as his cock twitched, and moved up his body.

He was a mumbling, groaning mess, his eyes wild with need.

"I don't understand you, sweetheart."

This time, his body shook with laughter, and again he tugged at the scarves.

It was obvious to her how much strength he was putting into the effort.

"You are going to break this bed. Just wait till I'm done."

He went off on another mumbling spree.

"I told you not to make me laugh, Jake. I'm not gonna untie you until I'm done," she said sternly.

He teased her with his eyes.

Turning, she lay on her back on top of him, and started touching herself again.

She knew it was driving him wild. She was so into it, she failed to notice how quiet he'd become. Her concentration was solely on making this birthday something he would never forget.

"You are fucking dead."

On hearing his voice, she turned her head and yelped—his one hand was free, so was his mouth, and he was, at that moment, untying his other hand.

She shot up off him and attempted to roll off the bed, preparing to run, when he grabbed her leg and yanked her back toward him.

"Hell, no...you started this. Now, I'm going to fuck you." He looked so serious that her heart skipped a beat before it began to pound desperately.

Holding her in place by her leg, he reached out and grabbed her arm, then pulled her closer.

Giving in to her fate, she giggled when he took her head in his hands and captured her mouth with his.

The kiss ignited every cell in her being, which was why she gave up on her pathetic attempts to escape and succumbed to his touch.

"Fuck me," he whispered in her ear, and she couldn't ignore his need anymore.

Positioning herself, she guided him inside her and lowered herself onto him, then rode him like her every breath depended on it.

TEN

HOLLY

THE SEX WAS ROUGH, POUNDING, SWEATY.

When he finally got his feet free, he repositioned her on her knees, ass up in all its glorious bareness.

This wasn't want or need anymore, it was pure carnal lust as he slammed into her from behind.

She was aching, and was sore in both a good and bad way, but he didn't stop.

He fucked her as if that was his very reason for living, and she relished the fullness and the pleasure coursing through her. He stiffened as he climaxed, jerking and driving in deep. Holly collapsed the minute he slipped out of her.

Jake dropped down next to her, spent.

It was a struggle for her to open her eyes, her body relaxed and exhausted.

"That was the best fucking sex I've ever had," he muttered, making her chuckle.

Her eyes refused to open. She needed sleep; she'd be back at work tomorrow.

She hated that he had to leave.

His lips brushed her shoulder. "I love you baby," he whispered softly.

So exhausted was she, she couldn't even say it back. She was already drifting away.

The next morning, they had an early breakfast, and then their paths parted in front of the hotel—his to the airport, hers to the hospital.

Tears stung her eyes, but she willed them away. In a few weeks, they'd be together again, until the New Year. She'd have Jake and Jamie with her for almost two months.

It was the silver lining to all these goodbyes.

Every moment away from him was becoming increasingly more painful. How had she done it without him for all those years?

"I'll see you soon." Jake's expression was forlorn.

"Stop looking at me like that, you'll only make me cry," she said as her lower lip trembled. She dropped a quick kiss on his lips and hurried away.

In the cab, she succumbed to her tears. She hated crying in front of him.

When she reached the hospital, she handed the driver some cash and wiped her face with her hand before climbing out. Once inside, she hurried through the hospital to the locker room, where she collapsed onto the blue sofa and waited for her sobs to subside.

Eva and Petra walked in minutes after her, and as soon as they saw her, rushed over. "What happened?"

Holly shook her head and wiped her tears away, but didn't answer.

She needed to stop crying, for heaven's sake.

He hadn't left her for good. He was coming back.

Get a grip, Holly, just get a grip!

A WAVE OF NAUSEA ROLLED OVER HER AS SHE MIXED HER shake. A week had passed since Jake left. He'd given her enough of Gus' shake, vitamins, and supplements to last her for the duration of her pregnancy. But even though she had been taking them diligently, something felt off. She was too scared to phone Gus and tell him—didn't want him to doubt his formula, to feel like he had failed for real this time.

It was just a bit of nausea and dizziness, which usually went away when she drank the shake.

It had to have been the birthday sex, and that's what she blamed it on. Some kind of delayed aftereffect; she was sure that no pregnant woman should be having that kind of sex.

She was still sore from her escapades, for crying out loud. The sickness was bound to happen.

After taking her shake and all the vitamins, she felt slightly better. She was surprised she could get the tablets down because it was literally a handful, but as it helped her with her condition, that's what she did.

By late afternoon, though, the dizziness hit her like a tidal wave in the elevator and she fainted.

She woke up with Bianca beside her bed.

"Holly, what's going on? Are you taking your supplements?"

She nodded.

"Then what is going on?"

"I'm just tired, drained, and I miss my family." She wanted to cry.

Bianca frowned. "Jake was here last week, Holly."

She chuckled through her tears. "I know, it was just very hard saying goodbye, and I still feel out of sorts."

"Oh, Holly. He will be back. You need to take it easy. You should go home."

She shook her head. "No. I'll be fine."

"Okay, just lie here for a while. Get some rest and I'll let one of the nurses come and wake you for rounds."

"Thank you."

"Do you need me to phone Gus?"

"No, no need. If it happens again, I'll phone."

Bianca nodded. However, just to be sure all was indeed well, she hooked Holly up to the sonar.

A smile spread across her face when saw the baby, but it soon froze when she noticed Bianca frowning at the screen.

"What is it?"

"I need you to go to the 3D scanning room. Something looks odd. Just odd, Holly, not wrong," Bianca reassured her.

She followed Bianca, and then settled on the bed while the doctor prepared the ultrasound. Her eyes looked down at her belly. She was showing more than she should be.

She knew what the odd thing was—twins. She could feel it in her bones. Flashes of her previous pregnancy played through her mind, and her heart ached at the thought of losing another child.

This was probably why she wasn't feeling well. The babies were taking too much out of her. And she hadn't been eating well, either.

The blue screen popped up above her, and she immediately saw the baby. Bianca started turning the hologram above her around.

A gasp filled the room at what she saw next. Another baby popped up, directly behind the one they'd just seen.

Tears formed in Holly's eyes and she covered them with her hands.

"It's just another one, Holly, not the end of the world."

Holly shook her head. "That's not it. Jamie is a twin. Her sister died at birth. You know, I was actually expecting this. I mean it's obvious...I look like an ox."

"You have to tell Jake."

"I know, and I will."

"You have to take care and rest as much as possible. These two little boys are relying on their...oops. Damn it!" Bianca was horrified at herself. "I'm so, so sorry."

"I'm having boys?" Holly asked, her voice breaking.

Bianca nodded. "I'm so sorry, I know you wanted to wait."

Holly smiled and touch her belly. Boys. She was having boys. "It's okay. Jake's the one who wanted to wait. I'm not good with surprises."

Jamie would be a sister to two brothers.

"Have you told Jamie you're pregnant yet?"

"No, but I sent a package for her with Jake—a story. I'll tell her soon."

"Sounds interesting. She'll definitely see the bump now, though, so it might scare her if you don't tell her. You have just reached the three-month mark, Holly. It's safe."

She nodded.

It was the first time she'd fainted since starting the shake, and hopefully, the next few days would be a walk in the park.

She was glad it was boys. She'd always wanted a brother, and boys seemed so easy. Girls were too emotional.

Bernie always said that she would raise ten boys before raising a girl, and now Holly was finally going to know what it felt like to have boys. The best thing was that her best friend was pregnant with one, too. She phoned Bernie immediately, too excited to keep the sex to herself.

Bernie was ecstatic about the news. She was due in less than seven weeks.

"How are you feeling about all this?"

"I'm fine, Bernie. I fainted, but I'm fine now. I'm sure it was because it's twins again, and I haven't been eating well. Please, don't tell Jake. Not about the fainting, or the gender. I haven't even told him it's twins."

"Holly, you should—"

"I'm okay, Bernie. Really. If it happens again, Gus and Jake will be the first to know, and I'm gonna tell Jake it's twins as soon as we speak again, I promise."

"Okay."

"Keep your mouth shut. Don't even mention it to Leo, he can't keep a secret."

"Okay," Bernie sang and gave a short chuckle. "Just look after yourself, please."

"I will. Promise."

"Okay, love you. Have you told Jamie yet?"

"I will, soon, tonight."

"I can't wait to hear what she is going to say. Tell Amelia to record it and send me the video."

"I will." She laughed.

"Love you, Holls."

"Love you more."

After the call, she sat with a grin on her face. She had her best friend back, and she was never going to run away again. She was here to stay.

But her smile soon disappeared when the two boys that were growing inside of her popped into her mind again.

Thoughts of Romy filled her head as she stroked her belly. She didn't know if she'd be able to carry on living if anything had to happen to these babies. They had to survive, no matter what.

When her shift ended, she let Bianca take her home. She was turning out to be more than just her doctor. Her concern for Holly showed every time she discovered something new with the pregnancy.

She reassured Bianca that if she fainted again, she would phone Jake immediately.

In her apartment, she heated up soup from a can and went to take a shower. Settling down, she texted Jake, although he was probably in surgery, and told him that she would set her alarm as they needed to tell Jamie tonight. He had to give her the present she'd told him to hide in his closet.

As she was more tired than usual lately, she went to bed early, after setting her alarm for quarter to one in the morning, which would be just before seven in Boston.

She'd barely slipped into a dream when the noise of her alarm woke her. Turning it off, she got up with a groan and ambled to the bathroom to wash her face and comb her hair, and then went over to her phone to Skype with her family.

It only rang a few times before Jake's face filled the screen. He was laughing at something Amelia said as the last few words of her sentence were audible.

"Hey, gorgeous," she said. "You with Jamie?"

"Yes." He gave her a sheepish laugh.

She smiled at him.

He was thinking about the birthday present she had given him; she could see it in his eyes.

"I promise, I won't do that to you again."

"Oh, fuck no, don't go making shitty promises like that. I loved every moment of it. I just didn't like saying goodbye."

"Yeah, I know. It's just harder for me."

"And you think it's any easier for me?"

"You go home to Jamie and your family, Jake. I have no one here."

"Sweetheart, you are part of my family. But I feel you. It's horrible. I want to rip myself in two and leave one half with you and another with Jamie."

"I'm sorry." She breathed deeply. "I'll try to be good next time."

"No, I like the naughty, slutty part of you."

She giggled.

"Maybe Jamie and I should just move there until your training is over."

"Over my dead body," Amelia's voice sang.

"Amelia, she's our child not yours," Jake snapped.

Holly laughed. "That would be really nice. But Amelia would miss her too much."

"I don't give a shit," he said on a laugh.

Amelia smacked him. "Hey, Holly." Her face appeared on the screen. "You're doing great over there. You don't need them."

Holly laughed again as Jake glared at Amelia.

"Would you really do that?" she asked Jake.

She heard Amelia whining in the background.

Jake shook his head. "Amelia, could you give us a moment?" He sounded agitated.

"Fine." Holly heard her say in the background.

"In a heartbeat, baby."

"What about Jamie? Don't you think the move would disrupt her too much?"

"She would be with us, we would be a family. Don't worry about Amelia, I know you're worrying about her."

"Jake..."

"I hate leaving you, Holly. I can't do that anymore."

"If you think it's for the best. I think it's time to give Jamie the package."

"Yeah?"

"Yeah, we've reached the twelve-week mark. It's safe."

"Great. Let me go get her."

He moved off-screen, and she heard him calling to Jamie.

Then suddenly their faces appeared on the screen.

"Mommy!"

"Hey, baby," she gushed. "Did Daddy give you my present?"

"Yes. What is it?"

"Open it and see."

Excitedly, Jamie opened her present and took out her T-shirt. She frowned at it, mouthing the words, then turned back to the screen.

"I'm going to be a sister?"

"Yeah, how do you feel about that?"

She could hear Amelia cheering in the background. "You are going to be the best biggest sister ever." Her face appeared on the screen and she kissed Jamie on the cheek. "Congratulations."

"When?" Jamie asked, and Jake started to laugh.

"Mommy is still growing the baby inside her belly."

"Your belly?"

"That's where all babies grow, pumpkin," Jake answered.

"How did the baby get into her belly?"

Amelia snorted.

"Oh, Daddy, why don't you answer that one?" Holly teased.

Jake blushed, but tried to suppress his smile. "Well..." he cleared his throat. "Daddy loves Mommy so much, so he gave her a tiny baby seed that can grow in her belly. You used to be a tiny seed, too."

"I'm not a seed."

"We started out as seeds, pumpkin, and when the mommy takes it..."

"When the daddy forces it on the mommy," Holly interrupted, joking.

"It wasn't forced," Jake snapped and Amelia shook with silent laughter. "As I was saying, the mommy grows the seed inside her belly. And after a very long time, it turns into a baby."

"Or two," Holly said.

"What?" Jake and Amelia said in unison.

"Don't tell me you are surprised."

"Twins again?" Jake hollered, which made Holly laugh. He did a funny dance and Amelia slapped him.

"Two babies, like me and Romy?" Jamie asked.

"Yes, sweetheart, like you and Romy."

"Is the one for Aunty Jamie, too?"

"No, baby. No. Aunty Jamie has Romy to take care of."

"So...I'm going to have two babies?"

"Yes," Holly laughed. The story about Jake and the little seed completely forgotten. "Are you happy, baby?"

"Yes." She pumped her hands in the air, and Jake and Amelia mimicked her.

"Okay, big sister. Mommy needs you to go play so I can speak with Daddy."

"Okay, love you, Mommy." They both kissed the screen, then she jumped off Jake's lap and went with Amelia.

"Twins again." Jake was grinning like an idiot.

"Yep, twins. I only discovered it recently, and it's been tough letting it sink in."

"It's not that horrible, Holly."

"Jake, I can't lose another child."

"You won't. Are you still drinking your shake?"

She nodded.

"I'm having twins!"

She just shook her head at his silliness. "I should've known as I'm carrying like an elephant."

"Well, you are my elephant."

"So sexy," she joked, making him laugh.

Their conversation drifted to Jake's and Jamie's visit, and he mentioned how Jane was driving him insane with wanting to see her daughter. He didn't bring up Mara, which ate at Holly. Their therapy sessions were over, and he still hadn't forgiven her. It was hard to accept that Jamie would never know her other grandmother—they kept to the story that Mara still had amnesia from the red part of the rainbow, not knowing who any of them were.

Gus was a different story, though. They had reconciled, and he'd forgiven her for what she'd done to him. But it was a whole other matter where Jake was concerned. She had to receive his forgiveness, and Gus refused to get in the middle of it.

Jake had been mad at his father at first, but came to his senses after he put himself in his father's shoes when Holly put herself in Mara's, wondering if Jake would forgive her.

He connected with that scenario, even though he was adamant that Holly would never do anything as fucked up as his mother had. Regardless, he was able to reason with it and started talking to his father again.

When they ended their call, Holly sank back into her bed. Just a few more weeks and she'd have her family with her again.

Her thoughts turned to the condition she'd been in with Romy and Jamie at twenty-four weeks. She was almost there now. But the difference this time was the fact that she knew she was carrying twins at the twenty-week mark.

She tried, but couldn't fall asleep.

Jake now knew that she was expecting twins, and Jamie finally knew about the pregnancy. Everything seemed to be working in their favor, but something nagged at her. And it was Mara.

She didn't know what exactly, but Mara was missing out on so much, and it irked her.

The last thing she should be feeling was compassion toward the woman, but she couldn't help it.

Sure, Mara had fucked up, lied to everyone, had gone off the deep end even, but surely she could be forgiven? She'd made a stupid, albeit monumental mistake, and then lied about it.

If she had to guess what Jake was struggling with most, it was the lying. The mistake, he'd come to terms with, because his mother couldn't have foreseen what had ultimately happened. But to continue lying for five years thereafter about it? That, he couldn't accept.

Exhaustion eventually kicked in and she drifted into a restless sleep.

ANOTHER WEEK PASSED, THE SEASON CHANGING FROM FALL to winter.

She woke up with tears stinging her eyes. She missed Jamie. It felt wrong not having her daughter with her. She shouldn't be alone, in her crappy apartment, with no one besides herself.

Her stomach turned, and she suddenly felt nauseous. Jumping out of bed, she ran to the bathroom, making it just in time.

She hated morning sickness, and unfortunately for her, it never seemed to dissipate after the three-month mark. But then, she wasn't the first to experience this, and she wouldn't be the last.

She took a slow shower, touching her belly that now resembled a melon. She dressed as warmly as she could—her wardrobe being limited, at best—stepped into a pair of boots, pulled on her jacket, and grabbed her shake before heading out.

On the bus trip to work, she drank her shake, which filled her, and by the time she got to the hospital, she was feeling slightly better.

Inside, it was warm and her cold bones started to return to normal. She went to the lockers to change into her scrubs and white coat. It was time she got a new top and soon, because her belly was taking up every available inch of space. There had to be maternity scrubs available. She made a mental note to ask the staff manager for one.

Her morning routine started.

She was present for all the cases that had been admitted. Most of them just had surgery, some of them were ready to be released, and others would be having surgery later.

After her morning rounds, she had a quick breakfast in the cafeteria, which left her with a few minutes to spare. She went to the staff manager's office to ask about the uniform.

On her way to the lower level, she started feeling light-headed and had to rest for her dizziness to calm down.

As soon as she felt stable enough to move, she continued on her way and upon reaching the manager's door, her feet gave way and she hit the ground hard. The last thing she heard were footsteps running toward her.

When she opened her eyes, she was on a bed again.

Bianca sat in a chair next to her.

She glanced around and noticed that she was hooked up to a monitor, which was regulating her heart, the boys' hearts, and all vital signs.

"They are fine, Holly, but you aren't."

"I don't know what is wrong with me."

"Gus and Jake are on their way." She sighed. "I'm sorry, but I had to phone them."

Holly nodded as tears filled her eyes. She hadn't wanted Gus or Jake to find out about this, but Bianca was right. Her babies had no one to rely on but her so that they could live, grow, survive.

She needed Gus to find out what the problem was.

"We need to draw blood. I'm not sure what's wrong with you. As your gynecologist, I highly recommend that we do all the tests there are, not just for you, Holly, but for them, too."

"Don't tell Jake that they're boys. He really wants to wait."

"I won't. Now, you need rest. You are in no condition to get back on your feet to work. Once we're able to identify the problem, we'll decide where to go from there."

"Thank you, Bianca."

"You're welcome."

As soon as Bianca left, she burst into tears.

From the minute she'd discovered she was pregnant, she'd had a pit in her stomach. She'd chalked it up to her pregnancy brain, but here she was, lying in a hospital bed once more.

This was real. She should have trusted her gut.

But it was too late for that now. Her main concern was for her boys. They needed to be okay.

Sleep took over and she drifted away, only to wake when Jake climbed onto the bed with her and wrapped his arms around her.

"I'm so sorry, baby." His voice was filled with sadness.

"Just the place I need to be, in your arms," she croaked, snuggling deeper into him.

"Holly." Gus was in the room, too. She blinked to clear her bleary vision—he was reading her chart. "Why didn't you phone the first time this happened?"

"It's happened before?" Jake looked at his father, then back at Holly.

"Because, at the time, I didn't think it was anything to worry about."

"Holly." Jake sighed, exasperated. He pushed himself

upright. "This is not just you anymore. It's us. You need to tell me about these things. How many times has this happened?"

"Just once. I told Bianca that if it happened again, I'd call you. Please don't be mad at me. I don't feel well." Her lower lip trembled.

"Baby, you need to let me in on these things. I can't help you if you keep me in the dark. Dad, what the hell is wrong with her?"

Gus shook his head. "There's nothing I can see here, Jake. On the chart, she looks great, her blood pressure is a tad high, but not like last time. It's manageable. Have they drawn blood?"

Holly nodded. "Bianca's really worried, but she promised me she wouldn't rest until she knew what was wrong."

"I agree. We need to know what is causing this."

Jake took her hand in his and kissed it.

"Where is Jamie?"

"With Amelia, which reminds me, I need to phone your mother. She's losing her mind."

He got up and left the room.

"I'm scared," she whispered to Gus.

Gus walked closer, looked at the monitor, then swung his eyes her way. "I'll find the cause, Holly, and I promise you I will do whatever is in my power to get you through this."

When she nodded, he bent down and kissed her on the forehead.

"Get some rest. We're not going anywhere."

She closed her eyes and fell asleep again.

HOLLY WAS SO SICK OF TESTS.

She didn't get to go home, because after the second time she fainted, she was admitted. Test after test was done. She felt like a pincushion from the amount of blood they'd drawn.

She was also sick and tired of her phone. Her mother, Amelia, Bernie, and Rodney had all been calling nonstop. She appreciated their concern, but their kind words were now grating on her. The only thing she was concerned about was in finding out what was wrong.

It all felt a bit too much like her last pregnancy, except her condition wasn't the same, and Jake hadn't been sitting in a chair next to her bed playing a game on his phone all those years ago.

His father was somewhere in the hospital, waiting on her blood results with Bianca.

She struggled to get comfortable, and gave up on trying to sleep when Bianca entered her room.

Jake slipped his phone into his pocket, and Holly sat up straight.

Bianca looked perplexed, which only increased her worry. Her heart rate picked up, the monitor she was hooked up to beeping her concern throughout the room.

"What is it?" Jake asked, noticing his dad had walked in behind Bianca. "Dad?"

"We picked something up that doesn't make sense, Jake. Holly needs to go for scans."

"Scans? Scans for what?"

"Jake, we don't know. Please, let us do our job, and then I'll have answers for you."

Jake nodded.

He helped wheel Holly's bed out of the room and into the next building. Upon entering, Holly froze when she saw Abigail.

The realization of what could be wrong with her washed over her, bringing tears to her eyes.

Abigail was an oncologist.

"No, please, not this," Holly cried.

"What is it, baby?" Jake asked.

"Why is Abigail here, Bianca?" Holly asked. She didn't know Abigail that well, but she was one of the top oncologists at this hospital.

"We have to turn over every stone, Holly."

She shook her head. "Jamie."

"What about Jamie?" Bianca looked confused.

"Not my daughter, my sister! Don't lie to me. What is Abigail doing here?"

"Your blood showed a shortage of oxygen, I consulted with her and she felt she had to be here."

Holly shook her head.

"Holly, if there is cancer in your family—"

"Her twin." Jake sounded so defeated that Holly barely recognized his voice.

"She has cancer?" Bianca asked.

Holly nodded, tears streaming down her face. "Had cancer, she died many years ago."

"I'm so sorry, Holly—"

"Let's just get her tested," Jake said firmly, taking control. "We will get through this. Just do the fucking test, Holly."

In shock, she just stared at him. She didn't have to do any test, because she already knew the result. Her twin had died of cancer, and now it was going to take her, too. What about her babies? She couldn't let anything happen to her babies.

She was wheeled into a room she recognized as being the same one where she'd found out she was carrying twins.

Had the cancer already been in her body back then?

She'd known something was wrong. Why hadn't she insisted in getting tested for everything?

What if the cancer was incurable? She should have demanded tests earlier, then perhaps they could have caught it.

If only she hadn't been so stubborn. If only she hadn't chalked it all up to paranoia.

She closed her eyes as Abigail worked on her. The woman was silent, there was no gasping or hitching of breath. Nothing that was giving off any vibes either way.

Holly's mind, though, went down a sad path, going back to when she was almost fifteen. When Jamie's cancer returned. It was a very dark time in her life.

She missed her sister, and wished that she were here right now holding her hand, but she wasn't. She couldn't be, because of fucking cancer.

Jamie had fought so hard, and Holly had fought with her. But in the end, Jamie had been taken from her.

Abigail tapped Holly on the shoulder, and she jumped from fright. Her eyes were still blurry from the tears she'd silently been shedding.

"You can get off the bed now."

She looked at Abigail, waiting for anything to come out of her mouth. "Just tell me."

"I found something on your kidney. It's hard to tell as you are pregnant, but we have to do a biopsy. I need to speak to Bianca so she can assist me."

"Please ask Gus."

"Holly, it's against protocol."

"The Peterses are not your run-of-the-mill doctors. Gus is *their* best chance, and Bianca would agree. Please."

"I'll see what I can do."

"Thank you." She climbed off the bed and took a seat in the wheelchair. An orderly wheeled her back to her room, where Jake and Gus awaited her. Jake immediately helped her get back into bed. Resigned, she slumped back with an arm over her eyes.

"Gus," Abigail said from the doorway. "Could I see you for a minute, please? Bianca will join us shortly."

When Gus stepped out, Jake turned to Holly with a somber expression on his face.

"Speak to me, please," he begged.

"She found something on my kidney. She has to do a biopsy, but she needs Bianca to assist her. I've asked her to rather ask your father, and that Bianca would agree with my request."

"Okay. That doesn't mean you have cancer. A biopsy is just another test."

"Jake..."

"You are not Jamie." His voice was harsh, making her jump. "Sorry. You are not your sister. Whatever happens, we will deal with it."

Leaning over, he kissed her on the head, his lips lingering there. Holly hoped it wasn't as bad as her mind thought it was.

Because in her mind, she was already in a casket. But she shouldn't think like that, couldn't afford to think like that. Her babies were too important. Her daughter was too important. She needed to be strong in order to cope and wait, like Jake suggested.

Only time would tell.

ELEVEN

JAKE

He was in the waiting room, waiting for Holly to come out of surgery. Fuck. At least his father was assisting Abigail with the biopsy.

He prayed, telling God that if he spared Holly, he would consider forgiving his mother. He hadn't prayed in a long time, but he needed to do it now.

She couldn't be taken from him, from Jamie, this way. She'd already dealt with cancer once too many times. And what about the babies?

The thought of losing her tore into his heart. What if this was his punishment for cheating on Kate? He never once regretted cheating on her, so this had to be his punishment.

He knew it sounded so stupid, but it was how he felt.

His phone rang and he looked at the screen.

Jane.

Everyone was either phoning or texting nonstop, wanting to know if he had any news.

Reluctantly, he answered the call.

"Jake, is she out yet?"

"No, Jane. I promise to give you a call as soon as she is."

"Okay." Her voice broke. "Tell her I love her."

"I will."

He put the phone in his pocket.

The hours ticked by, and he paced like a drunk sailor up and down the corridor.

Finally, his father walked out.

"She is stable, the babies are stable, and Abigail got her biopsy."

Jake nodded, his throat too clogged up with tears to get anything out.

"Whatever it is, Jake, we will get her through this."

Taking a deep breath in order to control his emotions, he replied, "Yeah, I know. It's just...she's been through this before with her sister and—"

"I'm really sorry, son."

He didn't want to think about cancer anymore.

All they could do now was wait. He phoned Jane to tell her that everything had gone well, but that they had to now wait for the results. He promised to call again as soon as he knew more.

HOLLY WAS AWAKE WHEN JAKE WALKED INTO THE ROOM.

"Hey, beautiful. How do you feel?" He smiled and put his hands on her stomach. Their babies were fine.

"Like I just came out of surgery," she joked weakly.

"Don't cry," Jake warned her. "We'll worry about the results when we get them. It might be something that isn't life-threatening, Holly."

She nodded.

To keep her mind off things—even though that was expecting the impossible—Jake collected some magazines that they went through together. When she eventually fell asleep, he left to go back to the hotel with his father. Once there, he phoned Jane the second he stepped into his room.

"Please, just tell me she is okay." It sounded like she was crying.

"We're getting the results tomorrow. I'll phone you the minute we know."

"I don't care what time it is, Jake. Just let me know."

"I will. Just hang in there. She—we all—need you to be strong for her."

Jane was sobbing by the time he hung up. He couldn't stand the fact that she was already behaving as if her daughter was dead, when they didn't even have a prognosis yet.

Sleep didn't come easy to him as his mind raced with things he didn't want to think about.

Tears filled his eyes, and before he knew it, he'd pushed himself up from the bed to sit on the edge. He buried his face in his hands and sobbed softly.

She couldn't have cancer. Not now that they had found each other again. Devastated, and devoid of any strength, he let himself fall sideways onto the bed. He must have dozed off, because a knock on the door woke him.

His side hurt, but that was because of how he'd remained on the bed. But he did feel better after his cry, which made him think about his mother, even though he didn't want to. She'd always told him that a good cry cleansed one's soul. He hated that she'd been right about that.

After a quick chat with his father, as that's who'd been at the door, they left for the hospital together, arriving early. He headed straight to Holly's room.

He found her asleep, so he collapsed into the chair next to her bed, taking her hand in his, and resting his head on the bed.

"I'll see if Abigail has the results yet," Gus whispered.

He gave his father a curt nod.

He kissed Holly's hand and felt her stirring.

"Morning, sleepyhead," she said.

"I'm not the one who was sleeping."

A hint of a smile touched her lips, but it soon vanished. She took a deep breath. He was sure that reality was weighing heavy on her again.

"Have you heard anything?"

He shook his head. "My dad just left to go find out if Abigail has the results yet."

She nodded, and it was clear to see that tears were close.

"You are not dying. I won't let you. You need to fight if you are going to beat this, Holly. I can't fight this alone."

The chuckle she let out was a tired one. "No one knows more about the fight you are talking about, Jake, than I do. I've been there." A tear rolled over her nose.

He wiped it away with his thumb. "I know. But I'm not going anywhere," he promised.

Bianca walked into the room. She was alone.

"Hi there, Holly. Jake." She smiled, but took a deep breath. Her eyes looked sad.

From the look on her face, Jake knew. Holly had cancer.

Abigail was next to walk into the room.

"What are our options?" Jake asked, before Abigail even had a chance to say one word.

"The cancer has progressed further than I thought. The only option is to abort the fetuses, then start chemotherapy and radiation. Without that, the chance of survival is slim."

Holly laughed sarcastically. "There is no way I'm going to get an abortion just for fucking chemo," she spat, the word coming out like it tasted bad in her mouth. "I lived through chemo with my sister, and I will not abort my babies, put myself, or my loved ones through that.

"It's just an option, Holly," Jake reiterated. He took a quick breath as Abigail started talking about treatment, and that the chances of beating the cancer would be greater if they terminated the pregnancy.

Without treatment, it would only spread throughout her body, as pregnancy, coupled with cancer, was a winning streak for going to one's grave early. The treatment Abigail was thinking of was harmful to the babies, hence an abortion being factored in. And if all went well, they were still young and could try again once Holly was healthy.

The words spun in his mind at such high speed, he couldn't see straight. Feeling weak, he forced himself to get up from the chair. "I'll just be a minute," he mumbled and walked out of her room.

He couldn't breathe.

The cancer had already spread, which meant that she'd had it for some time now and had been none the wiser. How the fuck hadn't she known? They should've picked it up when they took out the IUD. He knew he was being irrational. IUD removals didn't come standard with cancer screening.

How had this gone so wrong so fast?

He phoned Robin.

When the possibility of cancer had first been touched on, he'd given Robin a call without telling anyone, and during that conversation, after she'd heard what he had to say, she voiced her concerns. It was more or less what Abigail had told him, too. She'd asked him to call her the minute he knew it was indeed cancer. She also wanted to know what her doctor had to say.

"Oh, Jake. Not this," Robin said by way of answering.

"Yeah. I can't lose her, Robin."

"What did her doctor say?"

He relayed what Abigail told them, and Robin sighed deeply.

"Abort. I'm sorry. I feel like a monster for saying it, but as an oncologist, I don't see how she can beat the cancer with the babies inside her. It's going to spread like wildfire if she doesn't get the treatment she needs right away, Jake." She sounded worried. Her voice was breaking, too.

"Nothing..." he started, but couldn't finish asking if there was anything that could be done for his babies.

"No, I'm so sorry, Jake."

"Robby, there has to be an alternative, one that won't harm my babies."

"Jake there are many, but not as effective as chemo. The longer Holly has cancer inside her with the babies..." She sighed. "Having cancer and being pregnant is a huge risk to take, and more often than not, the outcome is fatal. There are other treatments that are not harmful for the babies, but the chances of them working are low."

"Percentage?"

"One you would understand in tumor terms; twenty-eighty."

No, fuck, shit!

"I'm talking to you as a doctor who works with this shit every day. You can't afford to was time in getting a second, third, or fourth opinion, Jake. I'm so sorry. It's her or the babies."

He nodded, although she couldn't see him. "Okay. I'll speak to you later." He cut the call.

He found the door that led to a small garden, and outside he sank to his knees, fighting to get air into his lungs. His body shook with sobs. He was going to lose his children.

A pair of arms wrapped around him, and from the masculine scent he knew it was his father.

"I'm so sorry, Jake."

"I know. I just spoke to Robin and according to her, the treatment that Abigail has suggested is the best way forward. The pregnancy has to be terminated, if Holly is to have any chance."

"I'm so sorry." Gus' voice cracked.

Fuck! Why couldn't Holly just have a normal pregnancy without any problems? Why this, why now when they were going to be a perfect family?

The tears continued to flow. Just thinking of killing his children was a painful stab to his heart, but it was them or her, or both.

And he couldn't live without her.

He didn't want to.

"It's going to be okay."

"It's not going to be okay, Dad. We have to make the decision that will take the life of two healthy children. Holly isn't a monster...and I'm afraid this is going to break her."

"It's going to be okay."

"No, it's not!" he cried into his father's shoulder. Why, why, why was God punishing him so much?

He wanted so many things for Holly. More children, another chance to have babies with her and now, now he was being forced to choose between his unborn children, or their mother. He was becoming the monster he'd thought her to be all those years ago.

And he knew, without a shadow of a doubt, that if he made her terminate the pregnancy, he would be the monster she'd thought him to be all those years ago. She would never forgive him—she'd end up hating him.

But he couldn't lose her. Not like this. What about Jamie?

As sad as it was, the pregnancy would have to be terminated. He couldn't think about the fetuses as babies anymore, as his children. He couldn't imagine a life without her in it, and if Holly died, their daughter would suffer.

Because he would be too depressed to look after her, wouldn't want to live without her, and Jamie would not just end up losing a mother, but a father, too.

They had to terminate. There was no other way.

Gus left him in the garden until he calmed down, and once he felt calm enough, he walked back inside and headed to the bathroom to wash his face before returning to the room.

Abigail was still in there.

Jake sat back down. No sign of a tear in sight.

"You okay?" Abigail asked.

He felt Holly's eyes on him, but he didn't dare look at her.

"Yeah, I'm fine. What's the plan?"

"There is one, but it's not going to happen right now Jake," Holly answered.

Jake frowned. "You said it's spreading?" He directed the question at Abigail.

Abigail spun to Holly. "Holly?"

"I'm not terminating the pregnancy."

Jake looked at Holly so fast, his head spun for a second. Had she lost her freaking mind? "Sweetheart..." he sighed, "...if you don't terminate, you will die and I am not okay with that. Jamie will not be okay with that."

"I know, which is why I will carry them until I'm six months along, and then I will fight."

"Holly, you don't know what you are saying. I won't take that risk."

"*You* won't take that risk? Yet you're fine with killing your children? Jake, we are past the twelve-week mark. You heard their heartbeat. That would be murder! These are no longer a bunch of cells inside me, they're fully formed babies! And I will not terminate this pregnancy. They are your children. *Our* children!"

"We don't have a choice!"

"There is always a choice, Jake. I've lived with this fucked up sickness. I know what it does. I'm not going to lose two healthy boys because of it."

Jake's eyes widened and his mouth fell open. *Boys?* He was going to have sons?

Holly closed her eyes. "I'm sorry. I know you wanted it to be a surprise, but Bianca slipped up when she discovered Cooper, I'm sorry."

"You already named them?"

"Yes, they are healthy and they are already little humans. Which is why I will not terminate this pregnancy."

"We can try again once you are back on your feet."

"You don't know that. This might be the last time, Jake."

"Holly, please."

"I am *not* going to kill my children." She screamed at him.

He stared at her, clenching his jaw. The muscles in his face pulsed, and he tried to contain his anger. "Then I can't fucking help you!" He pushed out of the chair and stormed out of the room.

Why was she being so damn stubborn? Her stubbornness was going to be the death of her. The only option she had to get better was out the window. He needed to think of ways to change her mind, and he couldn't do it while he was in her room. She made him so furious.

He would find something, and he would present her with a plan, a good plan, and then she would have no choice but to hear him out.

HOLLY

"WHAT IF I LOSE MY UTERUS, JAKE? YOU DON'T KNOW cancer the way I do."

"Then we will do a uterus transplant," Jake stated.

"*That's* your brilliant plan?"

"Yes. Then we'd still be able to have children."

"And what if that doesn't work?"

"Holly, please." He begged.

"No, Jake."

He stared at her. "Fine. Surrogate."

"Hell, no," she growled.

"You are not listening to anything I'm saying."

"That would just be humiliating. And I wouldn't be able to stand having another woman carry our child. No, Jake."

"Fine, adoption."

"Not the same."

"Damn it, Holly. You need to terminate this pregnancy if you are to live."

"I am not going to die. Stop being so negative," she said through clenched teeth. She was too tired to argue. "I've worked it out all in my mind, and your negativity isn't helping at the moment."

"It's facts, Holly."

"No, it's not. I can beat this, but I won't abort Bradley and Cooper. I need you to help me."

"This is me trying to help you. Fuck!" he screamed.

Holly wanted to yell at him. He was being so fucking stupid right now. It was his boys he wanted her to abort. She just couldn't. She'd hate him for it. Why couldn't he fucking grasp that?

"Get out."

Flabbergasted, he looked at her. "Excuse me?"

"If you are not going to support and help me to see this plan through, then get out."

"You are making a fucking mistake. Jamie and I are going to suffer because of your stupid decision." He stormed out, leaving her alone in the room.

She sighed. She wanted to go home so she could fight the fucking cancer where she was comfortable, but she had to wait to hear from the board. They were deliberating on whether to postpone, or terminate her contract. She needed her mother, needed Jamie at her side if she was going to survive this.

Even her mother had asked her to terminate the pregnancy. Why couldn't they all realize that she was doing this for her own well-being? The grief would kill her before the cancer did.

It had taken a lot out of Holly to tell her mother *no*, that she wasn't Jamie, and that she would succeed in fighting this.

Before they'd ended their call, her mother, still teary, assured her that she would be by her side all the way.

Rod phoned, Bernie phoned, begging her to consider a termination.

Holly was furious. First, they'd believed that she'd aborted Jamie and Romalia, and thought she was a monster because of it, and now they were begging her to do it. She couldn't handle it anymore. How did they expect her to fight the cancer after she killed her children? Were they somehow delusional? The grief would suck away at her will to live.

The boys were going to live. She needed all the reasons in this world to fight.

As for the others? They would have to make a choice over whether they were going to help her fight it or not.

The Peterses, apart from Jake, were the only ones who hadn't begged her to abort.

And that was a good sign.

She was counting on Amelia to be there for her.

Gus popped in a few minutes after Jake left and sat down on the chair next to her bed. He just sat there, looking at her.

"Please, don't leave me, too."

Holding the bridge of his nose between his thumb and fore-finger, he sighed, shoulders sagging. "He's not leaving you, sweetheart, he just doesn't know how to handle this right now as you keep dismissing his ideas."

"He needs better ideas, ones that don't involve killing the boys."

"I know you desperately want them. Believe me, we all want them."

"I can't and won't terminate this pregnancy." Silent tears streamed down her face. "Why can't he grasp that? If I kill them, I might as well die, too. I might not know your son as well as I should, but I do know myself. I'm not wired that way. Please don't ask me have an abortion."

Gus got to his feet and wrapped fatherly arms around her. Even if he wasn't her father, he showed her more fatherly love than Charles ever had.

"Now that, I understand. You should tell him that."

"He knows. I almost died with Romy. I will die with them, too, if he doesn't help me."

"He will. With men, it's only black and white, Holly. Always has been. They're of the mentality that it can either be fixed or it can't."

"Jake isn't like that," she said. "Otherwise, he would've never become a neurologist."

"Yes, he is. He takes every death he deals with very hard."

She knew that. She'd seen it at Downsend.

"You're telling me that he always goes into the OR confident he's able to save them?"

"It's the Peters syndrome."

She laughed.

"Or a godly one. He doesn't strive on the ifs. It's not how Mara and I raised our children."

"Well, he has to now. Because if he isn't going to be there for us, he will lose us."

"It's a lot for him, Holly, and I'm not making any excuses. I'm telling you who my son is."

"So he's already condemned me. Someone he is supposed to love."

"I'm not saying that. The cancer has spread. He's spoken to Abigail. He's also contacted Robin and she has your files. And she's the best at what she does, even if I say so myself. She's given him two scenarios. But he's not interested in two...he only hears the one."

"That's not how it fucking works. Where is his faith?"

"Jake creates his own type of faith."

"No, I don't buy that he is like that. He's not like that."

She refused to believe it. Jake had faith. She'd seen it before, and he'd told her that he had faith. Had he just been humoring her all this time, thinking she was stupid? If that was the case, she had no idea who he really was, then.

Resignedly, she slumped back down on the bed and let her tears flow freely.

"Just take it easy. The state you're in is not good for the babies, Holly. Or you. You need to surround yourself with happiness if you are serious about keeping these babies. I'll speak to Jake and try to make him see it your way, okay?"

She didn't even nod, but before he left, he patted her twice on the shoulder.

At around noon, Dr. Paulson entered her room. He was one of the hospital's owners, as well as a board member.

When she sat up straight, he smiled.

"The board has decided to postpone your contract, Holly. Most importantly, get better. Thereafter, you can complete the remaining time when you are healthy again."

"Thank you." She was so happy that she wanted to hug him. The training here would boost her career.

Even though he was just standing there, staring at her, looking a little uncomfortable, he managed to add, "I'm going to see you again. I just know it."

"Finally, some positivity."

That made him smile. Winking, he left the room.

She reached for her phone and reluctantly texted Jake.

I can go home.

Bianca and Abigail checked her over one more time, each had a report to fill out, and then they signed the release form.

She had no idea if either Jake or Gus were even at the hospital anymore. Thankfully, Gus came to collect her.

He drove her to her apartment and once there, helped her out of the car.

She felt weak, but she'd noticed lately that she was out of breath more easily. Of course, as anyone would, she tried to convince herself that it was all in her head, but her lungs told her otherwise—she just couldn't take in the amount of air her body needed.

The elevator ride to the apartment felt like it was taking eons, which only made her think of the memories Jake had left her with in this elevator, even though she was trying hard not to dwell on them.

It finally came to a halt, its door opening slowly.

Gus led her to her apartment and opened the door, and the first thing she noticed was that her bags had been packed and sat lined up on the floor.

"Jake packed them."

She felt embarrassed he'd had to do that.

While Gus carried the bags down to his car, which took two trips, she took a seat and waited. On the third trip, she accompanied him back down.

Why was she feeling so weak? She wasn't even that sick yet.

When she took a few deep breaths, she felt Gus' eyes on her, but she looked away and got into the passenger seat.

The fact that Jake wasn't here nagged at her. He'd promised that he'd be with her, be there for her. She didn't want to ask Gus where he was, but irritation won and the words rolled from her lips. "Where is he?"

"At the airport. He's not in the mood to talk right now."

There was nothing much she could say or do about that, so she nodded and fell silent again, staring out the window as Gus drove to the airport.

Gus led her to one of the lounges, where Jake was sitting, typing on his laptop. It was obvious to her that he was sulking, but she really didn't have the strength or the fight to argue.

Neither greeted the other, so she drank Gus' shake in silence and kept her back to Jake. Not once did she turn around to look at him, scared that she would start crying again, and she definitely didn't want to cry in an airport full of people.

No matter what, she refused to abort their boys. If he didn't understand that, maybe they weren't meant... Tears pricked her eyes. She couldn't even think about him not being in her life.

She took a steadying breath and blinked the tears away.

The wait for the flight was long and quiet. Gus apologized to her, saying that if it wasn't for the training some of the P&E staff had to take in California, they would've been on his jet by now, comfortable and on their way home.

They had a fucking jet. How rich were they?

Gus brought her something to eat and she smiled her thanks, but inside she was seething. Gus wasn't the one who should be bringing her food; he hadn't gotten her pregnant.

They boarded the plane. She'd never flown first class before, but it was definitely the way to travel. The seats were luxurious and reclined into beds.

Holly stole a look at Jake, but he was still focused on his

laptop, alternating between typing and reading.

With the amount of time he spent on his laptop, he really needed to get glasses. The image of him wearing glasses filled her with heat. He'd kill that look as well.

Would he ever make peace with her decision? She shook the thought from her mind as it wasn't something she needed to think about now. What she needed to do was carry these babies until the six-month mark and then...then she would cross all the bridges she needed to.

In a few hours she was going to see her mom and Jamie. It was almost Jamie's birthday, and according to her mother, Jake and Amelia had everything planned down to a T.

Bernie wanted to be there for her, but since she was close to her time, they'd decided against traveling.

She fell asleep watching a movie after lunch was served, and only stirred when the stewardess woke her with a gentle hand to the shoulder to tell her that they were getting ready to land. She even went as far as to help Holly into a sitting position.

When the plane touched down in Boston, Jake didn't even wait for her. However, Gus gave her a hand out of her seat, a soft smile splayed across his mouth, and then helped her off the plane.

Inwardly, she was all kinds of angry, wanting to yell at Jake and tell him to go Google moms who were pregnant with cancer, just so he could find out how many of them actually aborted their babies. But she didn't. He needed to deal with whatever issues he was having in his own time.

"Really? This is how it's going to be from now on?" She looked at Gus.

"Give him time, Holly."

What if she didn't have fucking time? But she was contradicting herself. No, she would fight and she would survive, with or without Jake. This time around, there would be no stories to tell her boys about their father being stuck in a fucking rainbow.

Amelia and Jane were waiting for them at the airport's entrance. Holly's eyes immediately scanned the surrounding area, but there was no sign of Jamie.

Her heart skipped a beat; she would kill Jake if he even thought of keeping Jamie away from her as a way to punish her.

Jane embraced her, gripping her tightly and sniffling in her ear. She and her mother had witnessed what cancer was capable of, and she needed her mother to be with her every step of the way.

"Don't leave me, Mom, please. I can do this."

"No one is leaving you, sweetheart."

On that, she was wrong. Jake was going to leave. She knew it.

She turned to Amelia, whose eyes glistened with tears. "Holly, what are you doing?"

"Amelia, please. I need you on my side."

A tear rolled down her cheek and she dabbed at it angrily. "Holly, I'm begging you to please terminate this pregnancy so you can fight this."

"I can't do that. I meant every fucking step I took that day, Amelia. And I thought you did, too."

"Fuck the steps, Holly! If you die, do you even have the slightest idea what it would do..." She shook her head. "Jamie needs you. And I don't want to lose you. Not like this."

Holly sighed. "Amelia, these babies need me just as much, if not more right now."

"Holly, you know me. I would never tell you to abort. It's against my beliefs. But you have a beautiful little girl, and a man who loves you to death."

"Really? Do you see him here? Because he's not, Amelia.

I'm not going to abort two healthy boys...I won't let the cancer win this time. But I need your help. Please. I need someone who will fight for me when I can't fight anymore. Don't let me do this alone. I can win this. I just need..." Her voice cracked and the sobs took over.

"Okay, okay. Shhh, I'm here." Amelia hugged her. "I've always been here." She pulled away and looked Holly straight in the eye. "Promise me that you are going to fight, or else I'll have to see someone about haunting your ass until the day I die."

Holly giggled, sniffling as she did.

"It's not funny, Holly, this is serious."

"I know. Of course it is. But that's not why I'm laughing. I said the same thing to a patient of mine. I promise you, I will fight. I have many reasons to live. I'm not going to lose this battle. Not this time."

Amelia hugged her. "You better not."

Holly sighed. At least Amelia was in her corner, it would have to be enough for now.

TWELVE

JAKE

Jamie's birthday party theme—Frozen—fit perfectly with the cold weather.

Holly was a vision dressed up as Anna, and she looked gorgeous. Jake had the privilege of being Kristoff, and his dog played a part, too, because they'd put reindeer ears on him so he could be Sven.

Jamie was an adorable Elsa, though with her black hair she was the complete opposite of the animation, but she looked beautiful.

Jane and Rodney were both dressed up to fit the era, but Gus...well, he'd dressed up as one of Cinderella's stepsisters, instead of a character from the chosen theme. But it had made them all laugh, nonetheless.

Jamie's cake was in the shape of Elsa's castle. Jake grinned as she closed her eyes to make a wish, then took a deep breath and blew out the candles.

Jake wondered what she'd wished for. Probably for Holly to

feel better. Jamie wasn't stupid. She knew her mother was sick. Or maybe she'd wished for her brothers to be okay—the ones he wanted aborted.

He hated himself for it, but he needed Holly to survive. He'd be broken without her.

He pushed those thoughts out of his mind, and concentrated on having fun with Jamie. It was the first birthday he got to experience with her, and he wondered what the others had been like.

He looked over to where Holly was sitting on the sofa. Her face looked pale and clammy, and she was short of breath. But they were all pretending that she was okay for Jamie's sake.

He was still so livid with her, with everyone who seemed to be okay with her plan. No one was happy that he was so distant with her, but what use was it when she was practically killing herself?

She'd made up her mind about how things were going to go a long time ago.

He wanted to scream whenever he saw Holly laughing and making jokes with Rod and Amelia. He couldn't stand it anymore, so after Jamie had been bathed and fallen asleep, Jake went upstairs and threw some clothes in a bag. He clenched his fists, his knuckles turning white as he walked into the bathroom to grab a towel and his toothbrush. Angry tears filled his eyes, but he grit his teeth together and willed them away.

Holly stood in the doorway of the bedroom, her eyes trained on the bag. He didn't look at her, just strode over to his bag, and dumped his towel and toothbrush into it.

"You're leaving?" she asked.

"I can't stay here, not while I'm feeling this way."

"I see. And what should I tell Jamie when she asks me where her father is?"

"Tell her I had to go away for work. I'll Skype with her at night"

"Damn it, Jake. Enough with this already!"

He looked at her. "You think I'm playing a fucking game? You better think again, Holly."

"Fine, if you want to leave, fucking leave. Just know that I'm not the one running away this time." She stormed out of the room.

He shook his head at her retreating back. He wasn't running away. He just hadn't made peace with her choice. And he didn't think he'd be able to. Couldn't she get it into her head that he wanted her to live? If he thought there was a chance that she could survive and keep their children alive, he'd be on her side? But he just didn't see how that was possible.

He took long, measured steps down the stairs, but came to a halt when he saw another cake with candles on it.

Holly was sobbing in Amelia's arms, and his heart clenched. He hung his head for a beat. He was being such a fucking jerk. Composing himself, he went over and took Amelia's place, wrapping his arms around Holly as he stared unblinkingly at the cake that was obviously meant for Romalia. Sobs wracked violently through Holly and Jake tightened his grip.

Everyone in the room was teary-eyed.

"I'm sorry I'm not wired like you. I can't do this, Holly. I don't know how." He brushed a kiss over her forehead, then grabbed his bag and left.

He allowed himself to cry all the way to the hotel. He hadn't known she celebrated Romalia. All those years when they'd thought Holly had gotten an abortion, Amelia had celebrated the baby with a cake on the estimated due date. Now, he saw Holly did the same for the daughter they'd lost. He knew that that was why she wouldn't terminate the pregnancy now. Regardless, he'd meant what he said.

He couldn't watch her give up and get sicker by the day. He just couldn't do it.

IT HAD BEEN THREE WEEKS SINCE HE'D LEFT. HE'D SPENT the first night in a hotel, but decided to move into the cabin for the time being. He'd taken the month's leave he'd planned on taking for Zürich.

Amelia was living with Jamie and Holly. She was pissed at him for leaving Holly so abruptly, but he couldn't understand how they were all so okay with it. They all thought she was going to survive.

Even his sister, Robin, had told him that if Holly believed she could survive this cancer without terminating the pregnancy, then she would carry out her wishes. She didn't give him her professional opinion on the matter, just that she wouldn't force Holly to abort the babies.

He'd wanted Robin to tell him that he was right, and that Holly's faith wasn't enough. Couldn't they see it?

Everything had been working against them right from the beginning. First, she was diagnosed with cancer while pregnant, and with her weakened immune system, it was only spreading faster than it normally would. Second, Holly's blood type was O negative, which made finding blood a bitch. Robin was already getting a supply stocked for when Holly went into surgery, but what if she needed an organ?

Everything was going according to Holly's plan, he was just not there to do his part. But others could do it for him.

He checked in with Melia and Jamie on a daily basis, and had spoken to Anna, who was going to take over the project on Jake's behalf. He refused to speak to her about Holly whenever she asked him.

He was certain this was God's way of punishing him for his ways.

His phone vibrated with a text from Holly.

I'm horny.

The corners of his lips curved up, but then he shook off the smile. How was it possible that she had no idea what she meant to him? He'd asked her to trust him and she hadn't. She'd made up her mind without even consulting him.

But he couldn't stop himself from dialing her number. He wanted to hear her voice. They hadn't spoken since Jamie's birthday.

"Finally," she said.

"How?" he asked, his voice breaking. "How am I supposed to do this, Holly? Please tell me." His voice came out harsher than he'd intended it to, and then his throat clogged up with unshed tears.

"Just be present. Help me fight this, Jake. I need you with me on this. 'Cause I promise you, if you are not and I kick this asshole in the butt, there will be no going back."

He didn't like what she was insinuating. "You're asking me to watch you fucking die."

"No, I'm asking you to be one of the reasons I have to live for. You, Jamie, the boys. That's all I need to fight this," she hissed, then started sobbing. "Right now, you're being a fucking asshole, and I already have a major one to deal with, I can't do two at the same time."

"Why couldn't you just terminate the pregnancy and fight like any other normal woman would do?"

"Jake, have you even researched the number of pregnant women with cancer who choose to terminate their pregnancies? Almost none of them take that option. I am being normal."

He grunted in response. He had, but he'd also seen the many losses. "Holly—"

"Look, I know it can't be easy not having everything go your way, but you need to trust me now. I will fight this. Just one more month, Jake. But I need to give birth to our children first. They need you. Your father has me on a regimen of steroids and vitamin C so their lungs will be strong enough at birth, as well as make their birth easier."

"Do you think I'll be able to tolerate anyone involved if they kill you?"

"They are not killing me. And neither is this fucking cancer. Make a decision, Jake. You're either going to man up and help me beat this, or you're going to turn your back on us—in essence, run away. Don't make the same mistake I did."

The phone went silent in his ear.

He felt totally and utterly useless. A jerk.

She wasn't the one running away this time.

He was.

She was right. He had a fucking choice to make.

HOLLY

She was taking a long bath.

Her stomach was much bigger than it had been with Jamie and Romy at this stage.

So far, the pregnancy was going really well, better than she'd expected, in fact. In another four weeks, her little boys would be able to come into this world.

She rubbed a hand over her belly and felt a small flutter of movement.

Robin had just left, and Holly had told her that she didn't want to know how far the cancer had spread. She knew it wasn't just on her kidney anymore. Robin's face, and the way Holly was feeling lately, confirmed it. But that didn't matter right now. All that mattered was that the boys were still safe in her womb, and that they were growing.

Sighing, she sank lower into the water. She hadn't thought that her conversation with Jake would go as it had. And she'd never hung up on him before. But how else was she supposed to get through to him?

What if Gus was right about who Jake truly was?

What then?

Would Jake leave her to fight this alone? And what about Jamie? Was he just going to leave her as well?

Jamie was already asking both her and Amelia to make her daddy come home from work; she constantly wanted to speak to him. She missed Jake, which was normal; she loved her father. But she couldn't understand why her mommy was so tired all the time, and why her daddy wasn't at home to make Mommy feel better.

There was a knock on the door.

"Holly, can I come in?" Amelia asked.

"Yes," Holly called out weakly. The bath was filled with bubbles, so all the important bits of her body were covered.

Amelia opened the door and walked over to the bathtub, sinking down to the ground next to it. She stirred the water with her finger.

"Give him time."

Holly nodded, but her heart ached. What if...no, she couldn't think like that. She had to beat this.

"Robin phoned when she got home. She wants to see you in a few days again."

"Why?"

"Holly, your hormones are like wildfire to the cancer. Why do you think my brother wanted you to terminate?"

"I can't."

"I know you can't, you crazy woman. I hope you'll be there —no, you better be there—to show those two boys that you loved them so much you were willing to die for them."

"What if it was you, Amelia?"

"What do you mean?"

"What if you were in my position now? What if you fell pregnant and then got cancer?"

"Holly, I'm different. I don't have a child that needs me."

"Look me in the eye"—Holly sat up in the bathtub, pulling her knees to her chest—"and tell me you would get an abortion. Amelia, I feel them, they are healthy. It's just fucking cancer."

Holly could see the doubt in Amelia's eyes as she looked up at Holly.

"Exactly my point. You wouldn't do it, either. You would fight with Armand every single day. So don't ask me to abort, not now."

"I'm sorry." She squeezed Holly's hand. "I still can't believe you told him there was no way back if you beat this and he wasn't here for you."

"Would you go through all this alone and let Armand back into your life when all the crazy was over?"

"I don't know."

"We are not so different, you and I, Amelia. I need your strength, so please stop being negative."

"I will, I promise."

"Besides, your brother is being a dick. If he keeps on condemning me, I will make it my master plan never to take him back."

"You are insane, you know that?"

"I'm not that crazy, really. Now, could you please help my fat ass out of this bath?"

Amelia laughed. "You better keep your promise, sister."

"I'm going to be fine, you'll see."

Amelia grabbed a towel and helped her to stand, throwing the towel around her body before helping her out of the bath. "I meant what I said. I will Ouija your ass if you die on me. If there's one thing I do not want to hear from Jake it's *I fucking told you so.*"

"He won't say it. I promise."

Holly went to her room, dried herself off, and put her pajamas on. She took a few calming breaths. She was still furious with Jake, but the anger wasn't good for the boys.

A cup of hot chocolate was what she needed, so she went downstairs and made herself one. She still didn't feel quite at home here, but Jamie did, and that was all that mattered. It also mattered that it wasn't the same house he'd shared with Kate, though Rodney had told her it was gorgeous.

This house was surrounded by big, beautiful trees. It also had two extra rooms, one for each of the boys.

They were already a part of her life. Why couldn't everyone just accept that?

She sat down at the kitchen island and opened her laptop so she could Skype with Bernie, something they did almost every night.

Bernie's new baby boy was so beautiful and healthy. She'd named him Donovan, and he was born a week after Jamie's birthday.

"Just give him time, Holly," Bernie said after Holly relayed her phone call with Jake.

Holly huffed.

"Don't you even dare think it."

She sighed. "Think what?"

"You know what. You promised to fight, and you do not have the luxury to think about *what-ifs* right now."

"I know. I just don't think he's ever going to get on board with this, Bernie."

"Then give him a fucking ultimatum. Be hard on him."

She laughed mirthlessly. "I have, and he's still not here."

"You go, girl. And if he is that type of idiot, fuck him."

"Watch it," Amelia growled upon entering the kitchen.

"He is an idiot, Melia!" Bernie snapped.

"I know he is...but he's still my brother."

They bantered back and forth playfully, until Bernie had to end the call because Donovan had woken up.

She missed having Bernie around, but she was glad and thankful that Amelia was with her. She was a great help with Jamie.

She assisted Holly to the couch, then draped a blanket over her as Holly rested her head against the soft armrest. She closed her eyes for a moment, but then felt Amelia getting up off the couch.

"Someone's here," Amelia said.

Holly opened her eyes. She hadn't heard anything, but she saw headlights reflecting through the curtains. "Probably Rodney," she said, closing her eyes again.

He'd said he'd come over either tonight or tomorrow. He was just as worried as Bernie, but they'd all promised to stand by her and help her fight.

The door opened.

"Amelia, can you please give us a moment?"

Holly's eyes flew open and her heart fluttered. He was home.

"Daddy!" Jamie ran into his arms and he picked her up and kissed her. A grunt left his mouth as she hugged him really hard. "I missed you so much!"

"I missed you more." He looked over at Amelia. "Go home. I'm sure Armand misses you."

"Jake..."

"You can come back tomorrow and be all jolly again."

"Fine." Amelia walked over to Holly and kissed her on the cheek. "Phone me if he starts acting like an ass, okay?" She squeezed Holly's shoulder, then picked up her purse from the coffee table and left.

Jake put Jamie down and gave her a doll.

"Look, Mommy."

"I see. And it's not even your birthday or anything," Holly said, raising an eyebrow a Jake.

"Thank you, Daddy." She reached her arms up and Jake crouched so she could wrap them around his neck.

"Go play in your room, I'll be there in a bit okay, pumpkin?"

"Okay," she said, running out with her present.

"You are spoiling her too much."

Jake didn't say anything.

Holly's eyes moved from Jamie's retreating figure and back to him. He was pinching the bridge of his nose between his thumb and forefinger.

Even when he looked like a horrible mess, he was still sexy.

She hated that.

"I swear if you die on me…"

Her lips started to curve, but she clamped them together to stifle the smile.

"It's not funny, Holly. This is serious shit."

"That it is, Jake. I've dealt with cancer before, as you very well know. But the difference is, I *know* I can beat this."

"What's the plan, then?" he asked, walking toward her. He sat down on the couch across from her.

Hope bubbled up inside her, but she remained calm and collected. "Deliver the boys, and then Robin will do what she has to do to get the cancer out of me."

"So, there's no fucking plan."

"Not yet."

"But it's spreading, Holly."

"Jake, I have four more weeks left. Just four more. Then you can hack away."

"I don't fucking want to hack away anything, Holly. That's my fucking point," he ground out between clenched teeth.

"So, you want me to hate you so much that I'll never be able to look at you again? Because that's what will happen if I get an abortion."

His face fell and he sighed. "No."

"You want me to fight?"

"Yes, hard."

"Then get my boys to live and I will fight, Jake. Don't become the monster your mother made you out to be."

"Holly, I'm not."

"Right now, you are, because you want me to kill our children."

"You are sick, sweetheart, it's a completely fucking different story."

"I won't fight if I kill them or lose them, Jake. Ever think about that? It will destroy me. I cannot go through that again. I won't. You have no fucking clue how hard it was for me after Romalia died, and that death wasn't planned. Do you have even the tiniest inkling of how much I will hate you, and myself, if I get an abortion? They are healthy, and they can survive this. *I* will survive this if I have them to live for. So stop asking me to abort them and help me." A sob tore through her throat and she covered her face.

She felt his arms around her, hugging her tight.

"I'm sorry," he whispered.

It felt so good to have his arms around her again.

"This is all my fault."

"No, it's not. You didn't force me into this."

"You sure about that?" he joked, eliciting a laugh from her, through her tears and all.

"I'll try to be more understanding, and I'll do whatever is in my power to get you through this."

Thankful, she nodded.

"But you have to do your part."

"I promise," she said.

"Okay." When he brushed a kiss over her lips, she darted her tongue out, urging him to deepen the kiss.

She hadn't been joking when she'd texted him that she was horny.

THIRTEEN

HOLLY

HAVING JAKE ON BOARD MADE EVERYTHING EASIER, AND Holly felt amazing during the two weeks Jake had spent with her.

They even made love, big bump and all. Not without difficulty, though. Jake had wanted to give up at one point, but Holly needed the intimacy, so refused. And because of that, they'd tried every position they could think of until they found one that worked perfectly.

For some reason, she'd thought that sex was even more mind-blowing during pregnancy. It had to be the hormones or something, she wasn't sure. Regardless, it was out of this world.

But his leave was almost up. Cases were piling up, which meant he had to get back to work.

Amelia would come back soon for good. She made sure to check up on Holly at least once a day, only to have Jake chase her away.

Boston was beautiful during the festive season. On one of

the days Holly felt well enough to leave the house, she and Jake took Jamie to go look at all the Christmas lights—their togetherness giving them a sense of being a proper family. For once, it didn't feel as if her cancer loomed over them like a dark cloud.

They had dinner at a small restaurant, but halfway through their meal, a strong wave of dizziness swept over her; she fainted yet again.

She woke up in the hospital, with her mother in a chair next to her.

"What happened?"

"You fainted, sweetheart. I need to go and get Robin."

She stared at the boys' heartbeats—fast and healthy. Not like Jamie's and Romy's had been. She glanced around to room for Jake, but he wasn't there.

Robin walked into the room shortly after her mother left. The look on her face said it all. "It's time, Holly."

"No. I need to carry them for two more weeks."

"That would be a negative. Holly, you have to face facts. It has to be now, or I can't help you."

"Robin, you are a Peters, and one of the best at what you do. Don't say that."

"You don't have to stroke my ego, Holly. This is insane. I'm not the type to give up, but we have to start finding organs."

"I don't want to hear it."

"You may not want to, but you have to. I might be able to save a part of your liver, and the one kidney might still function, if I can remove the cancer with laser treatment. Holly, in another two weeks you will die, because the cancer is spreading to your pancreas. If we wait these two weeks out, I won't be able to help you anymore. But if you deliver now, there's hope."

Holly swallowed hard. Hearing Robin say what she had to say out loud weakened her resolve.

"Please, I'm urging you to deliver them now," Robin begged her.

"It's only five and a half months."

"It's more than what your daughters got. I'm trying to save *your* life for your children. I can't do that if you fight me on this."

"Phone your father," Jane said to Robin. "Hear what he has to say, and I'll phone Frank."

Holly nodded. "Where is Jake?"

"In the middle of a surgery. He said he would try his best to be here."

Tears blurred her vision, but she managed to nod.

Jane left the room to give Frank a call. Holly knew her mother was scared, but she needed them to stay positive.

Even if Frank got on the first flight out, he wouldn't make it here in time. Armand was her boys' best hope right now.

Gus walked into her room, and the first thing he did was look at the monitor to see if Bradley and Cooper were doing fine.

"Will they make it if I deliver now?"

"We've done all we could for them, it's your turn to fight now."

"I'm as ready as I'll ever be," she whispered.

"Armand will be present during the surgery. He's just occupied with another situation at the moment. But he promised he would do whatever he needs to do to save the boys' lives, Holly."

She silently wrung her hands, the worry making itself known through her action.

"Don't be scared. Be safe with the knowledge that you have a really great team of doctors assisting you, who also happen to love you."

She managed to give Gus a wobbly smile.

"All you have to do is fight."

Taking a deep breath, she nodded, then released it.

Along with the boys, her own heartbeat was beating like crazy.

"Can I give her something to calm her, Dr. Peters?" Gus asked Robin.

"You sure can, Dr. Peters," she replied.

This time, instead of tears, Holly snorted.

"You're going to be okay."

She looked down at her stomach, sad that she couldn't give them more time.

Please, don't let me lose them, she prayed as tears filled her eyes. She couldn't go through that pain again.

Romy was one too many.

"Where are Amelia and Jamie?"

"At home, packing your bag. They'll be here soon. I have the OR booked and ready to go. It's time, Holly."

"I guess it is," she said.

"I'll meet you there." Gus turned on his heel and hurried out, but called over his shoulder, "Text your brother, Robin."

Robin grunted in reply.

Holly smiled.

"It's not funny. He's like a bear with a sore tooth and a huge stick up his ass," Robin said, pulling her phone out of her pocket.

Holly reached for her own phone from the bedside table. She needed to let Jake know that she was going to make it out of surgery. And, he had to make sure the boys would pull through.

I love you. Make sure my boys are fine.

Smiling, she hit *send*.

She knew he wouldn't get it in time, but hoped that he'd know how much she loved him.

Surprisingly, her phone buzzed with a voice note from him. She hit play.

"They are my boys, too, and you better wake up, woman."

Holly burst out laughing. And then a text came through.

I love you more.

She doubted that.

But she didn't doubt that she wanted to live—she needed to live.

Robin broke into her thoughts. "We are taking a huge fucking chance, Holly. I'm not going to lie to you. My dad is going to deliver the babies, and I'll try to remove as much I can. I'm hoping to save one of your kidneys, and a piece of your liver, then target it with radiation and a dose of chemo." She nodded to herself. "Yes, that might work."

"Solid plan."

"It has to be...for now."

She was glad that Robin had a plan, and she was glad that her mother was here. She just wished she could see Jamie and Jake before going into surgery.

Bernie, Rod, Frank...everyone she cared about flew through her mind.

What if she never woke up? What if that happened and she'd never said goodbye to them? What then?

I can't think like this. I just can't.

She should have made love to Jake one last time.

You can't think like that, she yelled in her head. *You are going to beat this. It's not going to take your life.*

She took a few deep breaths.

"You okay?"

"Just peachy," she said in a shaky voice.

"It's okay to be afraid, Holly."

"I can't afford to be afraid, Robin."

Robin had tears in her eyes. "You listen to me and you listen good. You have to fight this. I'm not losing my brother like that again, you hear?"

She studied Robin's face. Even though she'd heard how hard it had been on Jake from so many people, it was different hearing it from Robin, especially since Robin's eyes shone with tears; she almost never cried.

"Robin?"

"No, Holly. You know what happened after your disappearance. You know he smashed up his BMW, and you know he went looking for you. But what you don't know is that when my parents and Amelia found him in Seattle, when that lie fell on him and became his reality, that was the day I lost my brother." She wiped her eyes.

"I guess I understand why he doesn't want to forgive our mother. She turned him into something he never was. She brainwashed him into never asking you about the baby, or what happened, if he ever saw you again. She tried to erase you from his mind. There was a time when I thought she'd succeeded. He eventually got better, but he was no longer the brother I'd known. He was a stranger who just looked like my brother. None of us talked to him the way we used to, and I guess it's one of the reasons why Amelia hated you so much." She sniffed.

"This continued for a year. And then, he bedded every woman he could, only because they had strawberry-blond hair. He did a lot of fucked up things. I was ashamed to call him my brother." She paused.

"Thankfully, he went to China, which is when we hoped he'd get his life back on track. And it seemed like he had because when he returned, he was the Jake we knew and loved. But as time went by, I realized it was all just an act. You see, I'm a great observer. When no one else was looking, it was obvious to me that Jake was still miserable."

One of the pictures in Amelia's house flashed through Holly's mind. The one where he was staring at nothing. Was that what Robin meant? One of the times he'd lowered his guard?

"He pretended for our sake, probably some Chinese wisdom he learned. I knew I would never get my brother back. Until about a year ago. At first, I didn't understand what the fuck he was going through."

Amelia had told Holly the same thing.

"He was so confused that even Kate worried about him. He was fighting against something none of us could see. Even my mother was worried about him. One Sunday, we were prepared to intervene, but when Jake pitched up, he was completely different. I thought he'd somehow cottoned on to what we wanted to do and decided to pretend again, but"—more tears pooled in her eyes, and she swiped at them angrily—"when no one was looking, I saw my brother for the first time again, Holly. He wasn't the sad person he'd been trying for ages to hide. To me, it looked like he'd begun daydreaming again, and he had a grin on his face. He was happy." She rubbed a hand over her face.

Holly swiped at her own eyes.

"I thought that Kate was finally enough for him, and that the past few years were over. We joked once more, and even my mother started seeing the real Jake. And then that breakdown happened."

"What breakdown?"

Robin blinked. "The one at P&E. Rodney didn't tell you, did he?"

Holly shook her head.

"I guess it must have been right after you gave him an ultimatum, except he couldn't choose you, because of us. I watched my brother being torn in two—by something that was invisible to us—and the stranger returned." She took a huge breath.

"That entire month, none of us knew what the hell was

going on with him. But I knew it had something to do with the wedding. He didn't want to marry Kate. I even told my mother to break the wedding off. To do something, but she just ignored it. I even mentioned your name, and that I was no longer going to just pretend my brother was okay." She laughed. "You know what her reply was? That Kate was the best thing to ever happen to him, and that we had to push him to see it. Push him! What type of a mother would push her child onto someone who was far from the right person for her child?"

"Robin, I—"

"I'm not done. He had a breakdown because he was torn in two, Holly. He wanted to choose you, I know he did. Look, I'm not saying that what you two did to Kate was okay by any means, far from it. But we all knew Jake would never get over you. As much as my mother wanted to believe otherwise, we knew the truth. I prayed for something to happen so that he wouldn't go through with the wedding—and then something did. That emergency got him off that plane. I now know it was a higher power. Because if he hadn't gotten off that plane, my brother would still be a stranger, married to the wrong woman, one he didn't love, and aching for another.

"And then there was a phone call from Amelia. She fought with my mother, rambling on about a little girl that belonged to you, who looked just like my brother. Of course, none of us knew you'd returned. But things just made sense somehow, and that's when we all figured out what it was he knew. Except Kate. I now know that it was never her who brought him back—it was you."

"Robin, why are you telling me this?"

"Because you need to know how much you fucked up my brother when you left, Holly."

Holly shuddered with regret, for all that had gone wrong,

for the life that was lost, for everything that happened, and for what she'd set in motion by leaving. "I didn't mean to."

"That's not my point. We all know the truth now. My point is that he was a mess when you left, beyond repair, and he lost himself completely, when in actual fact you were still alive. Can you imagine the alternative? You can't die. You have to fight, please."

Holly nodded. "I made him a promise, one I intend to keep."

"I cannot lose Jake, Holly. Because if you die, there is no coming back for him this time. Not only will Jamie lose her mother, but she'll lose her father as well. And those two boys might as well become Amelia's, because Jake would never be able to look at them."

"Okay, I get it! Just do what you have to do and keep my heart beating. I will do the rest."

"Deal." Robin sighed, wiping yet more tears away, just as Aggie walked into the room.

"No time to waste, Aggie. I need her prepped and ready to go. Bring her to OR two, ASAP."

"Sure thing, Dr. Peters." Aggie smiled at Holly. "You ready to fight, baby?"

Holly didn't answer. She was finally seeing the whole picture of how she'd broken Jake.

"Baby?" Aggie spoke again.

Giving her head a slight shake, she smiled. "Sorry, Aggie."

"You ready to fight?"

"I have no choice."

"I'm glad you know that."

As Aggie adjusted the IV, the door opened and in walked Amelia with Jamie. The images in her mind had to be pushed aside.

"Good, you're awake."

"Mommy!" Jamie shrieked. "You okay? Is Cooper and Bradley coming, Mommy?"

"Shhh, baby. It's a hospital." She smiled as Amelia helped her onto the bed. Jamie snuggled into Holly's arms. "Yes, they are. I need you to be a good girl for Aunty Amelia, okay?"

Jamie nodded excitedly.

"That's my big girl."

Amelia rummaged in her bag and pulled out some crayons and a coloring book, as well as some story books.

Holly took one from her and began reading it to Jamie. Her voice was on the verge of breaking.

You okay? Amelia mouthed.

Holly gave her a sliver of a smile and nodded. But she was far from okay. The very real picture Robin had painted of the time she'd left was embedded in her mind. She now understood why Jake had reacted negatively toward her for choosing to keep the boys.

A part of her felt like a horrible mom. What would happen to her little girl if she didn't make it? Girls needed their mothers. Was she being selfish in wanting it all, that she was prepared to risk it all?

Aggie returned a few minutes later. "It's time, sweetheart."

"Let's go, pumpkin." Amelia reached out her hand to Jamie and she hopped off the bed.

Holly touched Amelia's hand. *Thank you,* she mouthed.

Amelia just closed her eyes and smiled, shaking her head.

"Love you, Mommy," Jamie said.

"Love you more," she said in return, exaggerating the tone of her voice, which made them all laugh.

Aggie and two other nurses started to wheel her out of the room.

"Where's Armand?" she asked Aggie.

"He's waiting in the OR."

"Jake?"

"He's going to try his best to be there, sweetheart."

Nodding, she asked, "Are the boys going to be fine?"

"They are Peterses, but most of all, they are Scallangers," Aggie stated. "They'll fight because they'll know how brave their mother was."

"I'm not dead yet, Aggie."

"Oh, don't even think about it, baby."

She chuckled. She was exhausted, but she knew this was just the beginning. The chemo was going to break her, but she had no choice. Robin's earlier words still haunted her.

Jake loved her with every fiber of his being—she owed it to him to survive.

Why hadn't she known the depth of his love for her? She should've known by now.

FOURTEEN

JAKE

HE RUSHED OUT OF THE OPERATING ROOM, TRUSTING ROD to close up and finish with the patient.

Out of breath, he pushed through the doors that led to OR 2. His father was already making the incision, and Robin was waiting. He grabbed a face mask and put it on, then squirted some disinfectant onto his hands, rubbing it in as he walked into the operating room.

"Dad, you couldn't wait?"

"No, she said she loved you," Gus told him. "Come, it's almost time to meet your first boy."

Armand was waiting next to an incubator. Jake's heart pounded a million beats per second.

She didn't even know that he was present.

He bent down and kissed her forehead softly as he took a seat right next to the anesthesiologist, who was monitoring Holly.

His eyes went to what his father was doing. Gus tugged and

pulled, and finally released the tiniest human being. When he cut the cord, the air in Jake's lungs evaporated. Glancing at Jake quickly, he stated, smiling, "Before you ask when I announce this little tyke's name, I did a sonar on Holly before the surgery and she named them in the womb."

Jake blinked a couple of times, his vision suddenly blurry.

"Nurse, hand me a tissue, would you?" Gus said, eliciting chuckles from everyone when Jake realized it wasn't for him but for his father.

"Hey there, Bradley," Gus said. "I'm your pops...welcome to the crazy bunch. I'm sorry we couldn't keep you in there any longer, but know this; we love you so, so very much. Be a brave boy and just breathe, okay?"

Gus handed the first boy to Armand, and Jake rushed around his father to Armand's side, who was trying to assist Bradley to breathe. Tiny, gurgling and whistling sounds finally came out of his mouth.

"It's all you are going to get, daddy," Armand said to Jake, who was discreetly trying to wipe his eyes.

Jake looked down at his son, and his heart felt like it wanted to burst. He was so tiny.

Armand put him in the incubator and waited for his brother.

And then Cooper came and it was the same thing all over again. Gus welcomed him into the world, and his uncle assisted him in taking his first breath.

Armand worked fast to intubate both boys, and then hooked them onto machines.

Jake's legs wanted to give out. He finally understood why Holly had wanted to keep them in longer. They were not ready to be in this world, and it would be his fault if they didn't make it.

"I've got them, Jake. You need to breathe and be strong for

your boys." Armand pierced him with a fierce, but calm look as he continued working on them.

They were wheeled out of the OR and taken to the NICU. Jake went over to Holly again—Robin had taken over.

He didn't want to look. He'd seen her scans, knew the cancer was taking over her body.

"Robin," he whispered.

"What is it?"

"Don't let her die, please."

"Not intending to. I've got this."

He rested his head gently on Holly's and prayed like he'd never prayed in his entire fucking life.

IT WAS HOURS BEFORE THE SURGERY WAS COMPLETE. JAKE was drained and exhausted.

Robin had managed to cut most of the cancer away, and she believed that with chemotherapy, the rest would be eradicated.

Holly had lost part of her liver, part of one lung, and one of her kidneys. Unfortunately, the other kidney still carried some of the cancer, but that would be dealt with, with what Robin had in mind. As the cancer had spread to all of Holly's reproductive organs, Robin had had to perform a hysterectomy. No sign of cancer was found in her breasts, so Robin felt it was safe to leave them be.

When she was taken to the ICU, Jake headed to the cafeteria. He needed some food to energize himself, and he needed some air, which he got by eating his sandwich outside, filling his lungs with as much air as he could.

When he was done, he headed to the NICU to go check on his sons.

"Congratulations on becoming a new daddy again," the

NICU staff sang when he entered. He was inundated with hugs and kisses. Dozens of blue balloons and flowers had been placed on a table to one side.

Walking over, he pulled a card off one of the huge balloons —it was from Bernie and Leo, another was from the staff at P&E. The card he pulled from the largest flower arrangement was from his mother. His nostrils flared with anger. He didn't want or need anything from her, including her stupid flowers.

Without another thought, he tore the card in two, aware that the nurses were watching him. Turning, he looked for and found the trash basket into which he threw the torn pieces.

Forcing a smile, he walked on and went to stand in front of the window, and there were his sons. Rodney and Teresse were helping Armand.

Rodney looked up and saw him standing right up against the window, and smiling, pumped his hands in the air in a *whoop-whoop* motion.

How's Holly doing? he mouthed.

Jake gestured that she was sleeping, and Rod smiled as he continued to assist Armand.

Jake trusted Armand, but he would be more at ease when Frank got here.

Just then, footsteps barreled down the hall. When he realized it was Frank, he sent a prayer up in thanks.

"Are they okay?" Frank panted, and Jake nodded. Smiling, he rushed past him and entered the room.

Jake watched Frank work—it was quite something.

Smacking Armand softly on his shoulder, Rod laughed before he turned around and walked out.

"Congratulations," Rod said, clapping Jake on the back.

"Thank you. How are they getting on?"

"Good. They're tiny, but Armand said they have the Peters will in them."

Jake laughed.

"She good?"

"Robin managed to get most of the cancer out. She said the rest would be gone when Holly went through chemo."

"Yikes, it's going to be tough, but whatever you need, I'm there."

"Thanks, Rod." Both turned to watch Frank and Armand at work.

"You think it's safe to leave them for a few minutes?"

Rod smiled. "They are in the best hands now, Jake. Go to Holly."

Nodding, Jake made his way to ICU.

Holly was still asleep, and Jane was sitting next to her bed. She had been with them when they'd gone to see the Christmas lights, but had left them to do some last minute shopping. Which meant that she hadn't been at the restaurant when Holly fainted.

His heart clenched at the sight of Holly's fragile body. She was on a ventilator.

He wiped at his burning eyes.

Jane got up to give him a hug. "We have to be strong now. She will fight, you hear?"

He nodded.

"How are Bradley and Cooper doing?"

"Good so far. They're tiny, but they are fighting." His voice was thick with emotion.

"Jake, what's wrong?"

"I wanted to abort them. I'm never going to forgive myself for it."

"We all wanted Holly to terminate the pregnancy. You are not alone in this."

He nodded.

Jane gave his arm a squeeze, and then went over to Holly

and bent over her. She kissed her cheek. "You have to fight now, sweetheart. Rest, as we both know you are going to need it."

Jake took the chair next to Jane, each occupied with their own thoughts.

"This really feels like déjà vu. Except that this time, you're here."

"I'm so sorry, Jane."

She smiled. "We both know that it isn't your fault."

"Yeah it is, I got her pregnant again."

She chuckled. "It takes two to tango, young man, unless what you're trying to say is that you forced yourself on top of her?"

He laughed, too. "No, that I did not do."

"Then there's nothing to be sorry about."

Jake sniffed. "They are so tiny."

"Yes, I can only imagine. Were you there?"

"Yes, they got the huge Peters welcome into the world."

She chuckled again. "Believe me, it's better than the Scallanger one."

Silence fell between them for a beat.

"Was she hooked up to machines the last time, too?"

"No, but then she didn't have cancer the last time, Jake. She had other problems. Her heart failed a few times, which scared the shit out of me, not to mention what she looked like. She is in much better condition this time around, meaning...you did good."

He smiled.

"You understand why I can't forgive my mother, right?"

"You don't forgive people because of what they did, Jake. You forgive them for you, for your sanity, for your peace of mind. It's one of the most important things Holly's taught me." A tear broke free. "She must have been in such a dark place when her sister died, and nobody was there for her. Not even me. That was the hardest thing I had to forgive."

He blinked furiously through his tears.

"Jake...please, find it in you to forgive your mother."

"I'll think about it."

"That's all anyone can ask you for."

How on earth was he going to even try?

But he watched Jane next to Holly, whispering soft words in her ear, smiling lovingly. She'd left Holly when her sister died, and so had Charles. Her twin had been the most important person in her life, a part of her soul, yet she'd found it in her heart to forgive her parents.

He had no idea how she'd done that, but he desperately wanted to learn how.

He was just so fucking tired.

HOLLY

She opened her eyes and heard her mother's voice.

"Sweetheart," Jane said, and Holly grunted.

"How do you feel?"

"Like I've just been sawed in two."

Her mother laughed. "You are going to be fine. Robin got most of it, and she truly believes that the chemo will destroy the rest."

"Chemo, Mom."

"You said you would do anything. If it's chemo she wants to go with, Holly, you have to trust her."

"Yeah. Chemo," she said tiredly. "Where are Bradley and Cooper?"

"Fighting, just like their big sisters."

"Jake?" she asked.

"He's been in and out, trying his best to be everywhere."

"So he's fallen in love with the two studs like I have."

"Head over heels."

"Music to my ears."

"We talked about a couple of things...Jamie and Romy for one. He asked if they were just as tiny, too, and who sat with them. Forgiveness was another. I think he's contemplating the whole situation. Perhaps he's trying to figure out how, in his heart, he can forgive Mara."

Holly sighed. *Finally.* She closed her eyes.

"Sleep. Nurse's orders."

Holly drifted away.

Her boys were still alive, still fighting. Jake was here. All was well for once.

The next time she opened her eyes, Jake was by her side.

"Hi," she said, surprising him.

He jumped up and touched his lips to her forehead, forcing a smile to his lips to hide all the turmoil within him.

"Plant them here, sucker." She tipped her head up slightly and puckered her lips, but the movement made her wince. Her body ached everywhere.

What the hell was the chemo going to do to her if she felt like this now?

Jake obliged, lingering for just a moment.

"Okay, love birds," Robin called as she entered. "I need a word with both of you."

"I just woke up, Robin."

"Yes, and we are helping you fight, Holly. Remember your orders."

"Okay fine, drill sergeant. What is the plan? What did you remove? And if you tell me that I will never enjoy a penis again, I will kill you."

Jake roared with laughter. "One particular penis only, may I add."

"TMI, Holly. You, too, Jake. Eww, guys! Keep it in check, will you? To clarify, I think you'll enjoy a penis...his penis...gah! —in no time. But you need to wait six weeks before you attempt that, Jake."

Holly gave a tired chuckle when she noticed Jake glaring at his sister. "So unprofessional."

"Moving on," said Robin.

Addressing Holly, she painted a disturbing picture of Holly's liver, and the remaining kidney. She'd had to remove part of her lung, too, but in due time, it would heal and would work again just as hard as her other lung. It was one of the reasons she felt so fatigued.

The one thing that hadn't entered her mind was the possibility of losing her uterus, so when Robin told her as gently as she could, she couldn't help but burst into tears.

Robin removed it due to it carrying a larger amount of the cancer cells, but she was positive that what still remained inside Holly would be eradicated through chemo.

"Okay," she said, her voice laced with worry. It was such a stupid word to say in this type of situation, but right then, it was all she could come up with. Not surprising, though, as there was a lot going on in her head. She was worried about the kidney— losing the one was bad enough, but finding out that the other still carried cancer wasn't hopeful, either. The complication of losing one of her organs was the part that really freaked her out. She was O negative, which meant she could donate to anyone, but finding a donor for her blood type wasn't easy at all.

"Holly?" she called, and Holly's eyes snapped to her. "Sorry. Didn't mean to make you jump. But you need to rest now, gain some strength back, because we'll need to start with the trial soon."

Holly saluted her tiredly. Robin in turn gave her a weary smile and walked out.

"As you were."

Jake chuckled at Holly's order. "We can really beat this, sweetheart."

"Don't let how I look fool you, okay? I'm not planning on losing this battle."

"You better not."

He kissed her mouth.

"How are my boys?"

"They're fighters. It's been three days and Frank is really hopeful. He said that Jamie was worse and she pulled through."

"It's a Peters thing."

He laughed. "No, I think it's a Scallanger thing. You survive when everything and everyone around you doesn't."

"Don't get nostalgic now, please."

"I'm just saying that you Scallanger girls are truly survivors, and I'm glad that it's a trait my children got from you."

"Okay, mister. If you say so."

He smiled at her, but her eyes were sliding shut.

"Sleep. Doctor's orders." His lips caressed her forehead softly, and she drifted away.

FIFTEEN

HOLLY

SHE REMAINED AT THE HOSPITAL. SHE WAS HEALING AND being assured by everyone that she was on track and that she'd be able to start chemotherapy soon. The twins were still in the NICU, but they were growing and gaining strength.

The first day she had a spike in energy, she demanded to be taken to the NICU so she could meet her sons. She was desperate to see them...just be with them.

It was beautiful and hard at the same time. Hard because they reminded her about the time with Romy and Jamie in the hospital, and beautiful because their father, uncle, and grandfather were present.

They all had a special bond with the boys, all except her. She chased them out when Jake wheeled her in between their incubators so she could have the life speech with her boys—the fight speech. She was fighting and they needed to fight too, because she couldn't do this if they gave up. She needed them to pull through.

After that day, the NICU became her new home.

Both boys had the Peters genes. They had dark fluff in the nape of their necks like their sisters had.

"You are going to break so many hearts, I can already see it. Just know that your mommy's heart is the most important, okay? Don't ever break it." She stroked Bradley's back.

Jake had told her he had been born first. And that he'd given each a big welcome into this world through tears. She'd laughed when he'd told her that. To tell the boys apart, Bradley's toe nail had been painted blue and Cooper's white.

The days turned into weeks.

She slept through Christmas and woke up on Boxing Day, but she spent New Year at their side. The boys had really improved. They were pulling through, but were still very small and needed a lot of tender love and care.

Frank and her mother were constantly at her side, and proved to be a huge support, just like before. Except that this time around, she had more support than just the two of them.

When Jake wasn't in surgery or consulting, he was with her and the boys. She'd found him many a time sitting with one of them, skin to skin, and it melted her heart each and every single time. The way he spoke to them, whispering sweet nothings in their ears. He even read medical magazines to them. Obviously, he was trying to make them fall in love with the family's profession from a young age, Holly thought.

Sitting with Jake and the boys, she reached out her arms to take Bradley from Jake when Aggie handed Cooper to him.

Silence permeated the room as Jake whispered to Cooper. Holly felt content at that moment; each holding a baby in their arms, just as it should be. She kissed Bradley softly on his head.

"I asked your mom if the girls were this small when they were born, and she said yes."

"They were, but they were even smaller."

His eyes grew wide. "Smaller?" he choked out.

She nodded. "And in greater danger. They had plenty of help, though, Jake. Something tells me our boys are going to be just fine."

"Their mother will be, too."

She sighed. "About that. Robin wants me to start the trial soon."

"That was the deal, Holly."

"I know, but I won't be able to breastfeed, Jake. They need it."

"Holly"—he closed his eyes for a beat, and when he opened them again, they locked on hers—"that was the deal."

There would be no reasoning with him as he wasn't going to listen. She'd begged them to keep the boys, and that thereafter they could hack away. They'd hacked away, but she was still not cancer free.

Robin had given her only a short time to regain her strength, and be with the boys. Now it was nearing the time for the long fight to become healthy again.

"Okay. You're right," she finally agreed.

"They will be fine."

She nodded, at the same time offering Philimina, the neonatal nurse, a faint smile when she took Bradley from her arms and returned him to the incubator.

She'd thought their names were fitting, but only realized after Jake made the joke about the actor named Bradley Cooper, how inappropriate their names actually were.

This time around everything was so much easier, everything except for one thing. Her father wasn't here. She'd really thought that the girls had changed him, but clearly she'd been wrong.

Still, she missed him. He was the only one not present from her original support group. Whenever she closed her eyes, she could still hear him reading *Sam I Am* to the girls in that soothing voice of his.

She mistakenly thought that their past differences were over, and that she could have a loving relationship with her father, but she knew now that she would never have what Jake had with Gus.

He hadn't phoned her once during her pregnancy, or even while she was sick, which told her that he had to be really fucking angry with her.

Cooper started crying and without hesitation, Jake immediately got to his feet. He was a natural. Just one of his hands was as big as their entire bodies. Watching him bounce their son at the same time humming a sweet lullaby, melted her even further. He was so fucking sexy right now.

Cooper finally quieted down.

"Oh, you are the spoiled one, aren't you?" Jake said softly. "It's not going to happen, Coop. You need to be tough." His gaze met Holly's. "What?" He smiled.

"You're a natural with them."

"You are, too." He chuckled, but it was short-lived. "This fear isn't going to ever go away, is it?"

She shook her head.

He took a deep breath and kissed Cooper on the head, his lips lingering. "I can't imagine the pain you went through losing Romy. I mean...I felt it, but to lose her at this age? I can't fathom it."

"Positive thoughts, Jake. No crying allowed in the NICU."

"Yeah, I know. I just missed so much with both of my girls."

"I don't wish that on anyone. A part of me was glad that you were not there to go through that."

"You can't possible mean that, Holly."

"Change the subject please," she requested softly, and on seeing the expression on her face, he gave her a nod.

They didn't speak for the remainder of the time they sat with the boys. Jake's beeper went off, and the nurse gently took Cooper from his arms and returned him to his incubator.

After clipping his beeper to his belt again, he bent and gave her a quick kiss on the lips and then turned to the boys and did some sort of a secret hand gesture that, knowing Jake, would probably turn into a shake later on.

"See you later, and get some rest, okay?"

"Yes, sir."

"It's doctor," he joked in a serious tone and she smiled, shaking her head as he walked away.

She continued to watch him through the windows as he threw his shirt back on and buttoned it.

The nurses were all drooling over his perfectly shaped body, but looked away when he said goodbye. She even caught one of the older ones fanning herself, who set the others off in a fit of giggles when she said something to them Holly couldn't hear.

She looked back at her sons, sad in the knowledge that she'd never be able to bear more children. She already felt like less of a woman now that her uterus had been removed.

She had no idea how Amelia went through every day of her life knowing she'd never give birth, never feel a life growing inside her.

Her mind took a sudden left turn and drifted to the married woman from Jake's past. She couldn't help but wonder if Jake still thought about her from time to time.

She remembered the first time she laid eyes on Amelia in the locker room at the paintball venue Jake had taken her to, before they'd even met, and how she'd spoken about the married woman. How Jake had felt about her, and how he'd struggled to get over her.

In a way, she still felt like she was second best to that

married woman, as Jake's standards had been too high at that time.

If Jake happened to cross paths with that woman again, would he want to stay with Holly and his children, or would he want to find out just how good life could be for him with her? She would be able to give him a bigger family, more children.

It was one of the reasons she still felt a twinge of insecurity about Jake. Even after Robin had recounted her version of what happened when Holly left. It hadn't sunk in how much she meant to Jake.

She pushed the woman to the back of her mind. She'd cross that bridge when...if...she got there. Right now, she needed to concentrate on getting both her sons out of this place alive and healthy.

"No more excuses, Holly," Robin said.

Sighing, she nodded.

The boys were still incubated, but were growing steadily, a good sign, and most of the tubes had been removed. They only had the oxygen nasal tubes in.

Not being able to breastfeed was downright depressing for her, but a promise was a promise.

Unfortunately, her remaining kidney wasn't doing well—chemo needed to happen soon, and it just had to work.

They walked into a large room where comfortable chairs were lined up, forming four rows. More than half of them were occupied.

Her heart broke when she noticed a young girl in one of the seats, because she reminded her so much of her sister.

"Sit," Robin ordered. "I'll be with you shortly. Mavis," Robin said, turning to the nurse, who nodded as Robin left.

Robin was so different from Amelia. Amelia was warm and kind. Robin, although beautiful, too, was very hard to read at times. Holly got the feeling that Robin still blamed her for all the mess between Jake and their mother.

"Hi there, Holly," Mavis greeted.

"Hey, Mavie," she returned with a smile.

"Good luck, baby."

"Thanks, I'm going to need it."

Mavis patted her shoulder in understanding. "Let me explain what we are going to do."

"No need. I know more about chemotherapy than you think."

Mavis frowned.

"My sister died from cancer a long time ago."

"I'm so sorry, sweetheart."

"It's okay. The sucker isn't going to claim me, too."

"I'm sure it won't. Not with Robin Peters as your oncologist. She has a tight plan."

"And the reason she isn't here to hold my hand?"

"Hold your hand?" Amelia's voice came from a few steps away. "Hey, Mavis."

"Hey, baby. How is that gorgeous husband of yours?"

"Still driving me crazy," she joked and plopped down next to Holly, while Mavis inserted a needle into Holly's arm.

Amelia looked at Holly. "You ready?"

"For chemo? Hell, no. But I have no choice, right?"

"Nope, no choice. Please don't ask Jake to shave his head. He looks awful bald."

She burst into laughter. "Where is Jamie?"

"With Jake. He'll bring her around later so you can see her."

"I wish she could see her brothers."

"I've shown her lots of photos, and she's seen them through the glass window a ton."

"It's not the same, Amelia."

"Of course not, but it's better than nothing. She'll get plenty of time with them. Trust me."

"I miss her. I feel like such a crappy mom."

"You are not a crappy mom. Believe me, she is getting spoiled rotten. Armand helped my dad put up a tree house in the huge oak that's right behind our house, and she spends hours in that thing."

"You're turning her into a spoiled brat, Amelia."

"She's our spoiled brat, Holly. I told you, you have to get used to it. It's a Peters thing, and talking about being a Peters...is it true that you are changing her last name?"

"Yeah, the green eyes forced my hand."

Amelia laughed. "Everyone is a sucker for them."

Holly grinned. Amelia was the female version of her brother. "Poor Armand."

Amelia laughed. "It's not that bad.

She opened a magazine and paged through it while Mavis was occupied with hooking her up to the IV—the poison carrier. She couldn't believe that she was going to pump that shit into her body.

If Robin hadn't revealed to her what it had been like when she'd left Jake, and how she'd realized that Holly's return was the turning point for him, she would have believed that Robin's intention was to kill her slowly.

"So...Robin mentioned something."

"Holly, I told you to not take everything Robin says literally. She is a drama queen, and still sucks on my mother's tit. I'm sure of it."

Holly snorted, but turned serious when she asked, "She's speaking to her again?"

"No, it's why she's such a little bitch lately. I could just slap her at times."

"She's not that bad."

"So, what did the brat have to say?"

She smiled. "If you're going to be mean about your sister, I'm not going to tell you."

"Okay, sorry. I won't be mean, Scout's honor."

"I doubt you were one."

"It's just a saying, but my promise is legit, Holly."

"She keeps mentioning that she doesn't want to lose her brother again."

"Yeah, I told you that myself, Holly," Amelia said, without taking her eyes from the magazine she was paging through.

"Amelia, she told me what your mother did."

Amelia closed the book. "Everything?"

She nodded. "Everything."

"Even about how she pretended he hadn't turned into a fucking stranger?"

She nodded again.

Amelia swallowed hard and stared at nothing. Tears welled up in her eyes, probably at a memory.

"Have you seen that picture on my wall?"

"The one where he looks like he's thinking?"

Amelia smiled and nodded.

"Yeah." Holly sighed.

"It was a good day, Holly. It's all I'm going to say."

She frowned. If that was a good day, what did the bad days look like? "It was *that* bad?"

"Yes, Holly, it was. I told you it was bad."

She blew out heavy breath. "I really fucked him up when I left, didn't I?"

"You can say that again, but you are here now, and you are not going anywhere."

"I regret not staying."

"Holly, it's in the past. You gave him a second chance, even though back then we all begged you to abort. I feel like a monster now that I've held my nephews, and..." She stopped and sighed. "Please don't ask him to forgive her. She was the monster, Holly."

"He needs to at some point, Amelia. And so do you."

"No." Amelia shook her head vehemently. "I don't even miss her. Her true colors came out the day the truth did. The fact that she lied about it, making me celebrate a make-believe birthday every year while I cried my eyes out, and then comforting me? That was the cherry on the top. She probably laughed at how stupid I was. How stupid all of us were. I should never have tried to drag his ass back to Boston. I should've helped him find you."

"Should've, could've, would've. It makes no difference, Amelia. It's like a *what if*, just ashes in the wind. Stop blaming yourself. We can't change it."

"Fine, then let us forgive her when we are ready. Stop pushing him, though, please."

"I will."

From the corner of her eye, she saw Amelia's lips curve into a soft smile.

But then her eyes caught on the shit that the IV was pumping into her body, and any glimmer of happiness she had just felt disappeared.

She was going to lose weight, her looks, her hair. She was going to put not just herself through hell, but Jake was going along for the ride, too, and the last thing she wanted to do was put him through anything close to hell again.

He didn't deserve more shit.

SIXTEEN

JAKE

He awoke with Holly puking her lungs out. She was home and had already gone through three chemotherapy sessions. This was not new to him.

He jumped out of bed and ran downstairs as soundlessly as he could to get a glass of water and juice, then ran back upstairs again.

Shoving the juice box under his arm so he could free up one hand, he pulled Jamie's door closed until it was only slightly ajar, and hoped she wouldn't wake up.

He never wanted to see the fear of her mother being sick on her face.

Shaking that thought away, he walked into the bedroom.

Holly was coughing and throwing up.

His heart wanted to break at what he not only was seeing, but at what she was going through. But he pushed that aside—he had to believe that she would kick cancer's ass.

He moved her hair out of her face.

"Please, don't," she begged.

"Look at it as practice."

"For what?" she asked tiredly.

"For the better or worse part."

"I'm not in the mood to laugh."

"I know." He was still holding her hair at the back of her neck. He couldn't even ask her how she felt. It was more than clear to see; like crap.

Her nausea eventually abated. Jake handed her both the glass of water and juice box, but she only took the juice, and then firmly pushed him out of the bathroom.

He hated the fact that she didn't want him to see her like that. It was his life, too. She was his life. She needed to get better, and he needed to believe she would.

Getting back into bed after placing the glass of water on the nightstand, he closed his eyes and waited.

The bathroom door finally opened, and he watched as she made her way steadily back to bed and got in.

She turned her back to him as she settled on her side, and he hated that she did that.

He put his arm around her and pulled her closer to him. "You know I love to cuddle, woman."

He was rewarded with a tired chuckle. He kissed her softly on her shoulder and closed his eyes.

Please, God, don't take her away.

She'd lost weight, he could feel it through her clothes, and he wished there was an easier way for her to get through this.

Robin had to know of another way that wouldn't be so hard on Holly's body. He'd talk to her in the morning.

Her body relaxed against his, her breathing slowed, and she started snoring softly. He could listen to her sleeping forever, wanted to listen to her sleeping forever.

He wished he knew when this would end. It was only still

the beginning, but it was already killing him to have to be a witness to it.

It frustrated him not knowing when it would be over. He'd always struggled with the unknown.

Everything he'd ever wanted in life, he'd fought hard and long for. But how the fuck did you fight for someone else's survival?

It wasn't up to you, it was up to them.

He tried to ease his mind and closed his eyes.

He was tired and needed the rest, especially for what was still to come.

⸻

THE NEXT FEW MONTHS WERE FILLED WITH UPS AND downs.

The ups were amazing; it gave him hope. And then she would go for chemo again, and it would floor her. She'd be sick for days.

He didn't know how much more she could handle.

She was terribly sick, and the expected happened—her hair fell out in large clumps, and it got so bad she eventually decided to shave it all off.

In support of her, Jake wanted to shave his head as well, but she begged him not to.

"I can shave it off if I want to."

She shook her head adamantly.

"Why not?"

"Because Amelia said you look awful bald. You need to woo me, baby. Bald head isn't going to do it for me."

He laughed. "Okay, fine, I'll keep the hair."

The boys were finally released and allowed to go home, and his sister 'sort of' moved in.

As much as he loved her, they really were not great roommates.

He could live with Robin, and they had, but that was because they were so alike; they just gelled. But Amelia irritated the shit out of him at times. Maybe they were too alike.

She was always extra chirpy around Holly and he could sense that it irritated her too, until one night, he just lost it.

"Melia, enough."

"What? I just said it's not as bad as everyone makes it out to be."

"Not as bad?"

"Jake, don't." Holly was tired.

"No!" He looked at his sister. "Stop being so fucking chirpy, because this isn't just going to blow over."

"Stop yelling!" Amelia shouted.

"Both of you just stop," Holly said and got up.

"You see what you just did?" Jake ran after her, hooked an arm behind her knees and the other around her back, picked her up and took her back to bed.

"Stop being so hard on her," she scolded.

"She irritates the living crap out of me."

"She's really helping, Jake."

"Fine, I'll try." He put Holly in bed and tucked her in.

Thankfully, as Jamie was already asleep, they hadn't woken her up.

He trudged downstairs and found his sister looking pissed off. He didn't have time for a fight. He was so fucking tired.

"Not a word," he warned, and went to get Holly's water and juice for the night.

But Amelia just couldn't let it be.

"Jake, you are not the only one who is trying to get her through this. I'm not blind. I can see it's eating her up, all that fucking poison Robin keeps pumping into her body, and you are not here during the day."

He looked at his sister. Her bottom lip was quivering.

"I don't mind taking care of her, but you are not here to see the things she throws up and the things she can't eat. Me saying it's not so bad, is actually me trying to help her think of this as something that can be manageable. It's not easy by any means, but she needs to think it is. So stop treating me like I'm all happy about this, because I'm not. It's just a front...a coping mechanism to help her cope." She started crying and Jake's heart melted.

Sighing, he walked over and wrapped his arms around his sister as she cried into his chest.

"I'm sorry. I guess I've just had a bad few days."

"I know. We all have them. We're all having them. But she needs to get through this, and sometimes you just have to let us do what we feel is necessary. She made us a promise that she was going to fight. We can't give up and allow her to give up."

"You're right. You want some cocoa?"

"I'd love some cocoa."

"So, what is it that I don't know?"

She shook her head. "It's better that you don't."

"Amelia, please."

"You need to stay positive. Robin said it's all great signs, but it doesn't look like great signs."

"Just two more weeks and we'll be done with this shit."

"Two more."

They drank their cocoa in silence, and then they went to bed.

Amelia was great with looking after the children. Her room was right next to Bradley's and Cooper's nursery.

Jake got up every time they cried, but Amelia was always right behind him with their bottles, shooing him back to bed.

She knew their cries.

He felt like a terrible dad, but he was actually grateful for Amelia being here.

Over the past two weeks, he'd thought Holly was going to die. She slept most of the time. The hardest was when Jamie asked him with teary eyes if Mommy was going to go to Romy.

A vice grip tightened around his heart. Jamie understood death better than he thought she did.

Kneeling in front of her, he gathered her in his arms, holding her tight against his chest and breathing in her scent. "I don't know, baby." He sniffed. "But we can't show Mommy were afraid. She needs to see us happy and laughing, not crying. She is trying her hardest to get better, sweetheart."

She nodded, but her little lip trembled, and tears flowed down her cheeks. She used her little hands to wipe them away.

He hugged her again. "You can cry with Daddy, just not with Mommy."

She let loose, her tiny body shaking against him as she burrowed her head in his neck. She sobbed loudly, inconsolably, and all he could do was hold her tight.

It had been hard when they'd told her Holly was sick.

Holly had wanted them to tell her. She'd answered most of Jamie's questions, and had even taken her to one of her chemotherapy sessions, telling Jamie that it was the same sickness that took Auntie Jamie to heaven.

Jamie had had tears in her eyes, sad and scared at the thought of losing her mom. But Holly had explained to her that she was getting lots of help from Daddy and Auntie Robin, and so many others so she could get better soon.

Robin was positive. It was the only thing that still gave him hope. His sister's positivity.

Every time she went in for chemo, it took about a week for

her to stop vomiting. By this point, she was extremely skinny and really didn't look healthy at all.

And then it was D-Day.

They were off to see Robin—she was going to do a few further tests and would then tell them if the chemo had worked or not.

There was a stress factor attached to the already stressful situation, because they were headed to P&E. He didn't know if his mother was at work, or if she had the day off. He hoped for the latter.

Once he found a parking spot, he helped Holly out of the SUV.

"You ready?"

"Ready to be back here, or ready to hear what Robin has to say?"

"Both." He smiled.

"I'm okay, I guess."

Ever attentive, he picked her up and carried her to the entrance.

"Such a knight in shining armor."

"I need to be someone's hero."

"Yeah, that is the problem. You are too many people's hero."

He planted a kiss on her lips as the doors slid open automatically.

Vanessa, one of the nurses, smiled and brought him a wheelchair.

"Never thought I'd see you again."

"I have no choice," he said, then wheeled Holly to the elevator, ignoring the worry on Vanessa's face. He didn't need that now. Today was going to be positive.

"See what I mean, her face just lit up," Holly said.

"Shut up," he murmured.

"Oh, just great," Holly muttered.

Jake's head snapped up.

His mother and Kate were standing at one of the boards, speaking to each other. Both turned at the same time, and when their eyes caught sight of Jake and Holly, their mouths dropped.

"Ignore them," he said and wheeled Holly into the elevator. He could feel their eyes burning into his back. He just hoped and prayed that they would keep their distance.

Suddenly, Holly laughed.

"What's so funny?"

"Kate seemed...hopeful."

"Fuck her. You are not going anywhere."

When they reached the oncology ward, he wheeled her out and they made their way to Robin's consulting room.

Her receptionist smiled as soon as they entered.

"Dr. Peters. So nice to see you again."

"The Wicked Witch of the West here?"

She laughed. "Just wait a few minutes. Holly," she greeted.

Jake frowned and pushed Holly to a corner right next to a chair and took the seat.

"See what I mean? So much hope from everyone, hero." She grinned.

Jake just shook his head with a laugh. She wasn't going to go anywhere. "I come with baggage."

"Oh, it's baggage none of them mind."

"You are not going anywhere, so stop making jokes like that. It's not funny."

"Fine, grumpy."

He smiled as he picked up a magazine and started reading it.

A few minutes later, Robin walked into the room. "Let's go." She didn't even greet them.

"I agree, she is the Wicked Witch of the West."

Jake laughed as he wheeled her into the room.

As Robin wanted to do a few more tests in order to make sure that the cancer was gone, they spent the entire day at P&E, ducking and diving his mother and Kate.

The result came in at around four-thirty. The good news was that Holly was cancer-free. However, there was also bad news—her kidney had stopped working, and she needed a liver transplant. With her blood type, getting part of a liver, and a kidney, was asking for too much.

All the air in Jake's lungs dissipated.

"Jake..." Robin said.

Holly was sitting next to him. He couldn't even look at her. He was so fucking mad. Not at her. He knew what it meant. Getting a kidney wasn't going to be easy. Not with her blood type.

"The positive side of this is if we obtain a kidney and liver that are a match, Holly has a chance of getting those organs, Jake."

"A chance? How big are those donor lists, Robin?"

She didn't answer. "I will fight for that kidney and liver, I promise."

"You are not a nephrologist."

"But I know a great one. I still have to speak to you about that."

Holly smiled. Jake didn't think it was funny.

"Trust me, please."

"I do, I just don't trust someone new."

"See it as bonus points you need to give out, okay?"

He shook his head. "So what now?"

She sighed. "You need a few minutes as I don't do grumpy faces in my office," Robin said.

Holly sighed deeply. He could hear the sadness in her voice.

He looked at her but she was looking at her hands.

"Don't even dare to feel what you are feeling now."

"Robin, enough," Jake warned.

"When we told her to abort, she didn't want to. She promised she would fight. So, she can't afford to look defeated. Am I right, Holly?"

"Yeah, you are right. So, I need a kidney and part of a liver?" Holly pushed back.

She was really strong in so many ways, stronger than him.

"Livers are sometimes easier than the kidneys," she said to Holly. Looking at Jake, she added, "She can go on dialysis, Jake. It's not the end of the world."

"Yeah, until her kidney or liver decide to not work together, then it's going to turn into a fucking nightmare."

"She's beaten the fucking cancer. This is different. Stop thinking of all the worst-case scenarios. We can overcome this. Live with the nightmare until a solid solution comes, Jake." She looked at Holly. "I took the liberty of asking Devenn Miller what the best plan of action would be. He said that if you went with him, he would admit you for the first few weeks of dialysis, Holly. Your kidney isn't in the best shape and you will be put on the transplant list. We will find you a kidney and liver, I promise."

Devenn Miller. He didn't know the guy all that well, but had worked a few cases with him. He mostly kept to himself, but he was extremely thorough in his work.

The door opened and Devenn walked in.

"Good, you're here," Robin said. "Devenn, Jake and Holly."

"I know your brother, Robin. We've worked on a few cases together before."

Jake chuckled. He was better than all of Robin's other choices.

The nephrologist went over to shake Jake's and then Holly's hand.

"I'm Doctor Devenn Miller. Good to meet you. Can we jump right into it, or do you want to get a second opinion, Jake?"

"No, I trust my sister's judgement, Devenn," Jake replied with a lopsided smile.

"Good. I'm sure Robin's caught you up with the situation. The positive thing about this is that we can test family members. One of them is usually a perfect match," he said.

"Okay," Holly said. In the midst of all her worry, she still managed a chuckle. "With my luck, it'll turn out to be my father."

"Can I test, too?" Jake asked, but he knew he wouldn't be a match. He just wanted to do something. He had no idea what the rest of his family's blood type was, but O negative was rare.

"I'm not taking your kidney, Jake."

"I'm not asking you to take it. It's just a test. We'll cross that bridge when we get there."

"Fine," Holly griped.

"Whatever is going through your mind now, it needs to stop," he said to her. "Robin is right. You promised, Holly. You need to fight. It's not over."

She nodded.

"I'm not going to be a match, sorry," Robin said. "You know I would give it to you if I could, Holly."

"I know." Holly managed a half smile.

"What are you talking about?" Jake asked.

"Nothing to do with you," Robin snapped at him.

He shook his head. When had she become such a bitch?

"Whoever is up for undergoing testing, all are more than welcome," Devenn said.

"I just have one request," Jake stated, looking at Devenn. "She won't be admitted to this hospital. Downsend has the same equipment. I'd appreciate your cooperation, please."

Robin sighed.

"Not here," Jake said again.

"Fine."

"I'll take her to Downsend, and you find the organs." He looked at Devenn. "When can you begin with the test?"

"I can do it at Downsend in an hour."

Jake nodded.

"Perfect," Robin said. "Now, can you please leave my consulting room so I can get on with my work?"

Jake shook his head, but caught Robin winking at Holly. "I'm the best. I'll help Devenn find you a kidney and liver. That is the least of our problems."

"Aye, aye, captain," Holly joked as Jake wheeled her out. "Do I really have to go back into hospital?"

"Doctor's orders, sweetheart. Just for a week or so, until he is happy that you're handling the dialysis well." He sighed.

"This is so messed up."

"Nope, it's not. It's just a kidney."

"And part of a liver," she added, laughing. "And you know it's not just a kidney or just part of a liver, Jake. It's ultimately my body deciding to either accept or reject both organs." Her voice broke.

"Holly, you are not going to die. Period. Please don't get yourself worked up. We will find you a working kidney and both you and your body better fucking accept it."

Despite everything, that made her laugh. Jake wheeled her into the elevator, then crouched down in front of her and took her hands in his. "Just trust me. You fought against and beat the cancer. You said you would. Now, let us do what we do best. Save lives."

"Okay."

"Okay." He squeezed her hands and got up.

The elevator stopped and he turned around.

His mother walked in. She froze as the elevator's doors closed, and stared at Holly.

"Just pretend we are not here," Jake said in the coldest tone he could muster without looking at her.

"Stop it," Mara hissed. "What the hell is going on here?"

"None of your damn business."

As soon as the doors opened, he wheeled Holly out. "Sorry about that."

"Jake, this has to stop."

"Holly, don't you start. I'm not going to fight with you."

He hated his mother. He knew it was a very strong emotion and word, but he wasn't mad anymore. It had gone beyond that now. He loathed her, and spat on the ground she walked on. Not to mention how embarrassed he was to be one of her children. But only on paper.

He would never forgive her for what she had done. Ever.

———

HOLLY WAS ADMITTED IMMEDIATELY. AND THEN THE SHIT hit the fan.

Mara wanted to know what was wrong with Holly. He had to give it to his old man for not saying a word. They were still together, still married. But he knew that his father wouldn't have been able to keep it a secret forever, and then messages would stream in from everywhere.

Amelia was devastated when she heard the news, but she managed to work through it. She wanted to put up a strong front. Everyone was tested to see if they were a match. Even Gus.

Jane came, and so did Frank.

His house was filled with people again, except with the

person he truly wanted there—Holly. He got a taste of what life would be like without her.

He could not fathom it. He couldn't breathe.

The vibration of his phone had him taking in a deep breath. Rubbing his hand over his face, he answered the call.

"You are not a match, Jake. None of us are."

Silence permeated the airwaves and Jake closed his eyes.

Why did she have to fall into the seven percent O negative blood type?

"I'm so sorry," Robin said. "Try her father. The chance that he's O negative is huge."

"Yeah, okay. I doubt that it would matter, but I'll phone him."

"Don't say that, Jake. Just phone him." He could hear her voice was thick with emotion. He didn't like that.

"Robin, please," he begged.

"I'm allowed to doubt a little, Jake. You are not the only one here that is tired of all this shit."

"I need you to be strong."

"I am, but I have my off days and I'm pretty sure I am allowed to have them."

"Yes, you are."

"Mom came by the office today."

"I don't want to hear it."

"She really sounded worried, Jake."

"Or happy that she would finally be rid of Holly once and for all."

"Be fair."

"No, I'll never be considerate to that bitch ever again."

"Jake!"

"Robin, if you want to run back to her, do so. But I don't want to hear about your happy little reunion." He cut the call.

He hated fighting with his sisters. Especially Robin. She'd pulled Holly through so much.

His heart sank. He felt depleted. He felt as if he was losing control of everything. He didn't want to be strong anymore, he just wanted Holly to be healthy. Why was it so much to fucking ask?

Her mother wasn't a match, but he had a funny feeling that her father would be. That she was right about the comment she'd made that it would be just her luck if her father had the same blood type.

With much trepidation, he dialed Charles' number.

"Charles Scallanger."

Jake sniffed. "It's Jake. Before you cut me off, you need to know that you have two healthy newborn grandsons, but Holly isn't doing so well." He was sure that Jane must have told him about the cancer.

"I know about the cancer."

That revelation shocked Jake to his core. "You really are not trying..."

"My daughter made her choice the minute—"

"I don't want to fight. This isn't about you, and it isn't about me. It's about your daughter. She is going to lose her life, she's going to die if she doesn't get a healthy fucking kidney and liver. That's all I wanted to tell you." Swiping his finger across the screen, he let out a harsh expletive.

The man was a fucking asshole. He hoped he never turned into anything resembling that bitter bastard who'd end up not caring about his children.

He prayed he was a better father than Charles Scallanger had ever been.

SEVENTEEN

HOLLY

She remained in the hospital for a week before she was allowed to go home. Dialysis took place three days a week, however, her liver was the bigger problem.

The yellowing of her skin increased to such an extent that Jake took her to the hospital again one night. She was in so much pain, and sick.

The search for an O negative match continued, but it was proving fruitless. Her father hadn't even bothered to come.

She was going to lose the battle, and not even due to cancer.

Left with no choice, she was readmitted and put on dialysis immediately, and felt better after a few days. But they wouldn't discharge her.

She could see that Jake was losing hope and Dr. Miller's face said it all.

All he kept telling her was that she was on the transplant list for both organs.

She tried to keep her spirits high, but it was almost near to impossible. Everything around her seemed to be crumbling to pieces.

No hope. Not even from her father.

But if Dr. Miller didn't find her a kidney and a liver soon, she had to face the facts. His surname wasn't Peters. She didn't have faith in him the way Robin had. She doubted that Jake even really liked the guy.

During one of his visits, Jake mentioned the black market. It was crazy talk, even for him.

"Are you insane? No!" She was horrified at that. She had no more strength left, wasn't even certain that dialysis was working as it should.

What did it mean?

Was what she was going through the reason their paths had crossed again? So that Jamie found her father before she died? Was that to be her fate?

She wanted to cry but she'd cried so much already, she wasn't sure there was anything left to expel. Putting on a brave façade was damn hard, but she had to try.

Sadly, not even her mother was a match.

Why did she have to be born with this blood type?

She was losing hope. Every day, when Robin came to visit, more hope went out the door.

She hated her room, even if it contained things from home. All she wanted was to be with her family.

A knock sounded on the door, and after calling out to whoever it was, she waited for them to enter.

The door opened up to a pepper-haired older version of a once-handsome man. He entered, taking a few steps into the room and stopped. He stared at her and tears filled his eyes.

"Dad." She smiled. "What are you doing here?"

"I came to see you." He walked closer to her, shoulders

hunched, head hanging low. When his shoulders shook, she knew he was crying.

"Dad, this is a no-crying room."

Charles sniffed. "Don't give me that crap. What do you need, Holly?"

"Your money isn't good here. And besides, it's illegal to buy what I need."

"Still the kidney and liver."

"Dad, it's not a packet of candy, or pocket money."

"You're my daughter. It's the least I can do."

"It's not your obligation."

"It's not an obligation, Holly. Damn it, I know I'm not the easiest man to have ever walked this planet, and I have made more mistakes than a normal person should. I promised myself that I would never set foot in a hospital again after Jamie, but I broke it when you came to me because he..." He choked on his tears.

"Dad he didn't know. He was told a lie, please." She begged of him.

"Yet, here I am again. Next to another child's bed." He ignored her pleading. "How many do you want me to lose, because I won't make it this time."

She stared at her father, having just realized that it was the first time he'd mentioned her sister's name in such a long time.

"I beat myself up every single day that I wasn't there for you or your mother when Jamie died. I took the easy way out. But I tried with Jamie and Romy."

"Yeah. You were a real role model for me, Dad. I know how it feels to run out of someone's life. I learned it from you. You're still running." Tears filled her eyes.

"Don't try to make excuses for him, Holly."

"Dad, I'm not making excuses. It really happened. He isn't talking to his mother, hates her for all the lies she told. Who do you think is trying to save my life? It's not your money this time. It's his, and his family's. I have the support I need. If you don't want to be here, please feel free to leave."

"That's not what I meant."

"I know what you meant, Dad. But we both know you are not the kind to stick around. Especially if things don't go your way."

He nodded, bent down to kiss her on the head, and then left her room.

She wept as he left. She loved her dad, even though he was such an asshole. She loved him.

Her mother walked in shortly after her father left, and immediately went to Holly's side and wrapped her arms around her.

"I'm so sorry. If I'd known he was coming I would've been here."

"Why is he even here? How does he know?"

"I told him about the cancer. It must have taken some time for him to realize how bad it had gotten."

"He hates Jake, Jake hates his mother, and everyone is just fighting with everyone. When is it going to stop?"

"Not with your death, sweetheart. It would do more damage than bring peace. You have to hold on. Dr. Miller is doing everything he can to get a kidney, and hopefully, that bit of liver for you."

"Mom, so far, every single kidney hasn't been a match. It's never going to be a match. I need to start preparing for the worst."

"Holly! I refuse to listen to this." With that, her mother stormed out of the room.

She needed a pen and paper, but she knew no one would give it to her, not anyone in her family, and certainly not the

Peterses, either. The Peterses would kill her if they knew that she wanted to be prepared for the worst.

HER FATHER RETURNED THE NEXT DAY, BRINGING WITH him a juice and a packet of candy, and what looked like stationary.

She frowned at the pack of envelopes and writing pad.

He sat down at the end of the bed. "I thought you might want to write...the things you might not..." He turned his head to wipe his eyes. "My blood type is not a match."

"What? How is that even possible?"

"I asked the same question, but apparently mine is just as rare as yours. I'm so sorry."

Her heart broke for her father. "I'm sorry, Dad, for everything." She sobbed.

He got up and wrapped his arms around her. It felt so good. "You have nothing to be sorry about. I wish I could give you a kidney. I wish I had been there for you. And I wish I could take on what you are going through right this second, but I can't, Holly. I can't do any of those things. I never was a great father to you, and still to this day, I continue to be a crappy one."

"Dad, you are not a crappy—"

"I can't stay, Holly. I've tried. I can't. I can't breathe knowing that I'm probably going to lose you, too. I only know how to deal with things one way. It's not in me to sit and wait."

She looked at her father. He was an asshole, but she understood where he was coming from. He didn't have a Jake in his life, only a Gabby who spent his money left, right and center.

"I'm sorry. I wish I was able to forgive the way you can. And I do hope you get what you need, sweetheart. So that one day when I'm old and bitter, and hopefully find my way back to you,

you find it in your heart to forgive me. I'm sorry, but it's just not in me stay." Tears streamed down his face as he got up, kissed her on the head and walked out of her room.

Holly shook her head in disbelief.

He'd just walked out of her life. He couldn't handle it, he couldn't handle watching her die.

He might be a bastard, but he was the only who saw the truth, and probably why he'd brought her the things she needed without her having to ask him for it.

She put the stationary under her pillow. Tonight, when she was alone, she would start preparing for the future. The future she wouldn't be a part of.

AGGIE CAUGHT HER LATER THAT NIGHT WRITING ONE OF the letters. She'd had to explain what she was doing. Aggie wasn't happy that she was giving up, but Holly told her it was just a precaution. That she would burn the letters should Dr. Miller find a match. Aggie seemed somewhat mollified by her explanation.

She'd written a few letters to the boys—they were the hardest as she had no idea what sort of personalities they'd have. They were still so young. All she could do was write about the things she wanted for them. She had to believe their twin bond would be strong all through their lives. She had to believe that they wouldn't resent her for not writing individual letters.

My dearest Cooper and Bradley,
For your 7ᵗʰ birthday

I love you boys so much.
Happy Birthday, my studs.
I wish I was there with you today to see the over-the-top
birthday party your father, aunts, grandpa and everyone else
threw you. But just know in your hearts that I'm there, watching
over you.
I can't tell you enough how special you both are to me, but know
I am always around you, watching over my two boys.
Love your sister, be nice to her. Be kind to her. She is the only girl
in the house, and girls cry easily. Always, my darling boys,
protect her.
Give Daddy hugs, even if you don't want to. He needs them.
Seven is a big year, my darlings.
Do your best with everything you guys take on. But most of all,
have fun. Nothing is worth it if it isn't fun.
Remember to laugh, be silly, be crazy, make jokes, run, play in
puddles, but most of all...love each other. Having a twin is
amazing, because they are the best friend you could ever have.
Love your sister for me. Give her hugs and kisses.
Know I'm always with you both inside your hearts and in your
dreams.

Love always,
Mom.

My dearest Bradley and Cooper,
For your 8ᵗʰ birthday

My boys are eight! You grow way too fast. I am sure your party is
packed with buddies. I hope you took my advice the last time I
spoke to you.
Eight is the year things start to get a bit harder. You might learn
how easy it is to fool the grown-ups around you by playing tricks

on them, and make everyone crazy by pretending you're each
other! See, I know you two.
But, listen to me and listen good. Stop it right now. I am not there
to tell you apart and save everyone from your shenanigans,
because a mother always knows her boys.
It's not nice, guys.
But today you will get a free pass as it's your day. So go crazy.
I hope the day is filled with happiness and love, I hope it's filled
with laughter, fun and games.
But most of all, I hope you know I'm right there with you when
you blow out your candles. Remember, I'm always close by, even
if you can't see me, and I will always be inside your dreams.
Love you madly.

P.S. Listen to your aunts, and don't give your dad too much
gray hair.

Love always,
Mom

AND SO SHE CONTINUED, THROUGH ALL OF THEIR
milestones; turning sixteen, eighteen, twenty-one, graduation,
and then marriage.

My dearest Bradley and Cooper,
On your wedding day

It feels strange writing this to both of you, not knowing who's
getting married, or if both of you are on the same day. So, I've
asked your father to handle it as fits the situation.
Today, I want to tell you how much I loved your father, and how

much he loved me. I don't know if anyone ever shared with you our love story, but it was one to beat the ages. I ran away from him, and for five years we never saw or spoke to each other. But your father was the man I loved with everything in my heart and my soul, the man I loved with every fiber of my being. I hope you've found that kind of love, a love that can withstand anything, a love that can withstand the test of time—for better or for worse.

I hope the woman you are marrying today is the kind of woman that you would search for to the end of the earth if she ever ran away. Because, my boys, that is lasting love, and I want nothing less for you.

Treasure your wife, and show her you love her every single day. Don't ever make her doubt your love for her.

I love you always,
Mom

AND A LETTER FOR THE BIRTH OF THEIR FIRST CHILD.

She even wrote them a letter for Jamie's milestones. Her first boyfriend, her wedding.

It wasn't as easy as she'd thought, because the Bradley and Cooper she was picturing in her mind's eye could not even turn out to be the Bradley and Cooper they would one day become.

She just hoped that they would be okay. She put the letters and stationery away as it was almost visiting hour. Tonight, she would continue her writing.

It took her two days to finish the boys' letters, and then she started on Jamie's.

The hospital was quiet. Jake had just left, thinking she was asleep.

Retrieving her pen and paper from her hiding place, she began on Jamie's letters.

As with the boys, she started with her seventh birthday, too.

My dearest Jamie, my peanut,
For your 7th birthday

Happy Birthday, beautiful girl! I hope you're having a magical day. I'm so sorry I cannot physically be with you today, but I am there in spirit. I bet you're wearing a beautiful princess dress, Rodney is dressed as some villain, and your daddy is, of course, a prince. I'm sure Cooper and Bradley are making a mess somewhere, and I'm sorry about that...but they're still young. Promise me you won't be mad at them if they break your toys. It's what little brothers do. I would give anything to hold you in my arms again, to kiss your head, and to smell the strawberry shampoo you love so much clinging to your hair...

She was crying when she started on Jamie's letter for her eighth birthday.

Then her ninth one came. She wondered what Jamie would look like. If she would be happy. Her birthday parties would be slightly different, themes would change.

She apologized again for her brothers; they would be at that impossible stage, irritating the living crap out of their sister.

The tenth, eleventh and twelfth birthday was just as difficult to write. Then the teenage years came. Her sweet sixteen.

My dearest, beautiful girl,
For your 16th birthday

Just know that as I sit here, writing this letter, I'm struggling to breathe just knowing that you are turning sixteen today. Happy sweet sixteen! To me, you are the most beautiful girl in the world, which makes me feel sorry for your dad...all those boys he's going to have to chase away! Tsk-tsk. I would give anything to be there, to laugh at him worrying about you. But that is to be expected, and I know that in his heart, he knows what an upstanding young woman you are. That you've been brought up to know right from wrong, and that you wouldn't do the things that all parents fear without careful consideration. I know you will wait for that special someone, because you will know when the time is right. And you'll know the time is right when that special someone enters your life, when your heart tells you it's right. You are such a special girl, and I hope you know how special you are. I'm sure Daddy tells you that every day of your life. Sixteen is a big year, baby. You've become a woman in a sense, you're just discovering where you fit in, but I doubt you'll find it hard to make friends. Don't classify people into categories because everyone, no matter how goofy, deserves a chance. Rodney was my most strangest, yet best friend. He changed my life—our lives. I hope you have someone like him in yours, someone who's always got your back no matter what. Don't fight too much with your father if he's strict in certain instances. It only means he loves you so much, that he feels he needs to hold on a bit tighter, and longer. Give him the benefit of the doubt, and try not to give him too many gray hairs. He is already too good-looking, but I'm sure you don't want to hear that.

SHE SMILED AS SHE FINISHED HER LETTER.

The letter for her eighteenth was just as difficult to write. She was sure that by this age Jamie would know what she wanted to do, or what she wanted to be become. Holly hoped it would in the medical field. She smiled. If Jamie chose a completely different profession, Holly would be surprised, especially as she was surrounded by doctors.

She also knew that by this age, Jamie would have had a few boyfriends, and perhaps even have met a special someone. If that were the case, she hoped and prayed that he would be her Jake Peters.

Putting pen to paper once more, she wrote another letter, one for the day every girl needed her mother. Her first broken heart.

My darling Jamie,

I know you feel like your heart is being ripped to pieces right now, and that you'll never love another boy again. I wish I was there to hold you as you cry, to stroke your hair and tell you that someone better will come along. To laugh when your father threatens to kill the boy who broke your heart.
Did your father ever tell you that he broke my heart? You should ask him about that story, baby. Let him tell you how we found each other again.
Love is strong, pumpkin. And with the right person, nothing can keep you apart.
I want you to wallow, baby. Wallow in self-pity and eat all the ice cream you can stomach until you feel better. And cry. A good cry is always healing.

There'll be other boys, and one day...you'll meet 'the one'.

I love you, sweetheart.
Mom

THEN SHE WROTE A LETTER FOR JAMIE'S NINETEENTH birthday. By this age, she knew that she was talking to a grown-up young woman. She couldn't imagine what Jamie as a young adult would be like. She wanted to be around for that day so badly, but she had to be prepared. Even if she received a kidney, the chances were slim that her body would accept it.

Then came the big one, her twenty-first. Jamie was a woman, and Holly wrote down the speech she would've given at her birthday party. The one that was going to make her feel slightly embarrassed, the one that was going to make her feel special, and the one that was going to fill her with so much excitement and hope for the future.

Her wrist was starting to hurt, but she carried on writing. But this one, too, came to an end and she put that letter in an envelope.

She didn't have the strength to write the next letter, but she persevered. It was a letter for her daughter's wedding day, although she didn't have any experiences to share as she'd never been married. Perhaps, by this time, Jake would have married, which meant that Jamie would have another woman in her life who she might call mother. That thought alone pinched at Holly's heart, but that was the way of the world. She wrote about Jamie's special day, and what she would've given her; something old, something new, something borrowed, and something blue.

My dearest daughter,
On your wedding day

Your very special day is upon you, and I know you've chosen the perfect day. I can smell the flowers in your room, I gasp at the most beautiful dress you have on, and there are tears of happiness glistening in my eyes.

I hope that the man waiting for you at the altar is everything your heart desires, that you didn't settle for less than you deserve. In my heart, I hope that the love of your life is someone like your father. Someone who is kind and loves you dearly, who wants to make your heart's desires come true, and is someone who takes your breath away every time he enters a room.

I wish I could have been there to help you get into your dress, to give you that final kiss, and tell you how beautiful you are and look.

This day will be one of the happiest days of your life, shared with loved ones all around you. I hope your brothers behave themselves and act like the perfect gentleman they were brought up to be. I'll make sure to mention this in their letters, too, I promise.

At your reception, remember to enjoy the dance with your father. Choose something silly, he can be so serious at times. Be happy, my beautiful girl. I hope that the love you share with your future husband grows and blossoms throughout the years. And may you love him as much as I love you.

Everyone should experience that unconditional love, the kind that God intended when two people come together in holy matrimony. Keep in mind that it won't always be sunshine and roses, baby, but in the end, I promise you, the fights and arguments are worth it. You'll both grow as people.

Promise me one thing? Don't ever run away, please. Unless it's for your life. In any other situation, stay and fight for what you believe in, for what you hold most dear, and for love. But if you have chosen correctly, as I'm positive you have, all will be just as you want it to be.

I love you, baby girl. You're forever in my heart. Don't forget me, please.

THERE WAS ANOTHER SHE WANTED TO WRITE FOR JAMIE, but she'd do that another day. Motherhood was something she knew a lot about, and it would also be her final letter.

EIGHTEEN

HOLLY

SHE GAVE AGGIE THE LETTERS SHE'D ALREADY FINISHED TO keep in a safe place.

If Jake, Amelia, or Robin found out, they would be upset, wanting to know why she was doing it if she'd promised to fight.

She didn't have the strength to fight with anyone anymore, and she needed whatever strength she had left in order to finish the rest of the letter she still wanted to write. Holly needed to tell all of them how she felt and what she wanted them to know.

So exhausted was she that she slept for almost the entire day. When she woke, she found Bernie at her side.

"Hey, poops," she croaked.

"Hey, babes." Tears welled up in Bernie's eyes, even though she tried to hide them.

"Don't cry."

"Just like fucking old times, huh?" Bernie wiped her face.

"Don't let one of the Peterses see you, they will chuck you out."

"They can try," she snapped, making Holly smile. "So a kidney, and a fucking liver, huh?"

"Yes, and please don't. We're not talking about candy here."

Bernie laughed. "I'm not a match, Holly. And neither is Leo. I'm so sorry. I don't want to lose you. Where's jellybean?"

"With Amelia, or Gus, or my mom. It upsets her to see me like this."

"I can imagine. But I doubt she would want to be anywhere else."

"I'm really trying, Bernie. I have so much to live for."

"I know. You know the boys are going to be little hellions, breaking hearts left, right and center."

"Yeah, that black hair and green eyes. Why do they have to look like him?"

"His genes are stronger, I guess."

Holly chuckled tiredly. "If only I could feel better while trying to hold on until Dr. Miller comes up with a match, things might not be so fucking difficult."

"So, you are really cancer free?"

"Yep, but what does that matter, because I'm going to die from organ failure. So fucking unfair."

"I don't get it, most patients live long on dialysis. I googled. Why not you?"

"First of all, my blood type is rare and although it's great at helping others, it's not so great at helping me. It's like it's stronger for other people, but not so much for me. Second, I need to wait for a donor with the same blood type, because I'm O negative. That's a bummer. Unfortunately, only about 6.6% of the population—Jake had kept yelling that at Robin—has it. You think we can find one of them? It's like I'm the only one on this planet with this blood type. The two times they managed to find a kidney or liver, there were others who needed them more than me."

"It's not fair."

"I know. But it's how it is."

"It can't end like this, Holly. It can't."

"Where's Leo?"

"With Jake at a bar downtown, probably discussing that percent you mentioned."

Holly burst out laughing, but then started coughing from her nausea.

"Sorry," Bernie apologized.

"Don't be sorry. Laughter is great. It's better than just lying in this fucking bed feeling sad and depressed."

"Jake needs to let it out, Holly. Leo's sort of been there for him before."

"I forgot. He helped get his fat ass back to how he looks now."

"Trust me, that was nothing compared to when you left."

"He got fat again?"

"No, worse. I should've never believed Mara."

"It's in the past, Bern."

"We could've had more time with you. It's not just something you forget, Holly."

"You can't do shit about it now. I should've stayed. I should've phoned you. I should've done something, it's my fault."

Bernie shook her head.

"I know you are mad. And I know things don't always work out the way you plan them to, but I need to ask you something—"

"Fuck, no. You are not saying your goodbyes. I won't listen to it."

"Bern..."

"No, Holly. I said goodbye once. I'm not going to do it again. You cannot force me to do this again. They will find organs."

Bernie's tears ran down her face. She jumped out of her chair and hugged Holly. "I can't. Please."

"Okay," Holly appeased her. She would just put it in her letter.

Her mother walked into the room, and in a stern voice said, "Bernie, no crying in this room." And then she took Bernie in her arms and gave her a hug.

"Yeah." She sniffed. "Don't mind me. It just feels like déjà vu."

"It's not going to be déjà vu. I will resurrect her, and then kill her if it is."

All three women laughed.

Bernie eventually stopped her tears and they started talking about each other's day, and the kids. The boys were growing and Holly hated the fact that she wasn't with them.

"Amelia promised that she would bring all three of them tonight."

"I don't think—"

"Holly, Jamie needs you still."

"I know, but it upsets her so much."

"She knows more about death than you think, sweetheart."

"I didn't want her to know about it, Mom. I wanted to protect her from what's going on. Why am I being punished for all of this? Is it because of what I did? I love him, Mom. And clearly he loves me, otherwise he wouldn't have stuck around." She started to cry. She was so fucking angry. "Everyone sees hope with me being this sick. Hope. It's so fucking wrong."

"I know."

"So why the fuck are we being punished?" She was out of breath and started to cough.

"Calm down." Her mother got up and slipped the oxygen mask over face. Her body ached. Everything was just becoming way too much.

"You are not being punished, Holly. I know that's how it feels, but the world isn't perfect or fair. Thousands of people go through similar situations every single day. You are not the only who asks that question. You know the Lord doesn't work that way."

"No, He works in mysterious ways, Mom. I just wish I could see the outcome of this one. I do not want to die, but I can't..." She started to sob.

"You have no choice, Holly. Your children still need you. We all still need you. Please, calm down."

"I'm going to go. I'll see you later." Bernie walked out.

Silence filled the room. It felt as if everyone was leaving her.

"It's not easy for her, sweetheart."

"I know. It's not easy on anyone. If I could make it easier I would, but none of you are letting me."

"Because you promised to beat this!"

"And I have. This is not cancer."

"It's part of it, Holly. Your organs gave up because of the cancer. You can't give up. Ever. I need you. Please, do not put me through this again. I've lost way too much already, Holly. Please." Tears filled her mother's eyes.

Resignedly, she nodded.

Her mother kissed her softly on the head. "You need to rest. I'll see you later tonight."

"Okay." She gave her mother a smile.

As soon as Jane left, she pulled the drawer open and carried on writing. She had two hours of alone time before visiting time. She would just have to put a smile on her face. That was still possible.

To my dearest Jamie,

Today you are where I've been before, twice. The second time was not so memorable, but hopefully you will only remember the joy of having brothers in your life.

I remember holding you in my arms when you were but a tiny little thing, much the same way you are holding that perfect little child of yours. He or she is going to bring you so much joy and happiness, and no matter the circumstances that you are in, as mine weren't perfect back then, you will be overjoyed at being a mother. It's so fulfilling, to feel that unconditional love, and I wish I was there to meet the special little person who is going to fill your heart with so much love. Maybe there'll be two, maybe only one, maybe even three.

You made me feel so many beautiful things during the time I was present in your life as your mother, but know that I will always be around.

I wish I was there to guide you, to give you advice on what to do when their stomach aches, and what not to do when a fever starts rising. But I'm sure you already know, as I have a feeling you might have been pulled into the family business and became one hell of a doctor.

But if not, you will still be the best at whatever you've chosen to do, as you are my child, and you are your father's daughter, too. Determination is the one thing you will know, among other great qualities.

I do not doubt your father, because I know he's raised you to be the perfect young woman you are today.

I imagine you reading this letter. Please don't cry when you do. But if you do, they should be tears of joy, not sadness. Always know that I am there in spirit, every step of the way, holding your hand, running the back of my hand down your cheek.

Take care of my grandbaby, or grandbabies, and know that I will always love you.

Mom

She'd reached the point, finally, where she'd told Jamie everything she'd wanted to. This was it. She was a grown woman.

Reaching for another clean sheet, she started writing a letter to her mom, saying how sorry she was that she had to go through all of this again, but that she'd given Holly her all. She had to know that.

She asked her to keep an eye on Jake, he was going to need a mother as his had failed him so badly, and that he would more than likely dislike her even more now that Holly wasn't around anymore.

She asked her mom to always tell Jamie and the boys stories about her and Jamie—their aunt— and how twins shared a special bond, one no one could come between. To continuously tell her children how much she'd loved them. She begged her to never let her children forget her.

By the time she finished her mother's letter, the tears flowed freely down her cheeks.

Bernie's letter came after that, in which she thanked her friend for being her rock after Jamie's death, and for the fact that she'd married Leo, otherwise she would've never met Jake.

She told Bernie that she would always be grateful to her for trying her damndest to fill the space Jamie had left empty.

She begged her to tell Jamie stories about her, to help her become the woman she wanted her to be. To teach her to be kind and not turn into a spoiled brat. She wanted Bernie to make sure that should Jake find someone again, that she was someone worthy to take her place.

Rodney's letter was also hard.

He'd taken Bernie's place when she wasn't there. She spoke about the day they met, how he called her *mother hen*. She asked him to continue to be a part of Jamie and the twins' life, to guide them and love them as much as he loved Jamie. To always make sure that they knew about their mother's goofiness and that it was okay to be silly. And that it was okay if they broke a girl's heart, not intentionally, but because things weren't going to work out. That it was okay to be angry and sad, because men needed to cry, too.

She wrote one to Frank, Gus, and Robin, thanking them all for having tried so hard, and that she was sorry things hadn't worked out according to plan.

There was one to Amelia, who had become like her own sister, always there for her children when she couldn't be. She was a great mother figure, and Holly wished with all her heart that just this once, the doctors were wrong. She wanted Amelia to feel what it was like to be pregnant, what it felt like to deliver a baby into this world. But should that never happen, she was a mom in so many ways to her children.

It hadn't been an easy letter to write.

She ended it with: *I would walk with you in high heels forever, sister.*

But now, it was time for her children to visit, so she put the letters away.

Jake stayed the night, which meant that she couldn't finish the letters. When she woke the next morning, he was gone.

She'd had an awful night, where she'd get cold then hot, and then cold again. Jake had tried to keep her warm by climbing into bed with her when she'd wake up shivering, and then he'd do everything he could to cool her down when she felt like she was burning up.

He was everything she'd ever wanted.

Unfortunately, though, she felt in her bones that soon she would leave this world. But not yet, not until she finished her letters.

She began her next letter. It was addressed to Mara.

Forgiving someone was never easy. But she wanted to have no regrets, no bitterness in her heart, and so she forgave Mara.

Mara,

I forgive you for what you did. I lost a child because of your lies, but my heart has forgiven you. I don't want to die with this blackness marring my soul.

I hope that someday you and Jake will be able to make amends, that he will forgive you and allow you to be a part of your grandchildren's lives. They already have a grandmother who loves them, but one more wouldn't hurt.

As a mother, I forgive you. I would never go to the lengths you did, but I know now that you were just being the kind of mother you thought you had to be. You raised great children.

Be easy on Jake. It will be even harder for him to forgive you now that I'm gone, but I hope that with time, he will realize that he has to if he's to have some semblance of a normal life. He's going to need you now.

Holly

THE LAST LETTER WAS TO JAKE.

My homewrecker and Hooligan,

I'm so sorry that I never got to tell you everything you meant to me. Words were always just that, words. I always tried to show you, and I know my mistake made you think otherwise. I just couldn't imagine a world where I would hate you.

I know that you must hate me for leaving you, but this time there is no coming back.

Just know that I will never stop loving you, not even in death. I will remember your smile that always had me weak at the knees, made my heart beat faster, and made me want to do things to you that I couldn't possibly put into words.

Even if heaven tries to wipe all the memories from my mind, I will find a way to remember you.

Our love was like The Notebook shit, and I know you probably have no idea what The Notebook is, but it's good so you need to watch it.

I didn't want to leave, but my stupid body was too weak. Probably your doing, too—but don't misinterpret my meaning, because when I was with you that was exactly how I felt; weak in my heart, weak at the knees, and weak in my anger when all I wanted was to rip your head off. And it's a weakness that will remain with me always—you are my weakness.

I could never say no to you, even if I'd wanted to so many times. It wasn't possible, and leaving you that day when I asked you to choose was the second hardest thing I ever had to do in my life.

I wish so many beautiful things for you as you are too precious to live this life alone. I want you to move on, to teach our children how good life can be. That it doesn't have to be spent in sadness or anger. That it's amazing to love, live, laugh.

I want you to laugh to your heart's content at least once a day, and I want you to not feel guilty in loving another. I will prob-

ably haunt her ass because that's how I roll, but I need you to move on.

Open your heart to possibilities. Love our children unconditionally. It's not the boys' fault that I'm not there, and they are going to need you every step of the way.

I know you're hurt, and I know you are angry, but please try to find it in your heart to forgive me.

The only mistake I ever made was loving you too much. Don't punish me or our children for that.

I'll see you in my dreams.

Always and forever,
Bee Puke

ONCE SHE PLACED HIS LETTER IN AN ENVELOPE, SHE pressed the red button.

Tears streamed down her face.

She didn't want to die, but she had no idea how to fight as she didn't have any fight left in her.

Aggie came rushing in, worried out of her mind.

Holly handed over the letters she'd written.

With her hand over her heart, Aggie pleaded with her, "Baby, don't do this."

"It's just a precaution, Aggie," she reminded the woman, wiping at her tears. "I'm still fighting."

"You better be." Aggie fiddled with the IV and the tubes she was connected to.

Holly closed her eyes and smiled.

Please, God. I don't want to die. If you could just put Robin on the right path to finding me a kidney, I'd be ever so grateful.

Why had she thought of Robin instead of Dr. Miller, she wondered? But, it was all really in His hands now. He knew how sorry she was for what she'd done to Kate, but she would never be sorry for loving Jake. He made her life extra special.

NINETEEN

JAKE

"It's going to be okay." Amelia hugged him tight.

He'd started shaking. He was in shock.

He'd left Holly early this morning to take a quick shower, make sure that the kids were fine, make sure that there was enough food at home, only to realize that he didn't have to make sure about anything as the support system he had was the best.

He returned to work to take his mind off of his worries, and just as he was leaving the OR, he got the call.

Holly had slipped into a coma.

Not a good sign at all.

Armand and Gus phoned everyone they could and passed on the news.

Robin took it hard, and was in such a state that she vanished. No one had heard from her since Holly slipped into the coma.

And there he sat, with nothing to occupy his mind except the ever-present worry.

A part of him wanted it to be over, but he knew he wouldn't be able to deal with it if it was. If Holly died, there would be no coming back for him.

She hadn't even said goodbye, because they hadn't allowed her to, even when she'd tried. He would never forgive his own stubbornness for it.

"I can't be here," Jake said to himself and left.

He went to his office and an anger he'd never felt before washed over him. In a vicious revolt, he threw an arm out and knocked all his certificates off the wall and onto the floor, then turned and swiped the contents on his desk to the floor as well, smashing his laptop in the process.

If anyone had to see him now, they'd think he was crazy, but he was beyond caring. With nostrils flaring, he picked up one of his paperweights and threw it at the window, shattering it to smithereens, the glass flying in every direction. He fell to his knees and screamed until his throat was hoarse.

The anger didn't dissipate, and neither did the sadness, but he felt spent, lifeless, useless.

A pair of manly arms gripped him strongly from behind. "It's going to be okay, bud," Leo said in a soothing voice. "Scream some more if you have to."

Jake screamed again and again until his throat burned, then he started to shake as he broke down.

Why her? Was it because of what he'd done to Kate?

Holly was his true love, his soulmate. He couldn't lose her.

Why was he being punished for loving her so fucking much?

She was the mother of his children.

Why, why, why!

He struggled to breathe. This was worse than the time he found out what his mother had done.

Ten times worse.

The same ache when he discovered that Romy had died crept into his heart and unseen claws tore at it.

"Jake," Leo called a few times, and getting no response, screamed for assistance. "Help!" He laid Jake gently on the floor and ran out of the room.

Jake was gasping for air, but it was all just a motion as no air entered his lungs.

People ran into the room, and during the confusion he felt something pierce the skin on his arm. And thankfully, his lungs began taking in air just as darkness overpowered all his senses.

ROBIN

HER PHONE BEEPED.

You need find a kidney. Jake is in the hospital. He had a panic attack. Love you.

The message was from Amelia.

Robin started to cry. In desperation, she hit the steering wheel hard, so hard it hurt, but she couldn't stop. It seemed like she'd been sitting in her car for ages.

"Why, why, why?" she yelled, hitting the steering wheel over and over again. This couldn't be the test. She'd lost many lives to get to where she was today.

They'd beaten the cancer, only to discover that both of her kidneys and liver were failing.

Devenn was trying everything in his power to get what she needed, and the two times they'd thought they had, the organs had gone to patients who'd needed them more. Why? Holly needed them, too. Life was so unfair.

Why was He doing this?

Why couldn't they fucking find a match?

Why was it so hard, so difficult just to save her?

What had she ever done that was so wrong?

But she knew why. It was because of whom she was fighting against.

No one could beat Him, not even her. Not this time. And she needed the win. Not for her, but for her brother, her niece and nephews.

Jake was going to become that elusive stranger again, the one she wouldn't recognize or love, the one that wasn't him at all.

She couldn't bear that again. The family couldn't bear that again. They couldn't do a repeat of him pretending he was fine when he'd be far from it. This time, it would signal the end.

"I need this win, please!" she yelled over and over through snot and tears. "You have one already, don't take the other one, too." She remembered Jake once telling her that Holly was a twin.

This situation was cutting her to the core. How was she supposed to summon the strength to go back into that hospital, into that room that already smelled like death?

She started her car and drove. The tears blurred her vision to such an extent, that at one point she'd had to swerve out of the way of oncoming traffic on the verge of slamming into her.

Wiping her eyes with the back of her hand, she took a corner and drove down another street, then up a hill and around a curve, eventually passing through gates that opened automatically when she neared. Security was such that it read her number plate immediately upon detection. Once inside, she came to a stop and cried some more.

The door opened.

So devastated was she, she was confused as to where she was until a familiar pair of arms wrapped around her.

"Robin?" her mother said.

Why here of all places?

She tried to speak, but all that happened was the opening and closing of her mouth.

"Shhh," Mara whispered.

She'd missed her mother so badly that in her distress, her heart must have guided her back home to the one woman who always had answers.

But she wasn't sure about that anymore, hadn't been for a while. It had felt as if that woman had died the day the truth reared its ugly head over what she'd done to Jake.

"Will you come into the house with me? Please," Mara begged, guiding her gently out of the car.

With no strength left, she allowed her mother to lead the way, her sobs uncontrollable. Once inside, Mara led her to a couch where they sat side by side. The one crying, and the other one comforting.

"What is going on. What's happened?"

Robin sniffed and tried to compose herself, shocked that she was home.

"I'm sure Dad's told you."

"We don't speak about you, Jake, or Amelia. I wanted to so badly, but he refuses."

"It's Holly. She fallen into a coma."

"What?" Mara sat up, shock spreading across her face.

"You got your wish, Mom. She's out of his life, and this time for good."

"I never wanted that!" Mara's eyes clouded over with tears. "I'm so sorry," she said, whispering Jake's name under her breath.

"Don't, he is not going to want to see you. I'll probably join your little corner, too, as he isn't going to want to see me, either. He'll blame me for not saving her life, because I couldn't help

Devenn find a damn fucking kidney or liver, and all because she is O negative!" she yelled, getting up and smacking her mother's lamp to the floor, breaking it.

Mara gripped her arms. "Calm down, sweetheart. Calm down," she repeated over and over.

"I failed him, Mom. He begged me to save her life and I failed him. We are going to lose him again."

"Shhh." Mara closed her eyes. "Calm down. You are laying a heavy burden on your shoulders, sweetheart."

"None of us are a match. Not even Jake."

"I'm sorry, baby."

"I'm so tired."

"Go take a bath, okay? And get some sleep. I promise you that you will find an answer soon. She will be fine."

She knew her mother was lying, was only trying to placate her. If her mother had seen Holly, she wouldn't be telling her these things. There was just no way.

But she took heed and went to have a bath, then had a glass of wine with the tablets her mother gave her. Which wasn't ideal in any situation, mixing those two, but sometimes one just didn't care.

She switched her phone off and climbed into bed—she was in her old room.

Somehow, she needed to make peace with the fact that Jake was going to hate her. She'd failed him, she'd failed Jamie, and she'd failed the twins.

She woke the next morning with someone gently shaking her. Her father.

"Sweetheart."

She started to cry when she saw the tears in his eyes.

"She's gone, isn't she?"

Gus hugged her. "No, she is still fighting, but you are breaking my heart."

That only made her cry harder.

"Mom said I would have the answer, but I don't. I failed him, Dad. I failed them all."

"We all did, sweetheart. Come. You need something to eat, and then I think it's time to pray."

"I doubt that's going to work. He doesn't like me, Dad. I've meddled in His business for far too long."

Gus stared at her, and then chuckled.

"It's not funny, Dad."

"Oh, I agree. It's not funny. But you have it all wrong, baby. We are not working against Him. We are the miracles He sends for people to receive. And it pains me you don't know that." He wiped her tears away. "Why do you think we all became doctors? That we all carry the statuses of being so good at what we do, sweetheart? It's only because He created us for this purpose. He made you to save His children from horrible sickness, Armand to save little ones, your mother, so that hearts could beat a little longer. He made us to give them more chances. He is really testing your brother, though, but Jake is more complicated. He needs challenges."

"We are going to lose him, Dad."

"We might, but God always has a plan, sweetheart."

"It's not going to work this time. Jake is going to fail whatever test he's being put through. I can feel it."

"Then we need to pray for his eyes to see, sweetheart."

She sniffed.

Her father's phone rang.

"Gus," he answered, sniffling. "Yes, she is right here. Devenn what is going on?"

Devenn!

She took the phone from her father. "What's happening, Devenn?"

"I found a kidney and a liver. Where are you?"

"Is it guaranteed ours?"

"Yes, it's ours."

"What?" she scrambled off the bed.

"Just get your butt here, stat! I'm going to need to harvest soon. I'll text you the pick-up location shortly."

"I'm on my way." She grabbed her clothes on her way out of the room. "They've found a kidney and a liver, Dad," she shouted as she entered the bathroom to get dressed.

"What?"

"Let's get going." She quickly got dressed and rushed out of the bathroom, screaming, "Mom!" Nothing. She yelled again as she ran down the stairs with her father on her heels, but there was no reply. Her mother had been right. The answer had come. And despite all that had happened, her mother still knew everything.

"Mara!" Gus was yelling, too.

"We need to go. Just leave her a note, please, and quickly."

Gus scribbled on something, while Robin put on her shoes.

On their way out of the house she dialed Jake.

"Jake's phone," Amelia answered.

"We found a kidney and liver. I'm going to pick it up soon."

"What, where?"

"Just let Jake know."

She cut the call as she started her car and drove like a mad woman. Not that she knew where she was going as yet, but Devenn would give her the address soon.

"You made me to give others their miracles, give me mine, please," she begged, directing her gaze upward.

"Watch the road, baby. Pray later." Her father steadied the wheel.

"Sorry, Dad." A chuckle escaped her lips.

The call from Devenn came—pickup was at P&E.

"Right under our noses!" She smiled and took the turnoff to P&E.

Practically skidding to a stop, she ran into the hospital, her father at her side.

"OR two," one of the nurses yelled. Devenn must have alerted them.

"Go," her father said. "I'll wait here."

Nodding, she ran to collect the organs and met Devenn at the entrance. All was good to go.

"Where are the donor's family?"

"Go, they know you need it. I'll be there soon."

"Okay. See you in the OR."

She ran back, but couldn't find her father.

"He said you must go, that he'll be there soon. There's an emergency."

"Just our luck."

Without wasting another second, she ran out of the hospital with the precious kidney and a part of the liver they needed in the container, to where an ambulance awaited her. They took her straight to Downsend.

Please just hold on. It's all you have to do.

She prayed to God to not take Holly, to help her fight, as her brother would lose this test if He called her unto Him. She asked God to give Jake another test, one with Holly at his side. Then, he would surely pass every obstacle God put in his path. Just not this current test.

The sirens wailed all the way to Downsend and when they got there, Holly was already waiting in the OR.

The operating nurses took the organs from her.

"Robin," Jake's voice was right behind her. He looked awful. But it wasn't a shock. "Please, just bring her back to me."

She hugged her brother. "I'll give everything I have in me, okay? Pray, like you never prayed before."

He nodded. Leo was standing right beside him.

"I need to get ready. Devenn is on his way."

"Good luck," Leo said, leading Jake away.

Please, God. I hope you are listening.

TWENTY

JAKE

He sat and waited with Jane, Bernice, Amelia, Leo, and his three children in the waiting room. And he prayed like he'd never prayed before.

Restlessness reared its head a few minutes into the operation. He couldn't keep his legs from bouncing up and down. He'd never been great at being on the other side of things—as a loved one waiting on the doctor's news.

The container with the organs and the huge P&E logo on the side kept playing like a movie in his head.

So close. The organs had been so close, right here in Boston.

He knew that the donor's family would still be at the hospital. "I can't sit here," he said to Leo.

"Where else are you going to go?"

"I need to go to P&E, the donor's family might still be there. I need to speak to them." He got up, told Jane where he was going, and kissed Jamie on the head. "I'll be back soon. Call me immediately if there's any news."

Jane nodded.

Leo stood up, too. "I'll drive you."

Jake handed him the keys to his SUV when they reached the car. They got in and sped away.

The traffic was practically nonexistent, but it was Sunday morning, so he hadn't thought there'd be any.

Please, God. Let her be okay. Bring her back to me.

Fifteen minutes later, they walked into P&E.

Rebecca smiled when she saw him.

He looked at the board. His mother's name wasn't on it. Thank God for small miracles.

Jake jogged to the elevator and headed up to the nephrology ward, Leo hot on his heels. Inside the elevator, he leaned against the wall. Fresh tears pooled in his eyes, and his body slid to the floor.

"You okay, bud?" Leo asked.

"Yeah, I just...I need to thank them. They need to know that their lost one's organs is going to someone special."

"I get it, bud."

When the doors opened, Leo helped Jake to his feet.

He sniffed and wiped his face with his sleeve as he strode toward reception.

One of the nurses, Florence, gaped at him in surprise.

"I'm here to see the—"

"—your mother didn't want you to know."

Confused, he blinked, then blinked again. "I'm sorry?" Jake asked. He could've sworn he heard her say that his mother didn't want him to know.

"You don't know. Why are you here?"

"I'm here to thank the donor and their family. What did you say about my mother?" he asked through clenched teeth.

"Give me a minute, Jake. I need to check with the patient to see if they will see you"

He was shocked that she didn't address him as Dr. Peters, but then he remembered it wasn't his turf anymore, it was his mother's.

When she returned, she led him to one of the private rooms. The door was closed and she knocked.

"Jake, just...be calm, okay?"

Still confused, he entered but stopped mid-step when he saw his father in the room. Odd. He was sitting next to the patient's bed. Who just happened to be his mother.

His mother closed her eyes, and he could see her jaw muscles clenching.

He looked to his father, who sighed.

"What the fuck is going on here?" Jake demanded.

His father shook his head. "Jake..."

He glared at his mother. "Is this one of your ploys to get me to forgive you?" He rounded on his father. "Did you put her up to this? Did you think I would magically forgive her if she did this?"

Mara was silent, and Gus sighed. "Jake, I didn't even know. I put two and two together when I accompanied Robin this morning to pick up the organs. Your mother wasn't home, which was strange. But I just knew that the woman I loved would do something like this. I guess she finally came home." He got up and kissed Mara on the side of her head. "I'll be just outside okay, darling."

She gave him a dim smile and nodded.

He squeezed Jake's shoulder as he passed him, but didn't say anything.

Silence lingered between them.

"Why? Why you?"

"I know...it's not fair, considering... I didn't want you to know."

Jake sniffed and wiped a tear away. "You raised me. You should've known I'd want to thank the donor and their family."

"I didn't think you'd want to do that while Holly was in surgery. I thought I'd have time to seal the records."

"Yeah...well, I couldn't sit in the waiting room." He paced around the room, then slumped into a chair. "I need the truth. I need you to be completely honest with me. Did you do this so I would forgive you?" His shoulders shook as a tear rolled down his cheek.

His mother gaped at him, a frown furrowing her eyebrows. "Sweetheart, no. I messed up, horribly so, and this was my chance to rectify that mistake when the opportunity arose. I had to do this; for me, for you, and for Holly. I wasn't planning on telling you, ever."

He shook his head, shoving his hands into the pockets of his jacket. His eyes were burning. He was so damn tired of everything.

He looked her in the eye and asked again, "Why, Mom?"

"I just told you."

"I need a better explanation than that."

"Robin was devastated," she said, sniveling. "I knew something was wrong with Holly. But nobody would tell me anything. Not your father, not her. But last night, she came to me, and she yelled at me. Robin has never yelled at me. She told me she felt like a failure. I didn't want another one of my children to hate me. You and Amelia already hate me enough that I struggle to breathe."

"So Robin asked you to donate?" He sighed. His mother still didn't get it.

"No, Robin just told me what she needed. But why didn't you come to me? Why didn't you ask me? You must have known I was O negative."

He shook his head. "Believe it or not, I didn't, and even if I did, you would have been the last person I'd have asked. I abhor you," he said through clenched teeth, the chords in his neck visible from the anger. "You lied to me when you told me you were on board with Holly's pregnancy, when I told you I wanted the baby. You tricked me. That was some premeditative shit. And because of that, one of my daughters is dead."

Tears rolled out the sides of her eyes and down her neck into her hair.

"Not to mention the lies after that, for years, even after I asked you, you still lied. You have no idea—"

"Yes...I do." She sighed. "Because you've made that perfectly clear. That's why I didn't want you to know about this."

"Oh, really? Because this is like a get-out-of-jail-free card. How am I supposed to hate you now? Be angry at you now? I'm fucking furious, yet I can't hold on to that anger anymore."

"It's why I didn't want you to know," she said again. "Be angry, Jake, hate me for as long as you need to. I messed up, in a catastrophic way, of that there is no doubt. I didn't do this for forgiveness. I gave her my kidney, and a piece of my liver, because of who she is to you." She swallowed hard and closed her eyes.

Jake stared at his mother.

"I knew I made a mistake when you vanished in front of my eyes. I pretended not to see it, and I tried to fix it. Instead, I created someone else that none of us knew. I pushed you to marry Kate, because I wanted to believe that she could bring you back to yourself. I should've left you to find Holly. But I was scared that when you eventually found any trace of her, you'd discover she was dead. And that would've been on me," she cried.

"Nothing I could ever say would justify what I did. I was just being your mother. I just wanted what was best for you, and at the time, I didn't know that what was best for you was Holly and the child you created together. All the lies, the pretending, was my punishment for carrying it so long. Seeing you turn into a stranger...that was my punishment. *I* did that to you. I'm sorry that I loved you too much. I was blind to how much Holly meant to you. I'm sorry, Jake." She put a fist to her mouth and bit down on it as sobs wracked her body.

Jake stared at her. Those were the words he had been waiting for. She finally got it.

"Robin was so angry with me last night. She told me that I had finally gotten my wish. That's when I realized you all thought I hated Holly. But, Jake, I never hated her. I thought she was trying to pin you down and I didn't want that for you. I never thought you loved her as much as you do. I'm not God. I missed all the signs, and because I was blinded by my love for you, I only saw what I wanted to see. I made a grave mistake, and I've had to live with that eating away at me on the inside for years. I honestly thought she'd get an abortion when she realized you and your money would no longer be available to her. You can be mad at me for as long as you want. I am the reason Romalia is dead. I live with it every day. I live knowing that I am your monster...when I should've been your mother."

Jake closed his eyes to keep further tears at bay. He couldn't cry anymore. He opened his eyes and looked at his mother. "Why wasn't I a match? You are O negative. Why aren't the rest of us O negative?" He covered his face with both hands.

"Sweetheart, please come closer."

Somewhat reluctantly, he walked over to the chair his father had vacated and sat down.

He felt his mother's hand on his arm. "Listen to me."

He pinched the bridge of his nose and nodded.

"When Robin told me Holly was O negative, when she said she wished someone was a match, I didn't think twice. I told her that she would get her answer soon; I knew I was O negative. I didn't think twice, baby." She touched his face. "I phoned Devenn and asked him to see me. We did the test and he was just as shocked as you are, asking me the exact same question. I was told that He works in mysterious ways and I never understood that, but it finally made sense. Darling, you are not her match because your heart already beats inside her. And that is the other reason I did it without even thinking. If she died, you would stop breathing, and I refuse to see you like that again."

Jake tried to push back the new wave of tears, but it was no use. Getting up, he bent over and hugged his mother.

"Oh, darling," Mara cried, wrapping her arms around him. She kissed him on the cheek.

At long last, his mother wasn't just saying the words he'd been wanting to hear all this time, she was showing him that she meant every single one. She hadn't done this just so he would forgive her, she'd done it because she'd wanted to. She'd needed to.

He didn't want to feel angry anymore, he didn't want to hate her anymore. And now, he finally understood what Holly had meant about forgiveness. Forgiving someone was not just for the benefit of the person involved—it was for yourself as well.

The bitterness toward his mother washed away, like a new dawn had broken. He still felt a tinge of anger at her actions, but it wasn't as piercing as it had once been.

His sobs continued as his mother embraced him. This was the woman he'd called mother all his life. Not the monster of the past five years. This was the woman he would do anything for, the woman whose advice and opinions he'd ask for. The weight he had carried on his shoulders from the moment he'd learned the truth melted into nothingness.

"I'm so, so sorry, baby," she whispered in his ear.

"Me, too." Straightening, he sat back down again. He felt as light as air.

"How is she doing?"

He shrugged. "I don't know, because I came to find the family of the donor, to thank them, give them some clarity, peace." He looked up at his mother. "But everyone knows to call me the second there is any news." He hung his head and whispered, "I've missed you."

"Oh, sweetheart. I know I've been the worst mother imaginable to you. And I know that I'll never be able to make it up to you—some things one can't take back, or fix—but I'll be darned if I'm not going to do my best and try. Even if it kills me."

Jake nodded. He took his mother's hand and kissed it gently. "Thank you, Mom."

"She deserved it more than I did. She is a great mother. Your father's told me how stubborn she was when you all wanted her to terminate the pregnancy. And I'm glad she didn't. From what I hear, you have two little studs now...and a gorgeous little girl. They all need her, sweetheart. I couldn't watch her go away again and leave you, because this time there would have been no return."

"I can't remember when last I prayed so much. It felt as if He was punishing me for what I did to Kate, for loving Holly."

"It's not how He works, sweetheart."

"I know, it still felt that way, Mom."

"I know..."

Taking a deep breath, he asked, "How are you feeling?"

"I'll be all right. I got back so much more, and I didn't even bargain on it."

He chuckled. "Really, Mom? You really believe that I wouldn't have found out?"

She managed a chuckled as well. "Yes. I figured you'd stay at Holly's side, and counting on that, I'd have sealed all records, but it wasn't to be." She took his hand in hers. "I really thought Kate made you happy, Jake. That's the only reason why I pushed you to marry her. I apologize for that."

"It's okay."

"It's never going to be okay, Jake."

"Mom, it's okay. I didn't marry her. But what I did do was help Holly make pretty amazing boys."

His mother snorted, very unladylike, but at that moment neither cared. "I'd like to meet all of them one day, if you'd let me."

He pursed his lips, but said nothing. He wasn't sure if he was ready for that to happen.

"I know...I'm pushing it."

His hand was still in hers, and his eyes roamed over her delicate features.

"When was the last time you slept? You look exhausted."

"Is sleep something I can eat?"

"You need to sleep, sweetheart. You have three children relying on you."

"I know."

"Why don't you close your eyes for a bit? I'll wake you if there's any news."

Jake sighed. The chair was so comfy. He rested his head against the back of the chair and set his feet on the frame of the hospital bed. "Maybe for just a couple of minutes."

As soon as his lids lowered, sleep quickly overtook him.

TWENTY-ONE

HOLLY

SHE WALKED OUT OF THE OR, THREW HER BANDANA ON the floor and screamed.

Everyone looked at her.

"You can't win them all," Missy said. She was one of the doctors, and was fantastic at her job.

"Something is wrong with this hospital," Holly said, looking at Missy in exasperation. The woman was magnificently beautiful. Her eyes were different colors. One was green, and the other was brown with just hints of green, and she seemed to stare right into the depths of your soul with those eyes. Her hair was dark, tied up into a high ponytail, and her lips were full and plump.

"No, there's nothing wrong with this hospital. It's actually a special place. It's just that some you lose and some you win."

"No hospital loses this many lives."

Missy sighed as tears of frustration ran down Holly's face. She'd taken an oath to save lives, not lose them.

"Come sit," Missy said, walking over to the beautiful white seaters that were stacked up against the wall.

Holly knew that soon she'd have to go to another room, with the exact same seaters. But she wouldn't sit on those. No, she'd have to look a family in the eye and tell them she hadn't been able to save their son.

She looked at the people around her, some were waiting, and some were consoling others, hugging them, talking to them in sad whispers.

It was like it was heaven's hospital. Holly laughed at that thought.

"This hospital is special," Missy reiterated.

Holly grunted sarcastically. "It's a killing machine, Missy."

"No, it's not."

Holly frowned.

"Saving lives, not saving them...that isn't what's key here."

Holly looked at her in disbelief, then shook her head. "You remind me so much of someone I used to know."

"Who?" Missy asked, her face unreadable.

Holly wanted to answer but realized she couldn't. She had no idea who Missy reminded her of.

"Who, Holly? Who do I remind you of?"

Holly shook it away. It was something that had started happening on a regular basis lately, and it was freaking her out. "It doesn't matter."

"Don't say that. Who do I remind you of?"

"Just drop it," she snapped. She got up and walked into the next room where she had to impart sad news to the family whose son she hadn't been able to save.

Missy was right. This hospital was different. They were happy when lives were saved, but even happier when lives were lost. One of the other reasons that she'd dubbed it *heaven's hospital*. Nobody was angry or sad.

"Is it Jake?" Missy called after her.

Holly turned around slowly. "Excuse me?"

"The person I remind you of. Is it Jake? Perhaps it's Jamie Bernice, or maybe it's Amelia."

Holly knew those names, but she couldn't place them. How did Missy know those names?

"Who are you?" Holly asked. "What is this place?" She was frantic now. Those names had triggered something inside her.

"Calm down," Missy said.

She had known something was wrong with this hospital. Who were those people Missy was talking about? Why did she know their names?

She paced up and down.

"Calm down."

"Don't tell me to calm down. Where the hell am I?" She couldn't even remember when she'd started working here. It was like she'd always just been here. "What is this?"

She ran to reception and started rummaging around the front desk. Not one form had been filled in. Doctors were writing with pens that didn't work.

They chatted to one another as if her tantrum wasn't taking place. They weren't at all affected by anything.

"Where am I?" Holly yelled at the one doctor. But the doctor simply looked at her before she continued filling in her paperwork, with a pen that didn't work.

"Calm down," Missy kept saying over and over, but Holly ran around the desk and pulled out the keyboard. She started punching keys, but no letters formed on the screen. She kept typing, but nothing happened.

She'd never worked on a computer here before.

"Calm down, Mom!" Missy shouted, and Holly whipped her head around to look at her.

Missy stood there, motionless, her face expressionless.

"What did you just call me?" Holly asked.

"You've been here too long. You have to go back."

"Go back where? And why did you just call me *Mom?*" She stalked over to Missy.

Who was this woman?

"You are forgetting. It's never a good sign when that happens. You need to remember them."

"Remember who?"

Missy reached out for her, but Holly backed away. She continued to reach out and touched Holly's face softly.

Suddenly, Jake's face, smiling at her with so much love flashed through her mind. Jamie's laughter when she tickled her.

Tears welled up in her eyes.

Bradley and Cooper, lying on the bed with her. They were growing up so fast.

Her family.

She choked back a sob and looked up at Missy, and her eyes were automatically drawn to the name tag on her coat: Romalia.

"Romy!" she cried, flinging her arms around her daughter. The daughter she had lost so long ago.

"You have to go back."

"Look at you, you are so beautiful."

Romalia smiled, but her expression soon turned somber. "Mom, listen to me. You need to go back."

"Go back?" Holly smiled, but Romy didn't return the smile. Instead, tears filled her eyes.

"I'm sorry I lied about my name. You've been given a gift. You received the organs you needed, Mom, but you are starting to freak them out because you aren't waking up. You have to go back."

"How? I just got here."

"No, you've been here too long. Time works different here."

"Where is here?"

"It's the place where some people come to when they fall into a coma, like you did. It's the place where people wait to die when they are under the knife. They just don't always remember when they wake up. Losing life here, is not what you think. It's the opposite. Where it seems we're losing a life, we're actually giving life back. Hopefully, you understand now what I meant by what I said earlier. And now, it's time that I give you back, Mom. I can't keep you here. I've taken up too much of your time." A tear ran down her cheek.

"No, Romy, if you knew how much I love you, you wouldn't say that."

"I know how much you love me. You almost died bringing me and Jamie into the world. I just wasn't as strong as her. But I am now. My sister isn't, though. She needs you, Mom. My brothers need you. And Dad needs you. He wouldn't understand Jamie. She may look like him, but she's like you. So please, go back. For me. Be with them, you have so much more to live for."

Desperate for more contact, she reached out and hugged Romy again. "I don't know how."

"Fight, Mom. Fight like you've never fought before."

Breathing deeply she inhaled Romy's scent. It was flowery, but so delicious.

Clearing her throat, she pulled away. "If you're here, where is your aunt?"

"She couldn't be here this time. She already had her chance when you brought me and Jamie into this world. We only get one chance per family member. Please, don't let me fail."

"Baby, you are not failing. Oh, you remind me so much of your father."

"I know, I'm just like him. That is why you have to go back, my sister needs you more than I do. I have Aunt Jamie to take care of me."

Holly brushed a strand of hair away from Romy's face and tucked it behind her ear.

"I'm begging you to please go back. It's not your time, Mom."

"How do I do this? How do I leave when I know I can stay with you?" she asked, and Romy released a huge breath.

"You can't stay with me. I was never meant to have anyone stay with me. I was always meant to be yours and Jamie's guiding light. Just think of them, Mom. Think how happy they make you, how much they fulfill your life. They are the key. Go back to them. It's what I want, Mom."

Holly nodded. She hugged the daughter she'd lost, her heart breaking all over again. "I love you, baby girl, so much."

"I know. Thank you for being my mother. Go be theirs now. And give this to Jamie." Leaning over, she gave Holly a big kiss on the cheek. It was heavenly and soft, and filled with so much love. "Tell her I'm always watching out for her."

They broke apart.

"I'll see you again...one day. All of you." She started walking backward, and Holly did the same. It wasn't a voluntary movement. It felt like she was being sucked backward and she couldn't control it.

"Romy!" She reached an arm out, but the hospital itself was beginning to move away from her. It started fading and flickering.

Intermittently, Holly saw children run around Romy.

"You guys ready for a game?" she sang to them.

"Yes!"

"Let's go, then." As she turned and started to run, the picture vanished altogether.

JAKE

WITHIN THE NEXT COUPLE OF DAYS, EVERYONE FOUND OUT that Mara was Holly's donor.

Robin cried, which Jake found surprising.

Jake felt sorry for Amelia. She knew that what Mara had done had practically saved Holly's life, but she was still struggling with the fact that her mother had been the one behind the lies that had led to a baby dying.

"You don't have to make peace with her, Amelia. She doesn't expect that."

"Romy is dead, Jake. How can you forgive her?"

"I know *my* daughter is dead. And you know what? Mom told me to my face that it was her fault. It pains her more than you think it does. But if Holly taught me one thing, it's that forgiveness is for oneself, not for the other person. And I realized that."

"I can't."

Jake hugged his sister and held her tight. "You don't need to make peace. Why don't you take the kids and go to the park? I'm sure Jamie could use some fresh air."

She nodded and Bernie got up, intent on joining her.

"I'll forever be grateful for what she did for my friend, Jake, but I just can't forgive your mother yet," Bernie said.

"That's okay." He smiled, and the two women left with his children in tow.

Holly was hooked up to a ventilator. Her heart had stopped beating in the OR, but Robin got it back. She'd assisted Devenn with the transplant.

He was glad that he hadn't been there to see it. It would've broken him beyond repair. But seeing her lying so still, her heart beating strong, not breathing for herself, was just another major concern.

He didn't really want Jamie around that, but what else could he do? Holly was her mother and Jamie both wanted and needed to see her.

Both him and Amelia tried to prepare her for the fact that Holly might not wake up, but Jamie simply told her that Holly was visiting Romy, and that she'd be back, because Romy would make her come back.

She wanted to buy her sister a teddy bear, and it broke his heart, but he bought the damn thing and gave it away to one of the children up in pediatrics.

Teresse asked him how she was doing.

He showed her that she was hanging on by seesawing his hand.

Then, his mother asked if she could see Holly. She wanted to speak to her, tell her to fight, apologize and ask her for her forgiveness. She believed that Holly could hear her and was so afraid that Holly would reject the kidney and the liver if she found out it was from her.

She wanted to prepare her.

It was why he'd sent Amelia and Bernice away.

Jane was outside Holly's room. She'd wanted to see Mara for a while now, but Jake had told her it was a bad idea. But she had to talk to his mother. He couldn't speak for Jane, or ask her to forgive his mother. That woman had lived through the worst nightmare imaginable, and now she was living through it again. She'd lost so much more than any of them had.

His mother just had to bear with what Jane wanted to say to her.

Bending over, he kissed Holly's cheek gently and left the room.

Jane was sitting, patiently waiting, as his father was going to bring his mother over. She wasn't even supposed to be going anywhere—she hadn't healed yet—but that was his mom. She never gave up, always pushed herself, even now right after a major surgery.

But Devenn had given her the all clear, as long as she stayed in the wheelchair and went back as soon as possible.

The elevator opened and his heart clenched when he saw his father wheeling his mother out.

Jane hadn't spoken a single word since the news got out that Mara was the donor. She'd just shed a lot of tears, both happy and angry for obvious reasons.

"You okay?" Jake asked.

She gave him a curt nod.

He was worried about Jane.

When his parents reached them, his father stopped.

"Mara, I want you to meet Jane, Holly's mother."

Mara merely stared at her. There was so much regret and guilt on his mother's face. She really had no idea what she'd just done for him, for all of them.

Then again, she'd never wanted anyone to find out.

Jane simply stared back at her, expressionless. And then her chin jutted out slightly and her lower lip trembled.

It was a mannerism she shared with Holly. Fuck, he missed her so much, missed her voice, her laughter.

Jane got up, and surprised him when what she did next was embrace Mara.

His mother looked confused, had clearly not expected that, but it took only a few seconds before she folded her arms around Jane.

"I'm so sorry. I wish I could do more."

Jane lifted her head and pulled back. "You did more than any of us could. For years I've held on to my anger toward you. I told myself that if I ever met you, I would make you wish you'd never been born. But when Jake told us what you did, all that built-up anger dissipated. You've given my daughter a fighting chance again. Something I couldn't do." Jane cried as she crouched in front of Mara.

Mara reached out and rubbed her shoulder.

"I need to ask something really huge of you, and I will understand if you don't have it in you, or are not ready," Mara said softly.

Jane looked up at her.

"Please, is there any way you can find it in your heart to forgive me for what I put your daughter through six years ago?"

Jane opened her mouth to speak, but then closed it. She cleared her throat and tried again. "It's almost seven, and it's already done. Your organs are the biggest gift there is. Holly was never one for promises, as I made and broke them so many times, but she was someone who looked at actions. Actions speak louder than words."

Mara started sobbing. "And here I was thinking I would get another scolding. I'm so sorry."

"Stop saying you're sorry. Help us to get her to fight."

Mara nodded, and the two woman hugged each other.

Jake was astonished. But by his father's expression, Gus was, too. He'd really thought that Jane was going to yell, as he had. But she didn't. Instead, she'd thanked his mother.

His mother touched his arm as Gus pushed the chair past him and into Holly's room.

Jane followed, and so did Jake. He gave Jane a sideways hug.

Gus pushed Mara's chair right up next to Holly's bed and stood behind his wife, hands to handlebars. Jake and Jane both took the chairs on the other side of the bed.

His mother stared at Holly. There was no hatred in her eyes, only regret. She touched her face gently.

"I don't know what to say to you. I've brought you so much pain. That day, I wasn't myself. I mean, I couldn't have been to tell you right to your face that Jake didn't want the baby. A part of me panicked, scared you would hear right through the recording, but I told you to phone him, anyway." Mara sniffed, wiping away the tears.

Holly had told him that she hadn't believed Mara when she'd told her that he didn't want the baby anymore. That a part of her had known he'd never have abandoned them.

"And a part of me bargained on you believing that phone call. You see, I know my son, so I knew he'd never have said those things to you." She shook her head. "He showed you in so many ways that he loved you. Ways that I was too blind to see. I'm so sorry that my lies caused you to say goodbye to one of your babies. I can only imagine the pain that must have caused. I will never be able to make that up to you, and I understand if you never want me near your children. But I need you to accept my organs, Holly. Not because it's from me, but for Jake and the children. Please." She paused to wipe her nose. "He is a mess without you, and I don't want him to turn into a stranger again."

Gus handed her a bunch of tissues, which she was thankful for and used to wipe her face. "And one day, I hope you can find it in your heart to forgive me for all I ever did to you." She grabbed Holly's hand and kissed it as she continued to cry.

His mother wasn't a crier. He'd always thought that she was so strong, and had often wondered if she was even capable of crying. He now had his answer.

She smiled at Jake, and then gripped Gus' hand that was on her shoulder.

"Your sister?" She was talking about Amelia.

"She's not ready."

She nodded. "I've hurt her so much."

"Mom." Jake sighed.

"No, a mother should never hurt her children as I have, Jake."

"And a mother should never leave her child while trying to

mourn the one she just lost. We all make mistakes, Mara," said Jane. "I know you think that I lost so much more than you did, but I could've done things differently. I chose the easy way out, and only taught her what she shouldn't do when things got tough. Everyone makes mistakes, some bigger than others. Holly taught me that, that we are all human. She gave me another chance, even though I messed up the other million. Your organs are something that she will treasure until the day she dies, which isn't going to be today, or tomorrow, or the next. I've spoken to Him, and He knows where I stand." She chuckled at herself, but the others chuckled, too.

Jane swallowed past the lump in her throat before continuing. "The hard part isn't asking them to forgive us, it's forgiving ourselves. And you should, too. One day, not now."

Mara smiled. "I'll try my best on that one day." She touched Holly's face again. "You can take me back now, Gus."

"See you later, Mom."

"Phone me, please?" she whispered to Jake, and he nodded. "See you soon, Holly."

ALMOST THREE MONTHS HAD PASSED SINCE THE transplant. His mother was back on her feet, and she was even drinking healthy green smoothies now. Said that a new lifestyle and diet was in order.

She was a constantly at Holly's side. She made sure Jake ate, went home to shower, all the little things mothers worried about. She was back to being the mother he'd always known. And every day, she sat and spoke to Holly. Sometimes even read to her.

Holly's condition remained the same, and even though her heart was still beating, she was not breathing on her own.

Her brain remained active, which had Jake wondering where she was, what she was seeing, what she was doing. Was his mother right? Could she hear them? He had to believe it.

A knock sounded on the door and Mara looked up, and so did he.

Amelia's head popped around the door, and then she entered. She stared at her mother. "I don't think it's a great idea, Jake." Amelia sighed.

"Amelia, they are—"

She held up her hand. "I know. But it's just my opinion. I can't be here, I'm sorry."

"I'll leave."

"No, Mom. Stay," Jake said.

When Mara looked at Amelia, she saw her wipe a tear away just before she walked out.

Leo and Armand walked in with two carriers, followed by Jane.

Mara's hands flew to her face, mouth hanging open. She looked at Jake.

"Make sure she's okay," he said to Armand.

He'd told Jamie that Mara had finally gained her memory back and she wanted to meet her granddaughter.

"They are so gorgeous. May I?" Mara asked, as Jane took Cooper out of his chair.

"Yeah, go ahead, Grandma."

She took Bradley out and kissed him all over his little face.

"Hello, baby! You are so beautiful. Just look at you. He is so beautiful, sweetheart."

"What can I say? I make beautiful babies."

His mother laughed. "Definitely a Peters," she said as she bounced with Bradley, smiling and cooing.

"And this is Cooper," Jane said.

Mara bent over and gave Cooper three quick kisses. "You

are going to be a handful, aren't you? Yes, you are." She had a huge smile on her face.

The door opened and Gus walked in. Jamie was clutching his hand.

His mother started to cry, and Jake took Bradley from her so she could focus on Jamie.

"Come here, buster," Jake held him in the air and Bradley gave a belly laugh. Cooper followed suit, which had everyone laughing at the twins, but Mara's eyes had not left Jamie.

Hesitantly, Mara walked over to her and crouched down in front of Jamie. She touched her shirt, and then ran her hand down her arm. "Hey, sweetheart."

Jamie smiled shyly.

"I'm so sorry, baby."

"It's not your fault, Nanna," Jamie said. "The red color was mean."

Mara frowned, but Gus mouthed that he'd fill her in on it later. "Very mean," she agreed, scrunching her eyebrows.

Jamie threw her arms around Mara's neck, and Mara melted like they all had when they first saw her. She hugged Jamie to her like there was no tomorrow.

"Grandpa was right. Your hugs are the best."

Jake smiled. He was happy that his daughter was finally meeting her other grandmother, the one who had been lost to her all this time. They started talking about everything under the sun, and when Mara got up to take a seat, Jamie clambered onto her lap, at ease with the new person in her family.

Despite the abundant happiness, Jake was still able to see the guilt and pain reflecting in his mother's eyes. She knew there should be another granddaughter. The pain of that loss was evident on her face. She was hurting.

He knew she wouldn't forgive herself for that for a very long time.

TWENTY-TWO

HOLLY

She found herself at the hospital again.

There was no one around her, but the weird part was that she kept hearing the buzzing noises of people working and talking to each other, like in a real hospital.

What was going on?

"And I'm telling you, that is what he said," a woman's voice close to her said. She looked around, but didn't see the woman, or anyone else, as the voice died out and faded into the distance.

"Just get me the damn results back!" A male voice said, this time right up close to her, but she still saw nothing.

Suddenly, a current ran through her body. She took a deep breath as she felt faintly out of place, but soon gained her normality back.

The deserted hospital and the voices weren't making any sense, but she did know which hospital she was at.

It was Downsend.

Curiosity got the better of her and she started wandering

around, passing by more 'people' talking, all the while experiencing those odd currents flowing through her body.

When she reached the elevator, she got in and rode it up to the sixth floor to where her room was.

The voices and currents continued, and now laughter was added to the mix.

But again, the place was completely deserted.

A shiver ran down her spine. She didn't like it, not one little bit. She was on the verge of freaking out.

"Maybe I should give them the letters." A familiar voice reached her ears. Aggie's voice, coming from behind the desk, but there was nobody standing there.

She closed her eyes. *No, Aggie, you promised!*

But of course, Aggie couldn't hear her. No one could.

"She is not dead yet," Sue pointed out. "She could still wake up."

"Could? It's been almost three months, Sue."

Three months? She felt a pressure on her chest and there, just up ahead, she saw her room. She ran toward it, but couldn't open the door. Her hand repeatedly penetrated through the handle.

Panic set in and she closed her eyes—she wasn't a solid entity. Was she even alive?

With nothing to lose, she walked forward.

Another current rushed through her body and it took a few seconds to dissipate.

Then she opened her eyes.

And gasped. She was looking at her body hooked up to a ventilator...she wasn't breathing on her own. Her heartbeat was being registered on an EKG.

No one was around. It was dead quiet.

On closer inspection, she noticed that she wasn't yellow anymore, and her hair was growing back.

A feeling of dread churned in her stomach, and it wasn't a good feeling. Where were her family? Where was Jake? They wouldn't just leave her here, all alone.

"Wouldn't it be great," Rod's voice filled the room, and the feeling went away, "if she woke up now and said *What's Up, Bitches?*"

Laughter surrounded her, tired laughter. She heard her mother and Leo laughing. Gus, too, and someone else she didn't recognize, but no Jake.

He was probably in a consultation, or in OR. Life did go on.

Three months. She'd been in this state for three months. No wonder the last time she saw Romalia, her daughter had been adamant she return.

How long had she been in that place? She couldn't remember if Romalia had told her.

Something touched her hand. It felt nice.

"Holly," Jake said, and she smiled.

He was here.

"You need to wake up, baby. You are scaring the crap out of me."

I'm sorry. I would wake up if I knew how. She was speaking to herself, because he couldn't hear her, just as she couldn't see him. She could only feel his presence.

"I can't do this without you, please," he pleaded with her.

A knock rapped on a door, and she whipped her head in the direction of the sound. She heard a door open, but the one in her room remained closed.

This was so weird.

"Amelia."

Now that was a voice she'd thought she'd never hear again. Mara?

Someone sniffed. "I need to speak to you," Amelia said, and the sound of a chair screeching against the floor filled the room.

What was Mara doing here?

She decided to follow the sound of Amelia's and Mara's voices.

She could still feel Jake touching her hand, but she walked through the door again, anyway.

Still, she saw no one. The emptiness made her feel so alone.

"Amelia," Mara said softly to her right, and Holly went that way.

"I don't know how to do this," Amelia cried.

"You don't have to do anything, sweetheart. I know I betrayed you," Mara replied.

She was standing next to them. Why couldn't she see them?

"This was my mistake, and you can be as angry with me for as long as you want to be. I never thought anyone would die, let alone a baby. I'm so sorry," Mara cried.

She heard Amelia sobbing.

"Why isn't she waking up?" Amelia asked.

"I don't know."

"She received your organs, Mom. She should wake up."

"I know, sweetie," Mara said.

She just froze. Was she a ghost? She had to be. Why else could she hear them, but not see them?

And then the significance of what Amelia had just said to her mother hit home. Mara had given her what she needed? Mara? Her organs? Was she hearing correctly? Could it be? She couldn't see Mara, but she started walking slowly, one foot in front of the other, until she felt a current. At that connection, a soft gasp escaped Mara.

"Mom, what is it?"

"I don't know," Mara whispered. "I just feel...I don't know." The tone of her voice depicted a calmness and perhaps also, contentment.

Thank you, she whispered, even though Mara could not hear her.

Just then, she felt something heavy in her chest, and a horrible beeping sound came from inside her room.

Both Mara and Amelia gasped.

The current dissolved as a long beep resonated from the room. Cries came from inside, mixed with panic and sobbing.

Jake was screaming. "No, no, no!" he bellowed over and over again. "You are not fucking leaving me, Holly! Do you hear me? I won't let you!"

He didn't sound like himself.

She felt a hard pounding on her chest. It was delivered with force, and it hurt.

"Please, God, please," Amelia screamed. She was hysterical.

It was at that moment that reality sunk in. She knew she had to fight. This wasn't over yet.

She ran to her room, right through the wall again, and saw her body lying motionless on the bed.

Fight! She was screaming at herself. *Just fight.*

But nothing happened. More stabbing pains pounded on her chest, but the beeping didn't recede.

"C'mon baby. Those new organs are healthy, use them, make them work for you. Just breathe," Mara begged. She was trying to save her life.

Please, God, please! Holly was down to begging as Jake's hysterical cries filled the room.

She hated that he was in pain.

Fight, fight, damn it! I don't know what to do!

She felt another stab in her chest, which was followed by more pain and agony all over her body.

Something wasn't right.

Fight! The more she yelled, the more pain she felt. She was going to lose everything if she didn't fight.

JAKE

He felt as if he was losing his mind.

Sounds came out of him that he never thought he could make. His father clutched him as he broke down and slid to the floor.

He couldn't even speak.

Fight baby, please. Don't leave me, he yelled in his head. *God, please,* he yelled some more.

Why wasn't He listening.

"C'mon baby. Those new organs are healthy, use them, make them work for you. Just breathe," his mother shouted as she tried to get Holly's heart to beat again.

He couldn't look. The beeping sound was still one flat tone.

Please, he begged tiredly. *I can't do this without you.*

Suddenly, the tone of the beeping changed; her heart started beating again.

Everyone's relief was so palpable, his included, he felt it in his bones. He glanced at his mother. She looked exhausted, her face wet with tears.

For how much longer was Holly going to scare him like this? She needed to wake the fuck up.

"It's okay, Jake. Jake, her heart is beating, it's okay." His dad mumbled the words over and over, not just to reassure Jake, but himself, too.

He heard a gurgling sound.

"She's waking up!" Mara gasped, her voice catching.

Jake pushed his father away and got up. He watched as his mother slowly began removing the breathing tube.

"I got it," Gus assured her. "Go for now, darling," he said, giving his wife a smile, and Mara hurried out of the room.

Holly coughed and gasped for air.

Jake rushed over to the bed and bent over her. Tears rolled down his face as he took her hand in his. Her mother was mumbling her thanks to God, and Amelia was sobbing in the corner.

Holly's hand tightened in Jake's, and relief coursed through him.

She took deep, raspy breaths.

"Don't ever scare me like that again." He smoothed her hair back from her forehead, repeating the motion over and over again.

She was awake. She was alive.

And she wasn't going to leave him. Not this time. Not for a long time.

EVERYONE WAS HAPPY TO SEE HER. JAMIE AND JAKE the most.

She didn't look as tired anymore, the yellow tinge in her skin was gone. She looked healthy.

Jamie climbed onto the bed and lay in Holly's arms.

"Hey, peanut." Holly sighed and kissed Jamie's temple.

"How is Romy, Mommy?"

Holly shifted Jamie in her arms and looked down at her.

"You went to visit her, didn't you?"

"Yes, I did, and she gave me something to give you." She smiled.

"She did?" Jamie asked, and Holly nodded as tears filled in her eyes.

Closing her eyes, she gave Jamie the longest kiss on her cheek.

"A kiss?" Jamie frowned in disappointment. "I bought a bear."

"Oh, baby, the bears in heaven can talk, so she wasn't allowed to give you one. She wanted to, she had so many, but they were very heavy and because they talk, Mommy couldn't bring them. Sorry, sweetheart. Just remember that she loves you so much."

"I love her, too."

"Of course you do and one day, far, far from now, we will see her again."

"Okay." Jamie was sulking, so Holly grabbed her again.

"I love you, baby girl, so much. Daddy needs to buy a big gun."

Everyone laughed including Jake.

"A gun, what for?" Jamie looked at her mother.

"'Cause you are going to be one hell of a hottie one day."

"I'm not." Jamie giggled.

Of course she would be a hottie, but from the way Holly was staring at Jamie, it seemed as if she knew exactly what she was going to look like when she grew up.

Jake wondered what she'd experienced while she'd been in the coma. Was there some truth to the lie he'd told Jamie to put her heart at ease whenever she came to visit Holly?

Jake caught Holly staring at him.

"What?"

"Thank you."

"For what?"

"For your kindness." She smiled. "And for your strength."

"I don't know so much about that one," he whispered to her when he leaned over to kiss her forehead.

He wished he could tell her what his mother had done for

her, but he was afraid that she would not accept any of it and her body would reject the organs.

But one day she would know.

HER STAY IN HOSPITAL LASTED FOR ANOTHER FEW WEEKS, and then she was released.

Jake was going to take her home, and he couldn't believe how lucky he was. It had been so close.

Often, he found himself wondering about a few things. Holly had changed since she'd come out of the coma, seeming more at peace with everything.

She'd never asked about or who the donor was, which was weird. Usually, patients were always curious about their donors. Then again, she hadn't asked him about his mother, either.

She was just a walking mystery, as if she hadn't been enough of a mystery before.

He pulled up to the house and parked the car, then rushed around to Holly's side and helped her get out.

Everyone was already inside the house. Including his mother.

"Holly," Jake said. She smiled at him. "There is something I need to tell you." He stopped at the front door.

"Go for it."

"I forgave my mother, but before—"

"Finally," she said with a grin.

He frowned. "That's all you're going to say?"

"Yeah. I asked you many times to think about it. I couldn't be more pleased you've finally forgiven her."

He nodded. But he wasn't done. He needed to tell her the that his mother was actually here.

"Sweetheart," he said as she was about to open the door. "She's inside. If you want—"

Holly didn't let him finish, merely straightened her shoulders and walked right on in.

He took a deep breath, resigning himself to the fact that she needed to get whatever she was going to say off her chest. His mother had told him that whatever she needed to do to get rid of her anger and her resentment, he should let her.

Composing himself, he followed her in and found her staring at his mother, who was sitting next to Jamie, reading her a story.

Mara looked up at Holly.

An awkward silence filled the room. Jamie continued to page through the book, oblivious to the tension.

"Please, say something," Mara beseeched.

"Come, Jamie," Amelia called, and when Jamie looked up, she saw her mother.

"Mommy!"

She smiled at Jamie, went down on her haunches and opened her arms. Jamie ran into them full on.

"You're back!" she said with glee.

"Forever and ever." She laid it on thick. Jake loved every word.

"Can we have Chinese tonight?"

Holly laughed. "We'll see, go with Auntie Amelia for a little bit, okay?"

Nodding, Jamie ran up the stairs behind her aunt.

Mara hesitantly got up from the couch at the same time Holly stood up straight.

Mara already had her handbag around her shoulder. "Look, I know what you said that time..."

She moved, taking the few steps needed so she could throw her arms around Mara's neck.

The silence was such, one could have heard a pin drop, and that was because no one had expected to see what they were witnessing. Not even Mara.

His mother looked at him, confusion playing across her face.

"Thank you," Holly said.

"For what?" Mara asked.

Holly pushed her away and chuckled. "Your kidney and liver, of course."

As one, everyone gasped.

"Jake," Mara scolded.

"Mom, I swear I didn't tell her."

She looked at Holly. "Then how do you know?"

"I know more than you guys think I do. And thank you for not giving up. I now know who to rely on if my heart acts up again."

"You what?"

She laughed. "It was a real journey. For a moment, I didn't want to leave. But then I saw her. And I don't know why I still remember it, it was so weird."

"Saw who, sweetheart?" Jake asked.

She turned around to face him. "I wasn't lying when I gave that kiss to Jamie and said it was from her sister. It was real, Jake. And you really do need to get a gun, because our daughter is going to grow up to be one stunning woman."

Everyone laughed, except Jake.

"You really saw her?"

"Yeah, and she wasn't a child anymore. It was so weird." She sat down and started telling them the story of how she found herself in a hospital after she must have slipped into a coma.

"I should've known that something was not right. The hospital was so beautiful."

They all listened attentively as she described the hospital. It sounded like heaven.

"But to me, it felt like something was horribly wrong. It didn't matter if I saved a life or lost it—the loved ones were always happy. I couldn't wrap my head around it. It frustrated me so much, because how on earth could anyone could be so happy for a loved one to pass on? I did not understand it. I lost more and more patients every day, until one day I just couldn't handle it anymore."

She relayed everything about her experience there, and specifically about the one doctor who helped her get back.

|She looked at them with shining eyes. "When she touched me, I remembered things...it all just came back to me, and during this 'awakening'"—she used her hands and did air quotes—"the doctor's name tag changed from Missy, which is what I knew her by, to Romalia. I was shocked. Romalia told me that I had to come back. She said that you wouldn't understand Jamie." She looked at Jake. "She said that Jamie was so much like me, and that she was just like you." She started crying.

Jake felt the sting of tears in his eyes.

"And she is, she's just like you. Adamant when she needs to be, and gentle when it's called for. She's set in her ways, and she knows everything. I was with the daughter I lost, at long last, and I didn't want to come back," she admitted.

Jake went over to her and wrapped her in his arms.

"It's okay."

"No, it's not, because I had so much to live for and she made me see it." She sniffed and pulled out of his arms.

"I asked her where my sister was, and she told me that she couldn't be there because she'd already helped me to fight back when the girls were born. I can't remember that, but something tells me that it wasn't the first time I needed a push. I just wish I could remember."

"I'm sorry that you had to let her go again."

She shook her head. "Romy was right, though. She didn't

need me, she was happy, so I had to let her go, hard as it was. When the hospital vanished, I found myself at Downsend, but it was deserted. Still, I could hear all the activity...I just couldn't see it. I didn't know what was calling to me, but I went up to my room. It was a really scary place. That's when I heard Aggie speaking to Sue, but I couldn't see them. I went to my room, right through the wall. All I saw was me lying there. All was silent. It was awful, because I really thought that you'd all abandoned me, but then Rodney"—she looked at him and smiled —"spoke. He said, 'Wouldn't it be nice if she could wake up now and say *What's up, bitches.*'"

Jake smiled.

"I wanted to, so badly. Then you spoke, Jake, and begged me to wake up. But I didn't know how. Amelia came and I only realized then that Mara was there when Amelia spoke to her." She touched Mara's leg. His mother smiled at her.

"When I heard their voices move away, I followed them. I wanted to know what she was doing there. And that was when I heard Amelia say that she'd given me the organs I needed. I didn't know what happened then, whether it was reality dawning on me in why I let go, but right then, my heart stopped." She closed her eyes. "Don't ever freak out like that again, please." She looked pointedly at Jake.

"I'm sorry."

"I felt this heaviness in my chest, and an agonizing ache everywhere else. I thought I was losing it, but it turned out that I was fighting harder and harder for my life. The rest, you all know."

Everyone sat in silence, staring at her.

"I know it's very far-fetched and something doctors never believe in, but there is something amazing out there."

"You didn't by any chance hug me when you discovered the truth?" Mara asked.

Holly laughed. "I couldn't see you, but I wanted to hug you. There was this current whenever I walked through things, things I couldn't see. So, I moved in the direction of where I heard your voice and thanked you. Not that you heard me, but I guess you must have felt it."

Mara shuddered, but then smiled.

"What is it, Mom?"

"I can't explain it. It was the most peaceful feeling I ever felt. Afterward, I thought it was the calm before the storm, a sixth sense, a higher power that was warning me about what was to come, but I know now that it wasn't that at all."

Holly hugged her. "Thank you for giving me your most precious kidney, and a part of your liver."

"It's the least I could've done. I'm so sorry. I will never be able to tell you that enough."

Holly pulled away and looked Mara in the eye. "Well, whenever you feel the urge to say it, just remember you're missing a kidney and part of your liver."

Laughter rippled throughout the room.

Jake was beyond happy. She was alive, more than just alive. She was perfect. The woman he'd always known her to be was now even better, and right at that moment, he knew he wanted to spend the rest of his life with her.

TWENTY-THREE

HOLLY

Jamie was talking about some sort of dance thing that she was participating in, and that it was going to be so much fun as Holly tucked her into bed one night.

"Am I going to see this?" she asked.

"Yep, just ask Daddy."

"Okay," she laughed, and kissed her on the nose. She hadn't been able to tuck Jamie in for such a long time.

Jake was adamant that he wanted to tuck her in, but this time she'd refused.

"Love you, baby girl."

"Love you too, Mommy," she said and they kissed each other goodnight.

She turned out the light and went to her room.

Jake was busy on his laptop, so she went into the bathroom.

Three months had passed since she woke up from her coma.

Shuddering, she looked at her hair. She missed her long hair, but Amelia had told her that she had a surprise for her tomorrow, and that she was going to need her for the entire day.

Robin and Mara had become her heroes.

She'd never thought that she and Mara would become friends the way they had.

Mara was really doing more than she should. She only had one kidney now and was supposed to take it easy.

Doctor's, and friend's, orders.

Squeezing some liquid soap onto her hands, she washed them, then cleansed her face, and followed that with her night cream.

She then left the bathroom and walked out into the bedroom, turning off the lights on the way. Lifting the covers, she climbed into bed.

"What is this dance Jamie is talking about?"

Jake stopped typing and stared at the screen. He smiled as he looked down at Holly.

"It's her recital."

"At school?"

"Yes, I can't believe she told you. It was supposed to be a surprise. Guess she can't keep secrets that well." He put the laptop down and grabbed Holly.

She laughed. "Stop that, Jamie's not asleep yet."

"Then maybe it's a good idea to practice to be really quiet."

"No. She could walk in here any minute, and I'm not going to explain *that* to her. Finish your work, we can play later." She kissed him softly on the lips.

"Fine, party pooper." He sulked and picked up his laptop again as she turned around and closed her eyes.

The mind was a powerful thing, and it truly never shut down. Like now, her thoughts went to all sorts of things. She didn't feel as beautiful as she used to; she was still struggling to pick up weight—she felt like a skeleton.

Surprisingly, though, Jake still looked at her as if she were the most beautiful thing in the world.

She still wondered what she'd ever done to deserve him. And on this thought, she fell asleep and woke up the next morning when Jamie rushed into the room.

Jake was still asleep.

"Shhh, let Daddy sleep."

"No, I'm up. I'm up," he mumbled, stretching.

"Go back to sleep, I've got this."

"No, go take a shower, Amelia is going to be here soon."

"Don't remind me."

"C'mon, it can't be that bad. I thought women liked shopping."

"Not this one. My finances are really bad."

"Then it's on me. I'll give you my credit card." Before she could object, he kissed her fast on the lips as he picked up Jamie and threw her over his shoulder, tickling her.

Jamie's laughter was like balm to the soul, because every time she laughed, it sounded like angels singing in Holly's ears.

The twins had spent the night with Mara and Gus. But Jamie had wanted to stay with her parents, and when Holly saw the disappointment on Jake's face, she couldn't help the grin that spread across hers. She'd slapped him, though.

He wasn't impressed. *My balls are turning blue,* he mouthed, and she blushed.

They hadn't had sex in ages, and it would happen soon, she just didn't want to feel like a skeleton when it did.

Amelia told her she was overreacting, that yes, she was skinny, but not skeletal.

Today's outing had something to do with making her feel like a thousand bucks again, or in Amelia's case, closer to a million.

She hoped that one of those stops would be to a magical place where she could walk in the front door, and by the time she walked out the back door, she'd have some meat on her bones.

Soon, she promised herself. She'd get there soon.

The diet she was on wasn't helping. It was all about the healthy meals—she needed to take care of her kidney. Doctor Jake's orders, and there was no way around that one as he watched her like a hawk.

When Amelia arrived, she quickly dressed in a pair of shorts and a yellow top, that used to fit her like a glove but now hung on her like a sack, and slipped her feet into a pretty pair of sandals. She combed her short hair with her fingers and went downstairs.

"You ready?" Amelia asked.

"Yep," she replied.

"Here," Jake said, holding out his credit card to her.

"I'm not taking it." She walked past him.

"Then I will." Amelia grabbed it. "We are going to need loads more money for this than what I have in my account."

"Thank you," Jake said, a broad smile splayed across his face.

The drive to the first stop was a quiet one as it was only ten to seven.

"Where are you taking me?"

"You'll see." Amelia smiled, and Holly rolled her eyes.

Amelia's phone rang, and as it was connected to the car's Bluetooth, she simply pressed a button on the steering to answer it.

"Hey, baby. Have you picked up Holly yet?" Mara asked.

"Yes, Mom, she's with me. You're on the car's speakerphone."

"Morning, Holly."

"Good morning," Holly sang, then smiled when Amelia just shook her head.

"The twins just had breakfast and we are going to take them to the park soon."

"You don't have to tell me everything you do with them."

"Just letting you know where they are."

"Jeez, Mom, you never did that with us when we were little," Amelia moaned.

"It was different back then."

"Okay, bye." Amelia laughed.

"Enjoy your day."

"Bye," Holly said before the call cut out.

They pulled up to huge gates.

"What's this?"

"It's a spa," Amelia said with humorous flourish.

Holly burst out laughing at how Amelia's face pulled when she did a little surprise reveal with her arms.

"Fine, spa it is."

"So, you and my brother done it yet?"

"Amelia!"

"Holly, he is a guy and a gorgeous one at that."

"He's your brother."

"Just saying. His balls are going to turn blue."

"Then he can help himself out. Not only does he have two perfectly functional hands, but I also happen to know that he is really good at satisfying his own needs."

"Eww...okay, *that* I didn't want to know," she said, driving through the gates as they opened.

Holly giggled.

"Still have something to do with the way you feel?"

"I don't feel pretty."

"And that is one of the reasons why we are here." She smiled.

"Did Jake put you up to this?"

"No, it's all me because of our last convo. You are beautiful even though you don't see it. I just want you to feel it again."

"Okay, fine. It's a spa," she mimicked Amelia.

"Yay," Amelia jiggled in her seat. Finding a space, she parked the car.

It wasn't just a spa day.

She even got hair. She was given curly, strawberry blond extensions, which not only looked but felt natural, and hung in waves down her back. The boys were going to love it, she just knew it.

They even did her makeup and nails while the stylist saw to her hair.

Amelia did the same with hers.

She laughed so much during their conversations, and when she was done, she hardly recognized herself.

"Yes?" Amelia asked.

"Yes. Thank you." She hugged Amelia.

Everyone applauded. "Our job here is done. You look like a princess," Neil, the stylist said. "And you tell that hunkalicious man of yours that he needs to come for a haircut. He looks like a baboon."

"A very sexy baboon, I might add," she joked.

"My bad." Neil rolled his eyes and gave Holly two kisses on each cheek. "Make sure she looks after that hair, Melia."

"You have my word, Neil."

"My stomach is growling."

"Have an oats bar. We'll grab something more substantial at lunch." She handed her a homemade oats bar, which Holly devoured.

"I need junk food."

"No, that's the last thing you need."

"I want to live, Melia. One burger isn't going to kill me. Even Robin understands that. And she's supposed to be the sucky one."

"Fine, you can have your stupid burger," Amelia teased.

"Yay!" She jumped up and down like a little kid.

The next stop was the mall, where Amelia went slightly nuts, grabbing clothes off of hangers.

She had never been able to fit into a size four before, but she did now. Every item of clothing Amelia handed her to try looked stunning and gorgeous.

"What am I going to do with all these clothes if I pick up the weight again?"

"Donate it. Who gives a shit?"

She rolled her eyes. "This is such a waste of money."

"Whatever, it's Jake's money."

"I'm never going to be able to pay him back."

"Then do what I do sweetheart, pay it off with your body."

"Ha-ha, great idea."

Amelia laughed.

"My stomach is grumbling."

"Okay, fine. I made reservation at the park."

She loved the park. It wasn't just a park, it was a gorgeous park filled with the most beautiful trees, a few select shops and restaurants, and tarred pathways that wound all around it. Picnics were held there more often than not, like for Mother's Day and movie nights.

She remembered the first time Jake took her there and read to her under the cover of one of the trees.

The drive was filled with music blaring and the two of them singing. Holly did funny little dance moves and Amelia copied her.

She missed days like these where it was just them, enjoying a Saturday without the kids.

The place was packed, and she quickly changed her yellow top for one of the new ones. It felt good to have clothes that fit her again.

"See? Gorgeous," Amelia said, walking ahead of Holly.

The place was buzzing with people, but they were helped immediately. A young girl led them to a table outside which was situated in front of wide steps that led down to one of the stone paths. From where they were sitting, they had a view that looked out over the entire park.

She ordered a milkshake, purposefully not looking at Amelia for disapproval.

"You know what, I'm looking the other way," Amelia said, smiling, and ordered herself a lime and soda.

"Are you on a diet?"

"Yes, because I'm really getting fat."

"Amelia, you are perfect."

"Whatever."

"Thank you for today."

"It's my pleasure." She smiled and they fell into easy conversation.

She barely got the chance to speak as Amelia babbled on, and when their drinks arrived, Amelia was still chattering.

And then, out of the blue, the sounds of an EKG heartbeat played over the speakers, and it was loud. They both looked around.

"What the hell?" Amelia snapped.

It was followed by the sound of a long flatline beep.

She hated that sound and the memories it brought with it.

Just as suddenly, Kelly Clarkson's song *Heartbeat* started to play.

Some of the waiters from the inside rushed outside and started dancing at and round all the tables.

"What is going on?" she asked.

Amelia started to laugh. "I don't know." She looked around and looked back at Holly again. "I think it's one of those flash mob things."

"Can we just go, please?" She hid her head.

"No, I want to watch." Amelia grinned and continued to look around. Holly eventually did the same.

A girl at one of the tables blushed, she was embarrassed. She shook her head, and Holly felt bad for her as a waiter took her hand.

But then, she must have thrown caution to the wind, because she eventually got up started to dance with him. This gave some other customers courage and they followed her lead, getting up to dance with all the waiters and waitresses.

What the hell? Holly couldn't stop staring.

Everyone continued to dance around them. She started chuckling.

"Please can we go?"

"No, c'mon...where is your spark of adventure, Holly?"

"Not for something like this."

One of the dancers came over to their table.

"Please, just go," she begged him, and Amelia laughed out loud.

The waiter was dumbstruck.

"We're not part of this...whatever this is."

Amelia got up. "Says who?" she yelled, going crazy with her own dance moves as the chorus played.

Holly gaped at her, but couldn't stop herself from laughing.

"Amelia, sit down!"

She was so wacky; she didn't even know the moves.

Holly looked back at the waiter again, who was still begging for her hand. "We are really not part of this."

"You sure? She seems to know the moves."

She looked at Amelia, and lo and behold, everyone had started dancing like her. "What the actual fuck?" *Oh, please. Don't let me be the idiot. I will kill her.*

When the chorus finished, the verse started again.

Her eyes caught yet more people coming their way, and shocked, she sat there with her mouth open.

Her mom had one of the boys in a baby carrier at her front, with Bernie and a group of others, and on the opposite side Mara had the other twin in the exact same baby carrier, with Robin holding Jamie's hand, leading another group of people.

"Mom?" She yelled and closed her eyes.

Amelia laughed.

"What's going on, Melia? No." She shook her head as her mother and Mara started dancing in front of her table. Bernie, Robin, and even Jamie knew the moves.

Shaking her head, she just started to laugh. "You are dead," she told them all.

A hand, asking for hers, popped between their bodies, and she caught sight of Rodney wearing a baseball cap.

"You know I hate this."

"Just go with it, baby," he said, wiggling his eyebrows.

With nothing left to do, she took his hand, only to be twirled into him so he could pick her up in his arms. And carefully, he walked down the steps with her.

She grunted playfully in his arms. "You are all fucking dead," she yelled as Rodney put her down and twirled her out as Kelly sang her heart out.

Next, she ended up in Armand's arms and he led the dance further.

She was probably red in her face.

"Just go with it, Holly," he said, and it was then that she realized this had nothing to do with Amelia.

"Jake is behind this, isn't he?"

Armand laughed, and Gus took over from him. She giggled as she danced with Gus. He sang along with the song, and frankly, she wanted to cover her ears. He was that bad.

When he twirled her out, she found herself in Leo's arms.

"I'm gonna go to jail for mass murder," she said.

"Nah, you love us," he teased.

He led her in a dance all the way to one of the big trees.

She just wanted to vanish into thin air. Without warning, the song ended and again, it started up with the sound of heartbeats, beating faster and faster, like hers.

Everyone applauded as she stood under the tree Leo had led her to.

"Okay, where the hell is he?"

"I'm right here, Bee Puke." His voice came from behind her, and she turned around.

She slapped him playfully. "Why would you do this? So embarrassing!" She failed to notice the headpiece he was wearing, microphone right at his mouth.

"You love me, I know you do," his voice boomed over the speakers.

"What the hell are you doing?" She covered her face, wishing the ground could open up and swallow her whole.

When she removed her hands, Jake was on one knee, holding up a box with a stunning diamond ring nestled within its satin folds.

She blinked. Blinked again. The air in her lungs whooshed out of her.

"Holly, my baby, my sweetheart, my life," he said into the mike. "My Bee Puke," he added in a whisper, although by the chuckles and giggles from the crowd, a lot of good that did.

"No one will ever love you more than this idiot, well except my mom—she gave you her organs."

The crowd behind her cumulatively murmured an *awww*, stretching the sound out for effect.

"Would you please do me the honor of becoming mine, forever and ever?"

Tears filled her eyes. "You're asking me to marry you?"

"Well, it seems that way, doesn't it?"

She just stood there motionless. Not for long. "Holy fuck, yes!" she screamed and threw herself at him, forcing them both to fall to the ground. Their lips met and she kissed him as she always did, vigorously and passionately.

Applause broke out, along with lots of whistling. Eventually, they separated.

Tears rolled down her cheeks. "I thought you'd never ask."

"You thought wrong. I guess you didn't see the pathetic attempt at the hospital. My mother stopped me. She said it wasn't appropriate, that you needed to be awake."

"I like her more and more," she said softly, and kissed him again.

She broke the kiss with a laugh, then stared at Jake with narrowed eyes.

"What?"

"This was what Jamie was talking about, wasn't it?"

"Yes, the little shit. I thought she almost gave it away."

Laughing, they kissed each other one more time.

HOLLY

THEY ALL HAD LUNCH IN THE PARK AT A BIGGER AND MORE private section.

She couldn't stop admiring her ring as she sat next to Jake.

This wasn't how she'd envisioned or dreamed he'd ask her to marry him, but he'd made it even more special by involving everyone she loved.

She had a burger and a salad while they talked about the flash mob.

"Mom's moves were the best. Why didn't I get to dance with you?" She looked at Frank, who was sitting next to her mother.

"Because Uncle Frank is one of the worst dancers there is," Jake teased.

"Two left feet, sweetheart."

"So when is the big date?" Amelia asked.

"Jeez woman, he just asked me."

"Soon," Jake answered, and Holly raised an eyebrow at him.

"Really, just like that?"

"I wanted to elope," he said in all seriousness. "But your mother threatened to perform my vasectomy with a butter knife if we did, so big wedding it is."

She giggled. It felt good to laugh.

The lunch continued on until two in the afternoon, and then everyone met up at Mara's and Gus' house. They swam the rest of the day and the kids had a ball.

Even the twins and Bernie's baby.

Jake and Armand took them in until it started to get too rough between Jake and Armand, so the two aunts took the boys and left the men to wrestle each other in the pool. Leo jumped in between them and joined the melee.

Jamie swam with Jane, who was teaching her how to paddle. Holly looked on from the sidelines.

Mara came to sit next to her and handed her an iced tea.

"Thank you. Exactly what we both need," she said and took a sip. She wasn't alone in this, and being around Mara, she would never forget about it.

"The ring is so beautiful," Mara said.

"Thank you. He really has great taste."

"Oh, that he has. He is marrying the bravest woman I've ever met, even if it took me a long time to see it. Thank you, Holly, for coming back."

"Thank you for giving me that chance," she said.

"Only my pleasure, sweetheart," Mara said, throwing an arm around Holly's shoulder and pulling her into her side to plant a kiss on her temple.

"No more sorries," she stated.

"I'll try."

"Okay." Holly smiled contentedly.

Gus strode over to them and picked Mara up, then threw her over his shoulder.

"You are going to pull a muscle. Your back, Gus!" she yelled.

"I'm as fit as a fiddle."

"Chuck her in, Dad," Ben yelled, egging him on. He was a younger version of Jake.

Gus jumped into the pool with Mara as she protested wildly.

Holly laughed. Never in a million years had she thought her life would be this perfect.

Mara was like a cat in the water, but still managed to dunk her husband.

They still had so much love for one another, and Holly knew that they would face anything together as she watched them share a kiss.

She wasn't just Holly's hero.

"Eww," Amelia bellowed.

"Eww," Jake and Robin, mimicked.

Then when the other three did the same, the kiss broke. But just to tease them a little more, Gus pretended to grab Mara and kiss her passionately, and laughingly broke apart when their kids splashed water at them.

Jake swam to the edge of the pool and hoisted himself up and out the water.

Her heart skipped a few beats when his perfectly toned body breached the water. He still made her body heat up with lust.

He took the chair his mother had unwillingly vacated, and kissed her.

"Have I told you how beautiful you look today?"

"No, and here I thought you hadn't even noticed."

"Oh, you can be glad there are people here," he teased, nipping her earlobe.

"Jake," she laughed as he grabbed her tighter so she couldn't get out of his grip.

"Toss her in the water," Gus yelled.

"No," she warned Jake.

"Oh? And, pray tell, who is going to stop me? You?"

"Jake, no." She laughed as he jumped up with her squirming in his arms.

"Please, don't, please, please, please," she begged, clinging to him for dear life.

"Okay, I won't. I won't, I won't." He stopped right at the edge of the pool. She relaxed when he kissed her.

"I lied," he murmured, then stepped into the pool.

She came up for air, gasping and sputtering, with the entire crowd laughing at her.

"You athhole," she said, intentionally mispronouncing the word so that Jamie wouldn't learn it, as she spat water in his face.

With her clothes clinging to her body, she swam to the edge of the pool, and just as she was about ready to pull herself out of the water, Jake grabbed her foot and yanked her backward into his arms.

She laughed as he played with her and when he finally let her go, she splashed him and turned to take Bradley from Amelia and cuddled him. He loved the water, so happy was he that he gave a belly laugh. Cooper mimicked his brother and she giggled.

There was just something between them. Whenever Bradley belly laughed, Cooper's laughter would follow, and it was music to her ears.

Most of the adults got out of the pool, leaving only Ben, Jamie with Sam, and Layla, Bernie's little girl behind.

She and Bernie dressed the boys in dry clothes, while Amelia kept them company and gave each a bottle as they lay outside in their portable cribs.

After dinner, Holly bathed the boys and put them down for the night. They were spending the night with Jake's parents. Her mother and Frank also stayed over, which led to Jamie wanting to stay as well. Jake and Holly said their goodbyes to everyone once Jamie had been put to bed.

Bernie and Leo went to her mother, as all three of her kids were tired.

On the drive home, she felt empty without her children.

Jake pulled her into his arms as soon as they got home and kissed her before she could protest.

His hands grabbed her ass firmly and squeezed, before moving down the back of her legs so he could pick her up.

Her legs wrapped around his waist and he carried her up the stairs without breaking their kiss. Her ears were already singing with the way he was kissing her, and she could feel her hormones levels rising as he took each step quicker and quicker.

At long last, she felt like she was ready for this, and tonight there were no little ears or cries to worry about.

The door slammed shut with the force of Jake's foot, and she found herself on the bed, him above her, holding her down with his body.

His kisses ignited her skin wherever he planted them, and she breathed heavily as he moved toward her shorts.

He swiftly unbuttoned them, and hooking his fingers in both her panties and shorts, pulled them off with the help of her wiggling her hips.

His mouth immediately zoned in on her pussy, and he used it to its fullest potential by licking and sucking at her swollen nub.

Her back instantly arched.

One finger slipped inside her as he flicked his tongue over her clit. Soft moans left her mouth.

She bit on her lower lip hard and grabbed her own hair as she succumbed to the pleasure he was wringing out of her.

He let out a guttural groan, as if what he was doing to her was his favorite thing in the entire world.

Panting, she closed her eyes as she gave herself over to the feeling of his mouth on her.

But soon his finger left her and his lips moved up to her stomach, his tongue gliding gently along her body, working his way up. His hands followed suit and when they reached the bottom of her shirt, he began pushing it up. Just as his fingers reached the underside of her breasts, he yanked it off and threw it across the room.

She flung her legs around his waist, lifting his shirt up so she could stroke his skin. Goosebumps flushed over his flesh, and he smiled against her lips.

A grunt left his mouth when his shirt was removed. He kissed her harder. His hands burrowed beneath her back to unhook her bra, and freeing it, he threw it over his shoulder.

As soon as her breasts were exposed, he cupped one immediately while taking the other into his mouth.

His free hand trailed back down toward her slick folds, and finding what he was looking for, he slipped a finger into her, and then a second.

All the while, her panting escalated.

He rolled slightly off her and admired her body, then devoured it with his lips, his tongue, his fingers.

She was on the brink of ecstasy, but she needed him inside her.

"Damn it," she moaned. "Fuck me!"

He didn't say a thing, but she felt his vigorous movements as he slid off his shorts, and then he was inside her in one swift motion.

She groaned as he filled her, his lips kissing and licking the side of her neck.

He penetrated her deeper, harder and faster, and her volume increased with every slam of his cock.

"Fuck" she yelled through clenched teeth. "I'm close." She bit his shoulder in desperation.

Jake grabbed her hips and pounded into her, again and again.

Her moaning turned to wailing, and then she screamed as her orgasm tore violently through her, digging the heels of her feet into his ass as her body trembled.

But he didn't stop. She knew he wasn't done with her yet.

He slipped out of her and pulled her toward the edge of the bed, turned her over, and slammed hard into her, eliciting a scream from her, not from pain, but from pleasure.

Grunts accompanied every stroke, and Holly moaned into the bedspread.

She could honestly have sex with him forever.

He continued slamming into her, hitting every delicious

spot inside her, his fingers digging into her waist, and then the feeling of wanting to explode, the tingling, returned.

"You've got to be fucking kidding me." She pushed herself up onto her elbows and looked at him over her shoulder.

Jake merely chuckled and slammed harder into her. "Ohh-hhh, yes," he grunted.

She screamed from pleasure as she came again.

He slipped out of her and rolled her onto her back.

"Still?" she said, and he laughed as he dropped down next to her.

Summoning whatever strength she had left, she rolled onto him and rode him fast and hard.

He titled his head back when she hit on just the right position.

"Fuck, yes!" he growled, biting his lower lip.

It was so fucking sexy.

She rode him faster, and just as her body gave out, he flipped her over and came inside her.

He groaned as she let out a long, satisfied moan.

"You are going to kill me one of these days, my heart is beating like crazy."

"As long as it's beating for me, woman."

He kissed her on the lips, slowly moving inside her.

The kisses were sweet and gentle, and she didn't want this to end.

"Time for a shower," he said against her lips. He grabbed her thighs firmly, her arms going around his neck, and lifted her up from the bed at the same time he got up.

He walked them to the shower and turned the taps on, then lowered her to her feet and stood directly under the spray as warm water cascaded down their bodies. It felt amazing.

They washed each other, in no rush whatsoever, and eventually made it to bed.

The room smelled of hot sex.

Jake pulled her up against him—both were naked, her back to his front—and cradled her.

She stared at the ring she was twirling on her finger.

It still felt unreal that he'd asked her to marry him, but in due time she knew it would sink in, and then it would be hard waiting for that day to finally arrive.

TWENTY-FOUR

HOLLY

The big day was finally upon them.

She looked in the mirror, hardly recognizing herself. She'd picked up about seven pounds, and was back to her old self. Her kidney was strong and her liver was now healthy. She had enough happiness to last her a lifetime.

It was still a dream come true to know that in less than an hour she wouldn't be Holly Scallanger anymore but Holly Peters.

"Suck it in, Melia!" Robin yelled, which brought Holly out of her happy thoughts. "Jeez, you are seriously becoming a fatty."

"Oh, shush!" She slapped Robin away from her as Bernie struggled to pull her zipper up.

"Girl, are you sure she made the right alterations?"

"Yes, she even made it a bit bigger. This is no use. I'm going to walk down the aisle in my underwear."

"Oh, heaven's no, please," Jane said in a serious voice.

Holly snorted.

Jamie was sitting next to Mara on the couch, laughing with the rest of them. She looked beautiful in her dress, and her hair was down in loose curls. Every time she saw Jamie, she saw grown up Romy with the beautiful eyes.

"One thing I can say, I love my new boobs. I don't know what the fuck I'm going to wear, but my boobs are perfect. Better than your little raisins," she teased Robin.

Mara shook her head in exasperation at her daughters.

"I'm sure the dress can't be that small. What the hell did you eat this week?" Holly stepped forward.

"Away with you," Jane said. "We do not want you to work up a sweat. There is nothing worse than a bride who smells."

"Mom," she whined.

"It's the truth."

"Nothing out of the ordinary," Amelia answered. "I've even taken extra yoga classes, for crying out loud."

"This is really too small, sweetheart," Jane said.

"Okay, we have a real emergency."

"Calm down," Mara said.

Holly stilled. She stared at Amelia, and happy tears suddenly pooled in her eyes. She reached for her phone and sent a text to Rodney.

Emergency! Need a favor. Go out and buy a pregnancy test, but do it discreetly, please.

She looked at Amelia again, who was still laughing with the others. Sighing happily, she wiped her tears and laughed with them.

Rodney texted back.

Why, you can't be pregnant? Those kinds of miracles don't exist, sweetheart. Plus, you've reached your quota.

Move! She sent back.

I'm in the car, chill.

It's not for me, it's for Amelia.

What?

Just get the damn thing.

"Who are you texting?"

"Twenty minutes, Amelia. I waited a long time for this, you have twenty minutes."

"Okay, fine. I'll just quickly zip down to my house and get another. It's not going to be violet, Holly, I'm sorry. My fat ass is ruining your wedding."

"Hurry," she said.

Robin went with her.

Holly sat down on the couch and started giggling. How could she not know? Perfect boobs was one of the first signs. They must hurt, she must feel sick.

"Holly, what is it, sweetheart? You are not getting cold feet, are you?"

"No, Mom. I think Amelia's pregnant."

"What?" The women in the room asked.

"Just think about it. We all know the signs. She said she wasn't eating much, and that she was even doing yoga. The only other reason you pick up weight like that is if you are pregnant."

"Her perfect boobs!" Mara gasped and cupped her face in her hands. "But the doctor—"

"Doctors have been wrong before. Miracle babies happen all the time. I believe she's pregnant. I can feel it."

"We need to get a test."

"Rod's bringing one. I already sent him out to get one."

"Oh, my word. My baby is going to have a baby!"

"We don't know that yet. Let's not get ahead of ourselves, even though I'm sure she's pregnant. I don't want to be wrong about this. Not this time." She closed her eyes and took deep a breath.

Rodney barged into room.

"Where is she?"

"She went home to get another dress. Give it here, before she comes back."

"She doesn't know?"

"Not yet. I'll be gentle."

Footsteps sounded on the landing and Gus' head popped into the room.

"What is taking so long? Oh, Holly, you look stunning."

"Thank you," she smiled, as Mara pulled her husband in and told him that Amelia might be pregnant.

"What? Where is she?"

"She'll be back soon. Her dress doesn't fit. She quickly popped out to go fetch another. She doesn't know. Don't make a fuss, we got the test. You know what, just leave. You can't lie. Just go." Mara pushed Gus out the door.

The women snickered at Mara's comment.

"He would give it away, truly."

Patiently, they waited for Robin and Amelia to return and finally, after what seemed like hours, both women entered the room.

"Okay, let's go," Amelia said.

"Not so fast."

"Please don't tell me you're getting cold feet. We are already twenty minutes behind."

"And five more won't kill them. Come with me."

"Holly," she protested running on high heels as Holly led her by the hand into the bathroom. "What is going on?"

"You need to pee on this stick." She gave her the pregnancy test, and Amelia frowned at it. She could already see the disappointment on Amelia's face.

"C'mon, Amelia. You have all the signs."

"I can't, Holly. It's going to be negative. The doctor said—"

"Oh, for heaven sakes, they're human, too. We're all doctors or nurses, except for Bernie—and we've all been wrong before. You have all the signs. You have to pee on the stick, Amelia, otherwise I'm not walking out that door."

"You're bluffing."

"Pee on the stick."

"Okay, fine." She grabbed the box out of Holly's hand, a lone tear rolling down her cheek. "But you are wrong."

Ripping the box open, she removed the stick, sat on the toilet and peed on it. "It should be morning pee, anyway."

"Oh, please! If you're pregnant, it doesn't matter what time of day the pee is."

Done, she put the stick down hard on the sink, and walked out the bathroom.

"Come here," Mara said.

Rodney couldn't wait, so he joined Holly in the bathroom.

"She's not pregnant?"

"Don't know yet. She didn't want to wait."

She stared at the stick, which was upside down. She was feeling anxious now. If Amelia wasn't pregnant, she was going to be devastated on her future sister-in-law's wedding day. She should've kept her mouth shut.

Jane joined them in the bathroom. "Holly, we don't have the entire day."

"I'm too scared to look."

"Don't look at me," Rod said.

"Fine then, shall I?" Jane grabbed it and turned it over. Her face was unreadable when she looked at it. "It has two stripes."

Holly screamed. "She's pregnant!" She ran out of the bathroom. "You are going to be a mommy!"

"What? I'm pregnant? How? I mean, I don't know...how is it possible?" Amelia cried.

Everyone shrieked, jumping up and down from joy.

"Look at my makeup now," Amelia said, ugly crying as she touched her belly.

"It's okay. We can try to fix it." Robin looked at it doubtfully.

Amelia was being congratulated, when Gus and Armand ran into the room, their faces as white as a ghost's.

"What is going on? What's with all the screaming? Women! Jeez. Could we get this going, please? Jake is going to get drunk if you don't hurry up," Armand was firing on all cylinders, but froze when he saw Amelia's face. "Babe, you okay?"

She flung herself at him. "You're going to be a daddy."

"What?"

"We're pregnant."

"What?" Tears pricked his eyes, and then it sunk in. "You're pregnant?"

She nodded, crying and sniveling at the same time.

Armand grabbed his wife around the waist and kissed her hard.

"My makeup!"

"Sweetheart, your makeup was ruined before I even got here. I'm going to be a daddy, for real?"

"Yes, for real. Look." She showed him the test, both had tears rolling down their cheeks.

"Congratulations, sweetheart." Gus hugged Amelia. "More grandbabies. I'm the luckiest man in the entire world."

"Okay. Best news, ever, Melia. But"—she looked at her twin boys making a mess of their outfits—"we have to get rolling. Look at those two! Robin, help Amelia with her face. The twins are busy tearing their clothes apart."

"Get your fat mommy ass in here, woman." Robin pulled her sister into the bathroom.

"Thank you," Mara said to the ceiling, contentment etched on her face, and a hand over her heart.

"Congratulations, Grandma." Jane smiled.

"Thank you," Mara whispered, giving Jane a gentle sideways hug so they wouldn't ruin each other's hair or makeup.

Armand and Gus left, with Armand yelling on their way downstairs.

"I'm going to be a father!"

"What?"

"She's pregnant?" Jake yelled.

"Oh...no, you stay right where you are, mister," Gus yelled.

Too much was going on, all good, but the tension was building. Eventually, Frank walked into the room.

"Holly, that boy is going to cry if he sees you. You are breathtaking."

She laughed.

Robin and Amelia walked out of the bathroom.

"Congratulations, baby," Frank said to Amelia, and they hugged each other.

"I'm not going to cry." She kept saying to herself over and over.

They all laughed. The hug broke.

"Okay, we have to get going. Nannas, the boys. Oh, my word." She ran to Bradley and Cooper. "What did Aunty Amelia say?" she scolded the two almost eighteen-month-olds.

"Bernie, see to Cooper, please."

She did, and Amelia handled Bradley.

When they looked almost as presentable as when they'd arrived, the two grandmas took them downstairs.

The bridesmaids followed shortly after them.

"See you at the front," Amelia said with a huge grin plastered on her face, then walked out the door.

"I need a quick word. It won't take long."

Holly nodded. "What is it, Frank?"

"I asked your mother to marry me, and she said yes."

"What, when?"

"She didn't want to spoil your beautiful day. I'm sorry that your father isn't here."

"It's okay."

"I know I'm not your real dad, and I've never had the honor to father children, but you and your mother and Jamie, and now the two boys, are what I call my instant family. I've loved you like a daughter, and I am honored to walk you down the aisle. You don't know how big of a deal it is, as I've known Jake his entire life. I've always said that the woman who steals his heart, will be one sent right from heaven, and here you are. No more surprises, Holly, please, because I fear my old heart isn't going to last if you ever scare us like that again."

"I promise to do my best." She had tears in her eyes, but suddenly grabbed Frank in a bear hug. Who, it now seemed, was going to become her stepfather real soon. She was going to kill her mother for not sharing the news.

Today was a good day. Everyone was happy. Life was happy. Her wedding would always be remembered.

JAKE

FINALLY, THE WEDDING WAS ABOUT TO BEGIN.

He was still sober, with Leo and a teary Armand at his side. His father had taken a seat, and soft music began to play.

"About time," Jake grunted, happy that his sister was pregnant, but thankful it was finally under way.

Mara walked with one of the twins on her hip throwing petals on the ground. Jake made his eyes at him and he laughed; Bradley. He had an amazing belly laugh. Then behind him,

Coop joined in. Jane was a few paces behind Mara with his second son in her arms.

The two grandmothers took to their seats. Jamie looked gorgeous in her violet dress with white stockings and violet shoes. She'd grown up so fast, and he knew she was going to turn into a beautiful young lady soon. Holly had told him that.

He continued to wonder what she'd seen during her coma. How lucky she'd been to have seen and spoken to Romy's grown up form. He wished that he could've seen her, too.

He winked at Jamie, and she winked back as she took a seat next to his mom, who gave her a hug and a kiss on the head.

Then it was Bernie with Robin behind her, and Amelia following both. She was beaming, her eyes still shining with happy tears.

He had tears in his eyes, too. She was finally pregnant. *Congrats,* he mouthed.

Thank you, she mouthed back.

He would hug her later.

And then finally, the woman of his dreams walked out on Frank's arm.

She was a fairytale, and he felt like the prince who was going to marry his Cinderella. He dabbed a tear away fast, feeling like an idiot that everyone saw it.

Her veil covered her face. He was antsy, and wished they would walk faster. Impatient, he mimicked walking quicker with his fingers, which had the entire congregation snickering.

Finally, they reached him and stopped. Frank lifted her veil off of her face.

His heart skipped a beat. But not because of the way she looked today, she would always take his breath away, no matter what she wore. It had been that way ever since he'd laid eyes on her that very first day.

His heart skipped a beat simply because he was over-whelmed with love and joy.

"Told you he would cry."

"Frank." Holly smacked him playfully, but he kissed her on the cheek, and slapped Jake on the shoulder.

No words of warning were spoken, because Uncle Frank didn't need to speak. He knew how much Jake loved Holly.

He took her hand. "You look so beautiful today."

"Not looking too shabby yourself, mister."

He chuckled as the reverend started with the ceremony. When they reached the part of the vows, Jake fumbled in his pocket for the piece of paper. He went first.

He cleared his throat as he unfolded the paper he'd written his vows on. "I promise to love you, for better and better"—everyone snickered—"as we've already gone through the worst. Nothing that comes our way could be worse than what we've already been through. It doesn't mean you will get free passes, though."

She smiled.

"I promise to give you everything you need, and will try not give you all the things you want."

More laughter came.

"And I promise that when we do fight, it will be something worthy to fight about. I promise to love you deeply and gently." *And sometimes rough,* he mouthed. Holly's eyes grew, but she giggled, anyway. "And I promise that you will always have a shoulder to cry on, even if it was the ass behind the shoulder that caused the tears."

A lone tear escaped at that moment and he dashed it away with his thumb. "See, already fulfilling them." He smiled. "I don't have to promise you to be there in sickness, as I've proven I won't be anywhere else, but I do promise that I will never abandon you, just as long as you are gentle on my heart. These conditions are forever, and ever, and not till death do us part."

Aws rang through the crowd. He rolled his eyes and took the ring from Leo, and taking her hand in his, slipped it on her finger.

She sucked in her lips as she looked at it and swallowed hard. It was her turn. Robin handed her the vows she'd been holding for her.

She looked at the gathering sitting behind them.

"I promise, I didn't know what his vows were going to be."

They chuckled.

Taking a deep breath, she unfolded her paper.

"I promise to love you for better and better."

"What?" Jake said, leaning forward on tiptoes to look at her vows.

"See, it's really there," she said. Clearing her throat, she started again. "I promise to love you for better and better, as we could never beat our worst. My vows aren't filled with promises, though, but they are filled with giving you my best all the time. I will love you like no other woman on this earth, well...except for your mom, the woman who gave me a kidney and a piece of her liver."

More *aws* followed.

"I will fight with you, and it's going to cost you loads of sucking up, but it wouldn't be because of something silly; it would carry meaning and something that is dear to my heart." He smiled. "So I'm glad we are in agreement on that one."

More laughter came.

"I won't take you for granted as I know what kind of diamond you are, and I thank my lucky stars every day that I found you." Her voice started to break and she cleared her throat. "Sorry."

"No fair, I didn't cry."

She smiled. "When Jamie died..." she took a deep breath, "... and I know I'm going to regret telling you this later on," she said and laughed. She took another deep breath. "She took a part of my soul with her, and I thought that I would never get it back. But I know she didn't take it with her, she kept it somewhere safe," Holly's voice broke and tears streamed down her face.

"You are going to make me cry, woman." Tears already shone his eyes. "It's humiliating," he hissed, and of course everyone heard, hence the chuckles that followed.

She sniffed and laughed. "Sorry," she said and recollected herself. "She knew I'd get it back one day, because she left it with you."

More tears flowed down her face.

"Don't ruin your makeup," Amelia whispered, but everyone heard.

They both grinned as Jake dabbed more tears away.

"So if you hurt me, I will break your balls."

This time, everyone roared with laughter.

"You definitely are a Peters," Jake said, because that was a classic Gus ending.

She slipped the ring onto his finger, and it was then that the reverend announced they were now husband and wife, and he was free to kiss his bride.

Jake grabbed her around the waist and dipped her backward, then gave her the loveliest kiss he could ever master.

The gathering applauded. She was his forever and ever.

TWENTY-FIVE

HOLLY

The reception was held at the venue by the lake.

It was stunning, and had been decorated with fairy lights hanging everywhere. And the food was amazing.

After everyone was done eating, the speeches were made.

She glanced behind her to where all three of her children were sprawled on a makeshift bed on the floor behind the main table.

So many people gave speeches.

Mara, apologizing again for what she'd done. Jake reminding her of her missing kidney and half her liver.

Gus, saying that Mara had finally let Jake off her boob, and that now he'd moved on to Holly's. And that he was proud of the man his son had become.

Amelia, she was just loving everyone tonight.

Robin making everyone cry, and Bernie right behind her telling Holly and Jake how much she loved them.

She wished her sister could have been here, but she knew she was in some way.

Rodney telling everyone about how he'd met Holly, and how, when Jake came back into her life, he finally had a face to put to the fake name Holly had told everyone—Steve. Jake was so not a Steve.

She blushed at that lie.

"See, Mom, other people also lie," Jake mumbled to Mara, who sat at his side. She smacked him softly.

And then it was time for the speech everyone feared; Leo's.

"I'll apologize right now for what he's about to say, because he refused to show me what he wrote," Jake stated.

"Go fuck it up, babe," Bernie called to her husband as he walked up to the podium.

Laughter rippled throughout the room.

"Loads of confidence that one has." Leo looked in Bernie's direction.

"I just know you so well," Bernie replied.

"I'm probably going to fuck this one up badly, buddy. Holly, I'm sorry if I say things you don't want to hear."

She laughed. "It's okay. I'll take it with a pinch of salt."

"He really does love you, more than you'll ever know."

"Please, I do not want to sleep with the dog tonight," Jake begged.

"She's very forgiving, Jake, but buddy, we have to set something straight. Something everyone wants to know, as you really didn't shed any light on this huge particular thing in your past."

"Oh, fuck," Jake swore.

"My speech is all about destiny tonight. I might not make much sense, but hopefully you will all get it after I'm done."

"No, dude, please." Jake sounded nervous.

Holly looked at him with one eyebrow raised.

"You are married now, so no more secrets, buddy. Holly fessed up to hers, and as you're her soulmate, you need to fess up to yours, too. And if I do fuck this one up, I'll keep you warm tonight."

Jake chuckled. "Okay, go for it." Jake shook his head and covered his face with one hand.

"Holly, everyone here loves you, and for those of you who don't know her the way we do, take our word, you love her."

More laughter.

"When Jake met Holly—" Leo started.

"Argh." Jake put his head down on the table and folded his arms over his neck, covering his ears with his elbows.

"What?" She wanted to know. What could be so bad?

"He's going to fuck it up. I know it," Jake whispered.

"Calm down," she whispered back.

"It all started with the married woman."

"No!" Jake groaned.

A collective gasp and soft twitters traveled around the room.

"You idiot!" Bernie hissed.

"No, go on. I want to hear about her. As you said, not a lot of light was shed on this topic," Holly said. "Homewrecker," she murmured out of the corner of her mouth.

Jake laughed.

"Just let me finish before you punish him."

Bernie shook her head, and Holly giggled nervously. He was going to fuck it up. Bernie could feel it.

"It was love at first sight for Jake when he saw her."

"Stop!" Bernie yelled.

"What?"

"You don't say things like 'It was love at first sight' at another's wedding, you idiot."

"I need to make a point, woman. Let me make it."

"Ugh. Sorry, babes."

Holly waved it away.

"He was fucked up after that," Leo said, drawing laughter from Jake.

"I give up, dude. I'm sleeping in the doghouse tonight," Jake grumbled.

"No, you won't. I've got it all figured out in my head, just wait for the punch line."

"Okay, go ahead. Dig my grave deeper."

Holly didn't like what Leo had chosen to say, and it was partly evident by the expression on her face. She couldn't look at Jake, but she wanted to know how he'd felt about this woman, and this was the moment.

"Okay, so Jake was messed up when the married woman wasn't available."

"Stop repeating it!" Bernie screamed.

"It was where I was last. Stop interrupting me."

"Fine, just carry on."

"Okay. So, married woman...messed up Jake."

"Please, shoot me now," Jake begged his mother.

"He's messing this up," his mother whispered.

"His heart is in a good place. I'll fix it later."

"We tried everything to get Jake to come and visit. Remember, baby?"

"Yes, just finish your messed up speech."

"It's beautiful. It's about destiny," Leo said.

"Okay, go on. Three months later..."

"Jake finally said yes to the music festival, and drove up in his RV." Leo pretended he was driving an RV and parked it, too.

"And then he saw Holly. Now, I'm not going to repeat what he said to me in the RV," Leo warned, and Jake just shook his head.

"Now he decides not to share," he said to Holly, who managed to force a half smile. "You want him to stop?" Jake had picked up on her uneasiness.

"No, it's fine. I know Leo. He'll make his point."

"I'd probably have to get up there to help, but okay." He sounded annoyed.

She patted his arm.

"But the married woman came up. I blabbered it out, my fault, again, very sorry about that, buddy."

"It's fine, just carry on."

"And Holly teased him about it, she called him a home-wrecker."

Everyone laughed.

"Still, they hit it off pretty strongly from the get-go."

"Yes, we did, and that's because she's my soul mate."

"That she is. Jake was happy. I can't recall when I'd last seen him that happy."

Jake blew out air.

"Then Holly left, and she fucked Jake up completely."

"Before she left or after?" Jake sounded confused.

"After buddy, focus. I'm talking about the inner kind." Leo tapped his chest.

The room practically shook with the combined laughter of everyone in it.

"We all laugh about it now, but it wasn't like that, Holly."

"Yeah, I heard. Sorry."

"Sorry?" was all Leo said. "Okay, moving on. But she came back just before Jake made the most horrible mistake of his life. Sorry, Kate. Is she here?"

"Hell, no!" Holly yelled, drawing more laughter from everyone.

"Okay, then I take it back. I didn't like her that much."

Gus shook with laughter. "I'm so getting you to speak at my funeral," he joked.

Leo laughed. "And Jake became happy again, Holly fell pregnant, almost a repeat of the last time, and then she was going to leave again. But this time, she wouldn't be coming back," Leo said, his voice somber. "What I guess I'm trying to say is, thank you, Holly, for fighting the way you did, for not leaving us a second time. Because this time around, if there was no coming back for you, there would be no coming back for Jake. He'd proved it, three times, how fucked up he was when you left, and I couldn't bear it happening again. So, eat healthy, look after yourself as you are more than a diamond to him. You are the air that he breathes."

"Ahh, bud." Jake laughed.

Bernie clapped, along with everyone else, but she looked confused. "I still don't see what the married woman had to do with this, or how destiny fits in at all."

"What? I fucked it up, didn't I?"

"Yeah, you did, and now I have to fix it," Jake groaned, getting up.

"And it wasn't three times, idiot, it was twice that she left. Almost left on the second," Bernie stated.

Jake shook his head when he joined Leo on the podium and grabbed another mike.

"Love at first sight is overrated, sweetheart," Jane whispered. "True love is real."

"It's okay, Mom."

"Okay, Bernie," Jake started. "When was the first time I met Holly."

"At the music bash."

"No," Jake chuckled.

"Yes," Bernie said, adamant.

"Not the first time she met me. I'm talking about the first time I saw her."

"Oh! My birthday party."

Holly remembered Josie teasing her about it. And that she

hadn't even see him. She really couldn't remember him being there. It was weird as he'd clearly stood out.

"And what happened at your birthday party?"

Bernie started to laugh. "I forgot, damn it! You hit what-his-face."

"Brandon," Jake answered.

"What?" Holly asked.

"I hit him because he kissed another girl. And he was with you."

"Seriously?"

"True," Leo said.

Holly laughed.

"And then, when did you see me again after that?" Jake asked Bernie.

"Music bash," she said.

"No."

"I saw him at the bar," Leo corrected.

"Yes," Jake turned to Leo. "Now, remember Holly is also part of this speech, we have to involve her, buddy."

"Go for it."

There was another ripple of laughter, but it was confused laughter.

"And when did you see me again?"

"At the bash, but it wasn't our fault. We invited you so many times," Bernie said.

"Yes, you did, and I should've just given in because then I would have met Holly sooner. But I was still heartbroken, fucked up"—he looked at Leo, and Leo nodded—"over the married woman. Just to make that clear."

Everyone laughed again.

"You two are idiots," Bernie groaned.

"He'll keep me warm tonight," Jake joked.

"The day I saw Holly at the bash, and I am going to tell you what I said to Leo as it was the key ingredient of that wonderful speech you tried to make..." he looked at Leo.

"Sorry bud," Leo joked.

"...my heart skipped a beat. I know it's not possible, but it happened."

Everyone was silent this time around.

"I pulled Leo into the RV and scolded him. I asked him what the fuck that dickhead Brandon was doing there. What did you say?"

"What?" Bernie was just as confused as Holly.

"I said that the dickhead wasn't there," Leo answered.

"The dickhead wasn't there," Jake repeated.

Holly tried to think what Brandon had to do with this.

"Then I asked," Jake paused to take a breath, "what the fuck his wife was doing there."

There were murmurs and gasps throughout the room.

"You've got to be shitting me. Holly was the married woman?"

"Thank you, Bernie!" Jake yelled.

"You did a piss poor job," Bernie told her husband.

"No, I didn't. I said she left Jake three times."

"Yes, you did," Jake agreed. "Now get off the stage so I can make my speech, you idiot. I just lost my fucking balls in this relationship."

Laughter erupted once more, but Holly was still in shock.

"So, sweetheart, my baby, my precious, my everything. How am I doing so far on the suck-up part?"

She didn't even crack a smile. Still looked very much confused, but then it started to sink in.

"You okay?" Jake asked.

Her lower lip started to tremble, and she covered her face. She'd been the 'married woman' all along. She'd been jealous and insecure over herself.

"Don't cry, please."

"Sorry," Leo said quickly, "finish your speech." He got off the stage and went to sit on Jake's chair so he could give Holly a hug. "I'm an idiot. I'm sorry."

Holly finally burst out laughing. "Yes, you are, both of you are fucking idiots. No wonder you are such great friends."

"But you love us both." Leo spoke.

"She okay there, or you going to fuck that up, too?"

"Carry on. I got this." Leo gave him a thumbs-up.

"Okay. So now that I have no leverage whatsoever, as she knows who she is to me, all I can do is continue and lose my dignity in the process."

"It's not that bad, sweetheart, you are doing great. She said she wouldn't take you for granted."

"Thank you, Mom. I'm going to tell you what my mother told me when she woke up after donating her kidney and a piece of her liver to you."

Jake had tears in his eyes, but wiped them away fast.

"I was pissed off, believe me, I was beyond mad. Because I wanted to stay upset, angry at her, but she had given me the perfect gift. Something that you needed, so that I could survive. I asked her...why her, why not me? And I will never forget what she told me. She said that you already had my heart beating inside of you, and that was the reason I wasn't your biological match for a kidney. My mother made a huge mistake, and we all forgave her as she became my hero by saving your life. But she was never a stupid woman. And her words that day were true. You do own my heart and I would give you my heart in a second, the real one, if it ever came to that. So you better take care of it, woman. And I know it's sad that I am saying it directly, but I hope I am the first to go, because then at least I'd know my children would still have a parent. Because if you go before me...I would pack my bags and..." He made a whistling sound, and pointed his index fingers up toward heaven. Our love is like *The Notebook* shit."

Everyone burst into laughter.

Oh...fuck. He'd read her letter.

"I meant what I said that night to you when you asked me to stay. I said that I know who I can live with, and who I can't live without. Sweetheart, I've proven it three times that I'm a fucked-up mess if you are not around. I'm begging you, don't ever leave me in any possible way there is, as I won't make it. And that is the truth. I will love you for eternity." Jake had tears in his eyes.

Leo looked at Holly, and quickly gave her a hug when she burst out crying.

"I take it back, love at first sight is the best," Jane said.

Holly laughed through her tears, and then Jake finally reached her.

"Go," he scolded Leo. "I'm sorry, he's an idiot." Jake crouched down in front of her and wrapped his arms around her waist.

She leaned forward and hugged him back.

"Great job there, mister," Jane said.

"Thank you."

She was the married woman. It was going to take a while for it to fully sink in. She didn't have to worry about another woman coming to take him away from her, she was his life. "It's okay. I just wish you'd told me that sooner."

"Really?" he asked.

"Yes, you weren't—"

"If it's not too much to ask," Gus said into the microphone. "My two beautiful children, one that came from my loins, the other through his heart, could you please open the dance floor for us? We want to party."

"Sure, since you asked so nicely," Jake teased his dad, and took Holly's hand.

She didn't have a clue what song was going to play as it was a surprise, although they'd practiced their dance to many other songs. She had no idea if he was even capable of choosing the right song, but she had to trust him.

And then *Shake It Off* from Taylor Swift began to play.

"Hell, no. Please tell me this isn't the wedding song you chose?"

"What is wrong with this song? I love this song."

"Jake Peters," she tried to suppress her laughter as he jumped up and down to the music, but couldn't. She just couldn't stay mad at him.

"Just joking. Play the song," Jake said.

"Thank you," she said, grabbing hold of his arm.

Jake wrapped his arm around waist and pulled her into him. She place one hand in his, and the other one on his shoulder.

"You are going to love it, it's so us," he whispered.

"I hope so, for your sake."

The music intro started and Jake widened his eyes as he stared at her.

"What song is this?" she asked.

"Just listen, you'll hear it soon. It's an oldie, but a good one."

"An oldie?" She frowned as the intro, which was being played on an acoustic guitar, started and it didn't sound like any song she knew. She loved the oldies.

And then when a male artist sang the first words, she closed her eyes and smiled as they glided slowly across the dance floor. A couple of people gushed, mostly coming from Robin's and Amelia's table.

"Yeah," he said.

"It's perfect." She opened her teary eyes.

Don't cry, he mouthed. "And don't look at the guests, either, as they have turned into goo," he whispered in her ear.

"Yeah, well, so have I." He guided her through their steps to the song. He'd chosen *Time after Time* by Cindy Lauper—except that this was the cover version by Rob Thomas.

It was perfect, and so them.

Jake mouthed most of the words to her, and when the song reached its chorus, they did their magic just as they'd practiced at the dance studio.

Everyone cheered.

Jake even played out the words 'I'll be waiting' very dramatically to her through one of their moves before they came together again.

Everyone gasped and clapped.

He was so goofy, but she was so madly in love with him. She couldn't believe that he was hers and only hers, forever and ever.

She wished Jake and her sister could've met, and when the song neared its ending, they slow danced again.

Something caught her attention, and her eyes moved to the doorway that led to the deck, and there she saw two figures, watching.

One of the figures had long, strawberry-blond hair, and the other one looked like Amelia. One waved, and the other one blew her a kiss before they disappeared.

Holly smiled this time, as the ache of missing both of them was light. She was happy, as she'd gained back that part her twin had taken through Jake.

As long as this man in front of her was by her side, the world could end.

Because she knew she would be just fine.

THE END

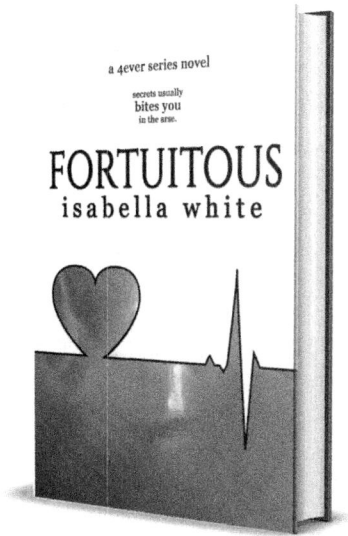

a 4ever series novel

secrets usually
bites you
in the arse.

FORTUITOUS
isabella white

Read Fortuitous Free, a What if Novel, that play off in the 4Ever series.

I've written 8 novels in the What If Series. All different scenarios how Jake could find out differently about Jamie Bernice.

Fortuitous play off eighteen months after Holly left and she runs into him at a medical conference.

Only a small change but with such a huge outcome.

If only Holly knew.

Get Fortuitous when joining my newsletter.

ABOUT THE AUTHOR

Isabella White recently reached USAToday Best Seller list with her title From a Jack to a King available in the Royal and Reckless boxed set.

She lives in South Africa, she loves life, loves her family and loves to write.

She writes under various pen names, but chose Isabella White to publish her contemporary novels. Imperfect Love was her debut novel released followed by Secret Love. Finishing with the third part Endless Love.

Finding Mr. Right is her newest and due for release in 2019.

To Join my newsletter to get Fortuitous go to my website
www.isabellawhitebooks.com

❤️ 🐦

Printed in Dunstable, United Kingdom